This book is dedicated to my family without them there would be no point. And to the ones who didn't make it.

Front and back cover photographs by Adrian Langley.
Cover design/layout by COBA Studios, Merrickville.

NW9productions@gmail.com

PROLOGUE

SUMMER 1974

It was a hot summer day, one of those days where the heat haze rose in wavy lines off the road, and mischief hung thick in the air. Terry, Dave, and Wobble were hanging lazily around, lounging in the park, as teenage kids do. Wobble swung lazily back and forth on a swing, dragging his feet in the dirty playground gravel. Dave was laying on the slowly rotating roundabout, staring up at the sky. The roundabout was one of those you see at nearly every playground, with the crisscrossing bars you hold onto attached to a wobbly, flat platform. The type that when the group of you would run as fast as you could, making it spin faster and faster, while you held on as long as possible, until the dizziness forced you to jump to a knee scraping crash on the gravel, that the council had so kindly provided, in their attempts to cripple as many kids as possible at an early age. Today, however, Dave lay on his back and lazily pushed the roundabout slowly in circles with one foot. He stared up at the few clouds in the sky, wondering how anyone ever saw the shapes of animals or buildings or whatever else in them. They just looked like clouds to him, big, white and grey, shapeless blobs in the sky.

Terry sat at the top of a metal slide, smoking a cigarette, keeping watch, when something caught his eye, the 183 bus coming down the High Road had stopped just short of the playground and the Baldwin brothers had jumped off. Terry watched carefully. If they turned to cross the street towards their house all was well, however, if they turned towards the park, not so much. The Baldwins were bullies of the first degree, and Terry didn't feel like an altercation. There were three of them, Jimmy the eldest, was seventeen and an aspiring biker. Doug was sixteen and idolized his older brother Jimmy. Then, there was Alan, fourteen and in Terry and Dave's class in high school. Wobble, who was the same age, had been held back a year due to time lost because of his accident. Of course, today, the Baldwins turned and headed straight into the park.

Terry jumped down from the slide, "Oi, you two, let's scarper."

Dave stopped the roundabout with his foot, "It's too hot, let's stay here."

Terry shook his head, "It will be if you don't get your arse in gear."

Terry started to walk out of the playground towards the corner of the toilet block, Wobble fell in beside him.

"What's the matter Tel?"

"The Baldwins, all three of them," replied Terry glanced nervously behind him.

"Shit, c'mon Dave, hurry up will ya?"

Dave ran to catch up with them and fell into step beside Terry. "Like you could get out of here faster than me, Wobs. What's going on?"

Wobble was stung by Dave's comment, he hated his nickname, almost as much as he hated the severe limp it referred to. He glared, "Fuck you Dave, maybe we should just leave you behind, see how you like that."

Dave rolled his eyes, "Calm down will you, what's up Tel?"

"The Baldwins, as soon as we turn the corner and are hidden by the building, we peg it, put some distance between us and them. Dave glanced over his shoulder, he could see the three figures, pursuing them, closing ground. As soon as they turned the corner they started to run, but not long into their attempt to flee Terry stopped to wait for Wobble, who, through no fault of his own, couldn't keep up with his able-bodied friends. Dave glanced behind him, noticing he was well ahead of the other two, before stopping and waiting for his friends to catch up.

"Fuckin' Wobble. C'mon will ya."

As the other two struggled to catch up, Dave looked back as the Baldwin brothers appeared around the corner. seeing their prey was eluding them, they too broke into a run. Alan, the youngest, shouted tauntingly behind them, "Run rabbit run, we're coming for you!"

"C'mon you two for fuck sakes, they're gaining on us." Terry and Wobble caught up to Dave, Terry was half carrying Wobble, and it was obvious to them all that they would soon be caught.

Dave looked desperately around, "I've got an idea, follow me."

The three of them crossed the park and disappeared, around the corner of an old church hall building. Dave led the other two around the far side of the building, to an old, wooden door, and roughly jiggled the handle before the door popped open.

"Get in quick," he pleaded.

Wobble looked puzzled, "How did you?"

"Never mind, follow me," Dave led the other two up on the stage and pushed an old carpet aside revealing a trap door. "Get in," he begged, opening it. The other two jumped into the space under the stage and Dave followed, closing the trap door behind them.

"Like Wobble said, how did you?" Terry looked confused.

"Boy scouts," Dave replied, cutting him off, "when mum made me go to the church scout group this was where we met."

The side door to the hall burst open with a loud crash. "Oi! Where are ya?" It was Jimmy Baldwin.

"Shit!"

"Shut up Dave, they won't find us here."

Terry tried to sound reassuring, even though the faces of his two friends showed they didn't believe him. They could hear the Baldwins whispering to each other, noisily opening and closing doors, searching. Terry, Dave, and Wobble lay back on the pile of large bulky sacks that were stored under the stage, listening to the sound of footsteps on the stage above them.

A disembodied voice called out, "Come out, come out wherever you are."

Then another. "Fuck it Doug, let's go, screw them I'm thirsty, let's go get a beer."

The footsteps above them hurried away and the three friends looked at each other in the semi darkness feeling a mixture of shock and relief.

"D'you think they're really gone Tel?" Wobble stammered.

"Sounds like it."

Dave smiled proudly, "Saved your bacon, didn't I?"

Wobble shrugged, "Whatever. What's this about you being in the boy scouts?"

Dave was embarrassed, "Wasn't for long, like I said mum made me."

"Dib dib dib, dob dob dob." Wobble held his fingers up in a Boy Scout sign.

Dave slapped his fingers down and hissed, still nervous about the Baldwin's somehow hearing them, "Fuck you Wobble, no wonder I never tell you two anything."

Wobble laughed. "You still got your uniform then?"

Dave was beginning to get really annoyed, "No I don't.".

Wobble looked around the space and then, "Tell me something Dave." Dave sighed,

"Here we go, what?"

"No, serious, what's in all these bags we're laying on?"

"Tents."

"Tents?"

"Yeah tents, scouts go camping, you know? It's kinda the point of the whole thing."

Wobble put his face against one and sniffed, "Don't half pong."

Dave felt proud to share his knowledge with the other two, "They spray them with a waterproofer at the end of the Autumn, ready for the next year."

Wobble nodded his head, then strained to listen for any sound out in the hall. "D'you think they've gone, Tel?"

Terry nodded, "Probably, let's stay here and have a fag to make sure."

Terry passed out the cigarettes and then pulled out a box of matches and struck one, lit Wobble's cigarette, then Dave's, before lighting his own. Without thinking and being used to carelessly tossing lit matches on asphalt roads and gravel playgrounds, Terry threw the match carelessly to one side. The tiny glowing ember on the match head landed on a nearby tent bag causing it to immediately burst into flames. The three boys stared for a brief second, watching in horror, at the rapidly spreading flames before they turned and then crawled as quickly as they could towards the hatch.

Terry flung it open and clambered out, before turning back and grabbing Wobble under the arms to drag him up onto the stage. He practically dumped Wobble onto the floor before returning into the cloud of smoke that was now pouring up from under the stage. Dave was struggling in the hatch as Terry grabbed him by the wrist and pulled him up. In the chaos, Dave's bootlaces caught on the trap door hinge, and he tumbled back down into the flaming abyss, his T-shirt immediately catching fire. The young boy screamed and tried desperately to pull it off. Terry reached through the smoke again, choking as he grabbed Dave by the wrist and pulled, as hard as he could, this time succeeded in getting Dave fully up onto the stage and beat out the flames that were hurting his friend.

The three boys ran for the open church door and burst out, gulping the fresh air once outside. They ran up the grassy slope toward Stag Lane and the South entrance of "The Poets," the sprawling council estate where they all lived. Reaching the road, Terry and Wobble turned to look back. Dave was halfway up the slope, laying on the ground, curled up in a ball crying and whimpering in pain. His back was red raw, and the skin was peeling off, it was clear he would need medical attention. The church hall was a ball of flame, sirens could be heard in the distance.

"What do we do Tel?" Wobble looked at his friend desperately. Terry hesitated for a couple of seconds, but to Wobble it felt like forever.

"Let's go."

“But Dave?” Wobble glanced around nervously before his eyes returned to his injured friend.

“He’ll understand.” Terry responded abruptly, cutting Wobble off before he attempted to change Terry’s mind. The two boys turned, crossed the road and headed into The Poets.

1

MONDAY, 20 JULY 1981.

Dave's eyes slowly and begrudgingly opened, the alarm was playing syrupy middle of the road music, the kind that Radio One and Tony Blackburn thrived on pushing on the teenage population who still believed there was hope and happiness in life. He is confused, confused to the point of thinking that he is still dreaming. But he has one eye open, so he can't be. The annoying Bucks Fizz drivel is still droning over the radio and the pink blinds covering the windows clearly aren't his, hardly, although the shade matches his hair, "Where am I?" He wanted to shout, but he was unsure who else was in the room with him, and there was a deep, innate fear that prevented him. A fear of being exposed, after all, he had no idea how he got here, wherever he was, or who else might be here.

Slowly lifting his head from the pillow, a pink, delicately scented pillow, that boded well for him at least, he turned towards the centre of the bed, the centre of the room, the centre of his fear. A face closed in, mouth puckered, ready for a kiss, ready to resume whatever passion he had clearly forgotten from the night before.

Bucks Fizz continued to sing about making your mind up, and the sudden realisation of who the nearing face belonged to, caused Dave to shout. "What the fuck!" and roll off the opposite side of the bed.

Kneeling on the floor, he raised his head and looked up, stared at the naked girl, as she knelt on the bed screaming at him. Her lipstick was smeared, black mascara running from heavily made-up eyes marking her cheeks with grey tear streaks, rolls of fat jiggling on her belly as she continues to yell at him. Dave scrambled and tried desperately to piece together the previous evening. The words slowly start to make sense, his eyes beginning to focus, but his brain can't keep up. The problem being the more his brain starts to function, the more his head hurts, the more the words start to come to him, clearer and clearer.

"You bastard, I wasn't too rough for you last night, was I? Oh no. You couldn't wait, you practically pulled it out in the minicab, couldn't wait to get me back here, you arsehole, you're just like all the rest with your morning after rethink, I should have known better..........."

Dave looked around the room desperate to find his trousers. He was wearing his t-shirt, he never goes bare chested, the burn scars had made him too self-conscious for that. Trying to figure a way out, he spotted them lying on the ground nearby. He stood, started to head across the room on wobbly legs, and scooped them up. As he was pulling his trousers up, he glanced down and spotted his morning glory standing tall and proud. He chuckled nervously as he looked up at the still yelling, still naked girl and asked, "No chance of a quickie before work then?"

It was early Monday morning, too early for much traffic even. A few cars, buses, and newspaper delivery vans passed Dave as he embarked on his walk of shame. He stopped in a cafe and got a cup of tea and a bacon sandwich to go. The girl, Vickie, had given him enough money for the train fare, but then he couldn't afford a sandwich and after all what was the rush? Dave never went to work on a Monday, most of his friends didn't either, hence their semi-permanent state of unemployment. It was becoming harder and harder to find employment and, if or when, they were lucky enough to, their generally lackadaisical attitude towards it, along with their love of drugs and alcohol, usually meant that it was fleeting at best. Instead, he would walk and enjoy his sandwich. And why not? Since, along with the money, Vickie had given him a packet of Resolve, a vitamin boost, so his hangover was receding, as it worked its mysterious magic.

As he walked, Dave looked around. This was a much nicer part of the city than where he lived and had grown up. There were detached houses with nice front gardens, walled in with brick walls. The kind of walls Dave's uncle, a brickie, had told him about building, for some quick cash jobs on Saturday mornings. These were the kind of places he could never afford. The type of district Dave could walk through without fear, yet the people who lived there were always in fear. They feared loss in a way that Dave, and his kind didn't, couldn't understand. After all, Dave thought to himself, what did they have to lose?

The 52 bus drove past and Dave jumped onto the platform at the back, hoping that, with luck, he'd make it most of the way to the estate before the conductor rumbled him for non-payment and kicked him off. The bus headed through Blackbird hill, left onto Church Lane. The conductor came down the stairs calling out, "Tickets please."

A passenger stood up from the bench nearest the back and stepped onto the platform, "Wanna read?" He said, giving Dave a nod, "Samantha Fox is a knockout today."

"Would I ever," Dave replied, practically snatching the copy of that day's Sun, "Thanks mate." Dave sat where the passenger had been sitting and held the paper up high in front of his face.

The ruse worked, the conductor passed by still calling, "Fares please," while Dave enjoyed what the topless, amply breasted Samantha Fox had to offer.

At the top of Church Lane, Dave jumped from the bus at the lights, the stop just before meant walking a little further, the stop after further still, so the gamble was to hope for a red light and jump then, as Dave did today.

"Hey", Dave turned to see the conductor's angry face, "That's not safe, did you even pay?" Dave laughed at him, shot him two fingers and walked away into the drizzling rain and the estate, unsure of which he hated more.

The outer rings of the estate consisted of row houses, the roads built in circles, all named after trees: Oak, Pine, Elm, Acacia. "What the hell was an Acacia?" Dave wondered for the umpteenth time, he had no idea and would never bother to look it up. He cut through the alleys that led directly toward the centre of the estate, between the high brick walls, the tops of which were studded with broken glass; he often wondered whether it was to keep people in, or out. As he turned a corner, the tower blocks loomed above him, some twelve stories high, six of them in total, all identical, all named after poets. There was Coleridge, Byron, Keats, Blake, Yeats and Wordsworth where Dave lived. Dave stopped and stared. He had lived here his entire life, and yet he was always dumbfounded by it, the sheer ugliness, the drabness, the lack of any craft or saving grace. He often thought that the lives of the inhabitants were doomed to the same drudgery and lack of imagination as these facades represented, and the thought always depressed him. From his room on the ninth floor of Wordsworth House, Dave could see beyond the estate, into the city. He would often find himself dreaming of a life out there, anywhere but here, but other than the literal tube ride, he couldn't imagine how to get there.

As he headed for home, Dave passed a milk float, slyly pinching a pint of milk as he did, gold top, the creamiest they made. With one jabbing motion with his thumb, he punctured the foil top and poured the thick, creamy liquid down his throat. He entered through the front glass doors of Wordsworth House, no buzzers or intercoms here, tossing the now empty milk bottle into the corner of the lobby. He grinned, enjoying the loud, echoing, clinking sound as he pushed the up button to the lift. The doors slid open, the stench of piss almost driving him back out of the door again, but Dave had no interest in walking up nine flights of stairs. The lift always stank so much worse on Monday mornings, after all the piss artists used it as a urinal on their way home from the pubs and clubs on the weekend.

"Fucking animals, they've got toilets in their flats, lazy bastards." As the doors slid open on the ninth floor to release him from the stench, Dave nearly bowled over Mrs. Bartrum, his friend Carl's mum. "Watch where you're barging you damn fool," she shouted at him.

"Sorry Queenie! It's worse than usual in there today!"

"Don't give you the right to knock me flat," Queenie tried to regain her composure.

"Carl at home?" Dave ignored her comment.

"No, he goes to work on Mondays, unlike the rest of you," the old lady glared at him, spitting out the words, clearly looking down her nose at what she perceived as Dave's lifestyle choices.

"He's a good man, your Carl, you should be proud!"

"I am, I don't need you telling me that!" She brushed past him, stepping on to the lift before continuing, "Now let go of the door and let me go, before this stink kills me."

"Sorry Queen, give Carl my best!" Dave half smiled and waved at her.

"Who you calling Queen, bloody cheek--" The lift doors slid closed, cutting off the remainder of her tirade.

At the front door of the flat Dave pulled out his keys and unlocked one, then two locks, "'Allo?" There was no answer, as he'd expected. Dave headed straight into his room, the walls bedecked with posters of The Clash, 999, Steel Pulse, The U.K Subs. The floor was carpeted with piles of dirty laundry, the dingy, glass windows covered in tape and newspaper in place of curtains: The Daily Mirror, full of stories about the miner's strike, unemployment, Jimmy Savilles latest good deeds for kids. Opening a bedside table drawer, Dave removed a joint, collapsed on the bed, lit it, and took a long draw, "This is the fucking life."

It was 11:22 when Dave surfaced from his Monday morning nap. He rolled out of bed, pulled off his dirty Siouxsie Sioux T-shirt and headed for the bathroom. A quick face wash, teeth brushing, deodorant application and he was set. A quick root through the piles on the bedroom floor, retrieval of one of his favourite shirts; a Tintin type cartoon on the front, with the title character throwing up in the street, his Bobby Soxer girlfriend looking on with text that reads, "WHAT'S THE MATTER STEVE IS IT TEENAGE ANGST OR TOO MUCH LAGER?" It always brought a smile to his face, not so much because he got the joke, but more because most of the people he mixed with didn't.

Stepping into the kitchen, Dave opened the freezer door. The freezer on top of the fridge hadn't worked for as long as he could remember. There was no food in there, but there was an old jam jar. Dave took it out, undid the lid and pulled out the contents. Money, five- and ten-pound notes, its familiar smell killed off from months sitting in the freezer and replaced by the smell of mould. His mum's rainy-day fund, Dave thought it a stupid name, this was England, and it was always fucking raining. After a quick count and discovering a hundred and eighty quid Dave took a twenty and put the rest back. He'd replace it when he could afford to, of course he would. What amazed him was that this wasn't the first time and yet his mum had never noticed, which he found strange, but maybe she never counted it. Oh well he'd make sure to return it before she did, but first he just had to get a better job that's all. He bolted out the front door and down the stairs. Going down the stairs was easier than facing the stench in the lift. Out the front doors he took a left turn and a short walk, yet again in the rain, past Coleridge house and Byron and there it was, the boozer.

The Laureate, not the most upmarket boozer you could find, despite the overly noble name the developers had shouldered it with. Why would it be? Considering where it was located, but it was home base for Dave and the boys. Somewhere to launch their sorties out into the grime and crime of London. To drown their sorrows if Arsenal lost, and to celebrate if they won. To party when there was an occasion, or to drink, as was the norm, for no reason other than the drink itself. Dave pushed the door to the public bar open, and there they were, as usual on a Monday, the cast of characters.

They were lined up along the bar like the characters in a western, if cowboys had dyed hair in a multitude of styles, cropped like Terry, Ray and Donnie, spiked like Alex, a pink crop like Dave, or if cowboys wore steel toed Dr. Marten boots and ripped T shirts or the Fred Perry, Levi's, boots and braces uniform of the skinheads. Dave sauntered in to join the ensemble.

"Afternoon gentlemen, oh and you lot."

That's when it began, first as a whisper, then slightly louder, "Vickie… Vickie… VICKIE"

"Hey Vickie, I'm gonna fuck you tonight!"

"Fuck you.... I didn't," they all start to talk at once, "You were doing the one step forward two steps back shuffle, you probably thought you were dancing but you were so pissed you couldn't stand still."

"Guns of Navarone was playing and as it ended you shouted, 'HEY VICKIE!'"

"But the song ends, and you know the way that wanker Kevin always leaves a long pause before he plays a U2 song?"

"As if it's a religious moment or something, Irish twat."

"Well, it was one of those."

"And in the silence, you shout… 'I'M GONNA FUCK YOU TONIGHT!!'"

"The whole bar freezes and then everyone starts to laugh!"

"Except Vickie, she was on you like David Jenkins."

Everybody stopped talking suddenly and stared at Donnie. Ray spoke up, "Who the fuck is David Jenkins?"

Donny looked stunned, "He was a famous Scottish sprinter"

Ray shook his head, "Well you're not in fucking Scotland now, for fuck sakes."

"Oh aye," Donny replied, "Name me a famous English sprinter then, I bet ye canny."

The others all stared at each other.

Finally, Alex spoke up, "Roger Bannister."

Terry piped in, "Yeah Roger Bannister."

Donny shook his head, "He was a four-minute miler, not a fucking sprinter."

Alex looked confused, "So what?"

"It's not the same, is it?"

"Why not?"

"'Cause a sprint's a hundred yards, a mile's a lot more than that."

Big Ray begins to get testy, "So what, at least he was English."

"Yeah, but a hundred-yard dash is what you do to get back to the lads after you've thrown a brick at those Chelsea scumbags, a four-minute mile's more like what you need to escape the pigs after you've been rumbled doing a B and E."

With the difference explained in clear terms they can all understand, they turn their attention back to Dave.

Terry is first to restart the assault, "She was on you so fast you didn't 'ave time to feel your 'ead spin and out the door you went."

The laughter washed over him like acid, stinging, unstoppable, then it hit him, the perfect retort. He ran his eyes along the line and then started at the left end with Terry, "You've had her!" Next were Alex and Donnie, "You two had her at the same time, I was there, remember? You even took her out on a date before you did her Ray, there's no one in this room has the right to act all high and mighty with me, not about that slag anyway."

Big Ray looked along the line, "What's this about you two at the same time?"

Alex and Donnie glanced at each other sheepishly. After a pause, Donnie started, in a thick, Glaswegian brogue, "Aah what the fuck, we were drunk one night over in Golder's Green at one of those college parties, you know how it is?"

"Apparently I don't, or I didn't till Dave here enlightened me, go on."

Alex took up the tale, "Well she, Vickie that is, was up in a bedroom with one of those college dicks."

Dave laughs, joins in, "It was a toga party!"

This is too much for Ray, "A fucking toga party? You wankers were wearing togas?"

Donnie laughed, "Ach no, we were in some posh boozer in St John's Wood, we couldn't get into The Music Machine to see The Clash, fucking middle class posers had bought all the tickets.

Anyhow, the place was wall to wall with strange tail and college boys, all dressed like Romans, we didn't fit in one bit."

Dave carries the story, "Those birds couldn't get enough, bit of rough on a Friday night like."

Donnie is really into telling the story now, "Aye, so they invited us to this toga party, but 'cause we had no togas we had to agree to strip to our undies like, Alex here was dancing up a storm."

"Yes, I was, it was a great crack, wasn't getting anywhere with these college birds though, then Dave comes across looking like the cat that got the cream."

"I couldn't believe my eyes, I come out of the upstairs khazi and there's Vicki slipping into one of the bedrooms with one of these stuck-up dickheads."

Ray's head swivels from one to the other as the story unfolded, "So?"

Alex shrugs, "We were already in our underwear, and we just thought we'd have some fun."

Donnie laughed, "Aye, a bit of a crack like, it was Dave's idea."

"That's right, put the finger on me why don't ya? Anyway, we gave them a couple of minutes, to make sure they got started like and then we stripped right down and burst into the room."

"It was freaking priceless, best crack I've had since I left Glasgow, this posh dickhead's pumping away with this deadly serious look on his face, like he was scared he was gonna shite himself or summat."

Ray looked amazed, "You all ran in naked?"

Alex laughed, "Like I said it was Dave's idea." Donny continued, "'cept he wasn't naked was he, oh no he had to keep his precious t-shirt on like always, didn't he?"

Terry looked uncomfortable about the t-shirt comment, it always bothered him when the subject came up. Dave continued the story oblivious to the crack. "Yeah, but we wasn't going to do anything, 'cept when we get in there dickhead starts shouting and yelling at us to get out, these two start rubbing Vickie's titties and she's telling him, "It's okay I know them, let them stay, let them stay" college boy storms out and these two climb on."

Ray's head was swiveling from side to side "And where was you in all this Dave?"

"Me? I was curled up in the corner, I couldn't stop laughing."

Ray shakes his head with a big grin spread across his face, "I guess Dave's right, not one of us has the right to give him shit on this one."

"I dunno," says Terry, "He did shout it across the bar on disco night and his mum and dad were here to see or should I say hear it"

Dave's face falls, "Fuck you, they weren't!"

Ray is now convulsed laughing, "Oh yes, they were!"

"Fuck you Terry, how much did that Vindaloo cost you to get in her pants?"

"Worth every penny, she blew me in the cab after!"

Alex shook his head, "Real classy. Like Ray said we don't have a lot of right to make fun of Dave on this one..."

"No, we don't, hey barkeep, bottle of Whitetop for my friend Dave here"

"Thanks Ray, I'll get you back later, shame Carl's not here."

"You're welcome, Dave, why's that?"

"Well don't let Sherry find out, but he had her bent over the shelves in his work van a couple of weeks back."

Ray froze, the beer halfway to Dave's hand, "You what?"

"Yeah, he was working in one of her neighbour's houses, bumps into her, she asks him for a ride and apparently that's what he gave her."

An uneasy silence falls over the group, broken, after a little while, by Ray, his voice clearly annoyed, "Wish you hadn't told me that."

"What? What's it matter? Like you said we've all had her."

Alex shrugs and says, "That's different."

Ray stared at Dave, "Here drink your beer."

"Thanks, like I said I'll get you back later."

Still with a face like a wet week Ray said, "Put something on the jukebox Alex, you cheap bastard"

Alex goes to the jukebox, slides ten pence into the slot and as he turns to walk away Bette Davis Eyes, by Kim Carnes, began to play.

Ray stared at him, and says, "Oh fuck off will you!"

Alex started to sing along, and the others, except for Ray, joined in. Dave grabbed Terry's hand and they mockingly slow danced across the bar singing loudly and out of tune. A tall muscular skinhead and a pink haired skinny punk rocker doing their best Fred Astaire and Ginger Rogers.

Gerry, the pub landlord, hurried around the corner from the saloon bar, to investigate the noise, "What in the name of God is going on, you're disturbing the lunch crowd in the other bar."

Ray stared at him momentarily, "Calm down Paddy, the boys are just having some fun, how about another round of lagers? "Oi Dave put Terry down for a minute, it's your shout, thought you'd've had your fill with Vickie last night anyway."

Dave released Terry, and headed towards the bar, as the boys began to sing, "She's precocious and she knows just what it takes to make a pro blush."

2

Three o'clock, the inevitable end of the party, the boys staggered out into the afternoon, into the rain-soaked brick paved courtyard, under grey foreboding skies. All of them with bar mats hanging from their back pockets, ready to be sown or pinned to jackets or jeans later. Gerry shook his head in disgust as he slammed and locked the pub doors. Alex staggered to one side, threw up over the side of a brick wall down into the loading bay below.

Terry turned to the others and joked, "We should tip him over."

Ray nodded in agreement, "Cost us a lock-in, useless twat."

Donnie chimed in, "You'd think he could handle a few voddies, you English poofs canny drink to save your lives!"

Ray, full of beer and not about to let his countrymen be besmirched span around suddenly and violently, "If it's so good in Scotland, why don't you fuck off back up there!"

"I would, but there's no work is there?"

Ray sniped, "There's no work here either you stupid fuck, what there is gets stolen by you fucking immigrants!"

Donnie spat back, "You can thank your darling Maggie Thatcher for both the lack of jobs, and for us coming south, her and her precious poll tax. Me dad had no choice but to kick me out, and I'm no fucking immigrant, I'm as British as the rest of ye."

Dave sized up the situation, there was no way Donnie, at only five foot eight but solid muscle, and an inheritor of a stubborn Glaswegian pride, that negated the possibility of backing down, as evidenced by the multiple scars that decorate his face will back down now. Similarly, Ray, who was six foot six, his upper body shaped like a triangle of solid muscle and covered in tattoos, and currently free after a two-year stretch for armed robbery, isn't exactly the negotiating type.

Terry watched, leaning on the window of a closed down store. The store was the last one, in the now empty precinct, to go, cut priced clothes of poor quality and higher prices than what can be bought a short bus ride, or a long walk away in the new Brent Cross shopping centre. Alex sat waiting for the inevitable explosion of violence, leaving Dave to feel as if he had little or no choice but to intervene somehow. Thinking quickly, Dave ran down the ramp to the loading bay where there was a pallet of bricks. grabbed one, ran back up the ramp and threw it through the store window, the explosion of the glass shattering shocked everyone into instant reaction. Dave laughed and shouted, "Whoo-hoo, c'mon scarper!"

Ray and Donnie stood there, chest to chest, almost touching, they span around toward the sound of the screaming alarm, and the whooping Dave. Alex, still in a stupor, and sitting on the wet ground, shook his head, trying to comprehend the situation. Terry, the only one, other than Dave, to fully understand what had happened, and why, looked at Dave and winked, and the instant before he started to run, shouted, "You crazy bastard!!"

Donnie ran to Alex, grabbed his wrist and pulled him upright, "Come on, you dinna wanna be left holding the can for that crazy fuck."

As they crossed the main courtyard, still running full tilt, Dave, Donnie and Alex whooped and hollered at the top of their lungs, they split into three factions. Why would they care about being inconspicuous anyway? The only people watching were a group of kids outside Wordsworth, twelve or thirteen years old, bunking off school, smoking cigarettes, trying to look tough.

Ray headed to the right, down the same alley Dave used to enter the estate earlier. A 183 bus going slowly behind a milk float provided a quick escape. Ray ran alongside, grabbing the silver pole on the back deck before jumping aboard.

Donnie and Alex ran to the left, Alex throwing up on himself as they did, one of the kids outside Wordsworth shouted, "That's fucking lovely, look at you, you fucking drunk." Turning back to a cute looking girl in the group chest puffed out, proud, "That told him, fucking wanker."

Dave and Terry barreled straight up to the kids; Dave grabbed a pack of smokes from the shouter's hand as they passed on their way into the tower block. "Oi, what the fuck, those are mine!"

Dave taunted him, "Call it a tax for your loudmouth you cheeky little git!"

"Fuck you Dave, my brother won't like this!"

Terry stopped, "Your brother's gonna do fuck all about it."

"I was talking to Dave, Terry, not you," the kid replied.

"Yeah well, you're talking to me now, got it?"

"Yeah, I got it," the kid grumbled, defeated.

In the meantime, Alex and Donnie disappeared down the winding alleys toward Colindale. After a while Donnie left Alex doubled over, throwing up against a brick wall, as he headed off to see his date for the afternoon; a married woman with time and conscience to spare.

Dave and Terry crossed the lobby and Terry pushed the button for the lift, "Fuck that, I'm not making that journey twice in a day."

"That bad?"

"Worse," they headed up the stairs, and Dave held out the stolen cigarettes, "Got a light?"

Terry pulled out a Zippo lighter, flicked it back and then forward again across his leg and held it up, lit, Dave laughed, "Flash bastard."

"D'you want a light or not?" Dave put a fag in his mouth and as he lit it, held out the pack to Terry, who took it and lit himself one. They sat on the stairs and Dave stared out at the city through a hole in the frosted window, "It always seems right in the rain."

Terry looked at him, "What does?"

"The city, the grey suits it, do you ever think about all the crime going on out there at any given moment, the evictions, the misery, the deaths?"

"Aren't you cheerful?" Terry rolled his eyes and took a drag of his cigarette.

Dave continued, "False hope is ultimately a far greater tragedy than no hope!"

"Who do you think you are, John Cooper Clarke?" he replied, flicking his ashes to the ground.

"No," Dave stammered a moment, "you know what I mean though?

"Yeah, I know,"

Dave continued, "I've been writing some poetry."

"You probably don't want the others to hear that."

"Probably not," the boy shrugged.

"Best to keep it on the Q.T. Between you and me."

Dave looked at Terry hopefully, "Wanna hear it?"

Terry scoffed, "No Dave, I do not want to hear your poetry."

"Okay then…" his voice trailed off, defeated.

"You live in your head too much, Dave."

"It's the only place I like, I mean look at the fucking world we inhabit," Dave gestured wildly around them, "that's not what I call living, hardly, what's the point?"

"And what the fuck was that with the window, you could've cost me my job!"

"You didn't do it!"

"No," Terry's eyes narrowed, "but if the pigs came, they'd pick me up anyway!"

"For what? You didn't do nuffin, there's no charge."

"They could pick me up on Sus though," Terry shrugged and attempted to blow a ring of smoke.

"That'd be a first," Dave chuckled, "I can just see the news headlines now, White man picked up on Sus, Thatcher outraged, plans to rewrite law to prevent any such barbarism from happening again!"

"You're crazy, you know that don't you?"

Dave puffed out his chest, "Proud of it!"

"Got any smoke?"

"I've got some sensi that'll leave you senseless, got it in Willesden when I went to see Linton Kwezi Johnston."

Terry folded his arms across his chest, "You know you're not black right?"

"I'm not?" Dave smirked.

"What the fuck are we sitting here for, if we could be getting stoned?"

The journey to the ninth floor resumed. Terry and Alex were the only ones with full time jobs, apart from Carl that is, but Carl wasn't a full-time member of the group, couldn't be, the colour of his skin prevented that. Terry worked for the Post Office, The Royal Mail, to be more precise. His workday started at two in the morning, which was tough if he allowed himself out on a work night and he only did that if someone he simply couldn't miss was playing at one of the many punk clubs in the city. On those occasions he would go straight from the club to work. The advantage was he was finished by eleven in the morning most days, allowing him to spend his afternoons drinking and smoking.

Donnie arrived in front of number 317 Churchill Terrace, a third floor flat in a low rise building in Grahame Park Estates, Colindale, the type where the front doors opened onto an outdoor landing. He didn't knock, he was expected, and Sandra didn't want him standing outside in full view any longer than necessary. Entering the flat he started to undo his boots when a voice called, "What's taking you so long?"

"On my way." What the fuck, it might be hot doing it semi naked he thought and headed upstairs. Sandra sat on the edge of the bed wearing only a man's shirt, "Hey, I wore this for you, d'you like it?"

"Is that his?"

"Yep!"

"Then I like it a lot, yeah."

"Show me!" The sex was the hottest it had ever been between them, and Donnie was about to climax when there was a huge crash, the front door bursting open. Donnie sat up quickly, "Who the fuck's that?"

Sandra scrambled off the bed, "It must be my husband!"

"What?"

"Get out!" She loudly whispered as she scooped up his clothing and threw them towards him.

Donnie gathered his things, peering around the room, "Where?"

"Through the window," she pointed towards a narrow window that Donnie was unsure would even open wide enough.

"You're fucking kidding me?"

Sandra ushered him toward the window, rushing in front to pull it open, "Quick!"

"You know we're three floors up, right?" Donnie desperately tried to pull his trousers up, gather his shirt and Harrington jacket in his arms and cross the room. At the same time as Sandra hurried to make the bed. when the bedroom door suddenly burst open and two police officers stormed in. Or to be more precise, a policeman and a policewoman.

The policewoman screamed, "Get down!" And rugby tackled the still semi-naked Donnie to the floor.

The policeman shouts at Sandra, "Are you okay?"

Sandra stared at them totally bemused, Donnie, trousers and underwear still around his knees hit the floor. The policewoman rolls over the top of him knocking over a stand with a vase and flowers on it, the vase shattered in the process, much to Sandra's chagrin, "My mum bought me that!"

Donnie and the W.P.C lie on the floor staring at each other, Donnie grins impishly at her, "'Allo sweetheart."

"Shut up," she turned to Sandra, "you okay love?"

Sandra snarled "Apart from the vase, yeah why?"

"You might want to cover up," she replied. Sandra looked down at herself, and realised she was naked. She glanced up at the young policeman who was staring, lasciviously, at her breasts, "Want a picture?" He blushed and turned away. Sandra picked up her husband's shirt and pulled it over her head, "What the fuck are you two doing here anyway?"

The W.P.C hoisted herself up from the floor, Donnie smiled, "Don't go."

"Constable Gardiner ma'am, we had a report of an intruder."

"From who?" Sandra looked confused.

"One of your neighbours and as there have been several break-ins on the estate recently we thought we'd take it very seriously."

Having recomposed himself, the policeman cleared his throat and asked, "Do you know this man?"

"What?"

"The man lying semi-naked on your bedroom floor, do you know him?" He repeated.

Sandra rolled her eyes, "No, I always shag strangers, what do you think?"

Gardiner tried to cut in and stop the inevitable argument that she could see coming, "We have to make sure he wasn't assaulting you; we're just doing our jobs."

"I bet it was that cunt in 307, wasn't it?"

"We aren't at liberty to discuss that."

"She's always sticking her nose in where it doesn't belong!"

"That's neither here nor there, now, do you know this man?"

"Yes, I know him, now if you'll get out of my way, I'm going to have a chat with my neighbour."

The policeman stepped in front of the bedroom door, "We can't let you do that!"

"I'd like to see you stop me," Sandra glared at him.

The two officers stared awkwardly at each other, Donnie shrugged, "Guess I'll get dressed? Unless one of you ladies...?" He looks at Sandra with a hopeful look on his face, her mouth falling open, "What do you think Donnie? Really?"

Donnie pulled on his shirt dejectedly, "I'll likely get blue balls otherwise."

Sandra and the male cop stood in the bedroom doorway in an awkward standoff, Sandra tried to step around him, "I'm going down the hallway."

He stepped back in front of her, "I can't let you do that... but I will tell you this, the person who called doesn't even live in this building." Sandra's face fell, as the truth suddenly hit her. "Are you okay madam?"

"I know who called, she's supposed to be at work."

Gardiner crossed the room toward her, "Who?"

"My sister-in-law, she lives in the building opposite, so I only let Donnie come over when she's at work... she'll tell him everything."

The other three stood in an awkward silence, broken by Donnie, "Gotta go."

Sandra is crestfallen, "You can't just walk out and leave me like this!"

The male cop stood in the doorway, "No he can't, we need to see some I.D."

Donnie stood firmly in front of him, "Unless you're arresting me, I don't have to show you Jack shit."

"You do if I say you do!" the cop broadened his stance.

"Just cause I'm not from here doesn't make me stupid you know, the laws the same in Glasgow as it is here and unless you've got a reason to charge me I dinna have ta show you shit!"

"Careful sweaty!"

Donnie smirked at the Cockney insult for The Scots, "Oh now you're a crafty Cockney, are ya?" The two now stood nose to nose. Donnie spoke first, "I'll tell ye what, you answer a question of law for me, and I'll cooperate with whatever you like."

"What's the question?"

"If I call you a cunt you can arrest me, can't you?"

He sneered at Donnie, "Of course, I can."

"But if I just think you're a cunt there's nothing you can do about it, is there?"

Constable Gardiner started to pay attention, "Don't let him bait you!"

But it was too late. "I can't police your thoughts, no."

Donnie sneered back, "Well I think you're a cunt!"

The officer grabbed Donnie and tried to pin him against the wall, but lacked the strength or technique, which allowed Donnie to easily twist free. Constable Gardiner joined in and tried to pin him. Sandra grabbed Gardiner by the hair. The two women fell to the floor screaming. At this point Sandra's husband came striding down the hallway, grabbed Donnie around the neck and swung at him, hitting him on the chin, but to no effect. Donnie headbutted the poor cuckold, leaving him senseless, sliding down the door frame, blood pouring from his shattered nose. Sandra had got the better of Gardiner and was sitting on her chest, hitting her in the face with the telephone. The policeman grabbed Sandra and pulled her off. Sandra screamed, "Let go of me you fucking bastard, I'll kill you too!" Donnie surveyed the room, muttered, "Fuck this," before he walked away down the corridor.

3

Ray jumped from the bus in Blackbird Hill, outside the Old Blackbird Inn, a pub that had seen better days and was renowned for the musty smell that hit you when you opened the doors. It always reminded him of how a cell gets to smell when three men have been locked up together 23 hours a day for weeks on end, and for that reason he avoided the place as much as he could. Ray's cousin, Mitch, who lived in the flats behind The Blackbirds was a regular in the snug bar, and Ray found himself with no choice but to go there when he had to see him. The other reason Ray avoided the place and the area in general was because directly across the road was the entrance to the sprawling Chalkhill estates. "The ghetto," Ray called it.

Chalkhill, the irony of the name always made Ray smirk, almost all the tenants were Black. The last white man Ray knew to live there was a guy named Gary. Gary and his family had moved out after one infamous night when Gary had gone upstairs to the third floor, at three in the morning, to demand his neighbours turn off the booming reggae music. Gary liked a bit of Dennis Brown every now and then, but this was ridiculous. After much banging on the door his neighbours came out and without listening to a word Gary had to say, they picked him up and threw him off the balcony. Three months later, after Gary came out of hospital, he moved as far away as he could, back to his native Manchester, and away from the supposedly gold paved streets of London.

The atmosphere in the Blackbird always smelt of violence. The snug bar was frequented by white working-class men, from the north side of the pub, the public bar was strictly Black only. The rules were unofficial but strictly adhered to. The men from the estate would play dominoes loudly and raucously at a dazzling speed. On Saturday nights, at closing time the police cars and paddy wagons would line the street waiting for the inevitable explosion of Red Stripe and whiskey fueled violence.

Ray strode down the street, straight towards the knot of young Black men blocking the pavement, he wasn't going to go round them. Why should he? This was his country. A young, Black woman, holding her child's hand to keep her safe from the rumbling traffic heading for the North Circular Road pulled the child closer to keep her safe from this more imminent threat.

The young men saw Ray approach, turned to face him, arms crossed, chests puffed out in defiance, one of them, Dejean Maitland, or "Mustard," to his friends, was Carl's cousin. He knew who Ray was, knew what he was capable of, but was determined to stand his ground. One of his sidekicks, Samson, only 14 years old, stood beside Dejean determined not to let him down, no matter what.

Ray was about ten paces from them, about to break into a run, to crash through the wall of humanity, when a car roared up behind him, half on the pavement, half on the road. The car screeched to a halt, the front bumper touching Ray's calf muscle. Ray turned and stared at the blackened windows, his eyes unable to penetrate through and see who was inside. His heart raced, his mouth went dry, his brain tried desperately to find a way out of the predicament he now faced. A wall of young Black men to his back, a car driven by God knows who, to his front. The engine roared, Ray's head swiveled from side to side, Dejean and his friends crept closer, the car window wound down.

"Get in you fucking wanker!" Relief crossed Ray's face as he saw his cousin, Mitch. He didn't have to be asked twice! Quickly, he ran to the passenger door, and jumped in. Mitch stomped on the accelerator, the car roared forward, Dejean and two of his cohort jumped backward, to avoid being run over. Mitch threw a half empty can of beer out of the window, spraying them with the suds and laughed out loud as he pulled into the traffic. In the rear-view mirror, he could see them gesticulating and shouting at him.

Ray laughed in relief, "What the fuck! Where'd you get the motor?"

"Is that your way of saying thank you, if I hadn't shown up Shaka Zulu back there would have skinned you alive."

"Fuck them, and fuck you, I should kick your teeth in for that little stunt you pulled back there."

"Shut up and have a beer," Mitch nodded his head to indicate an open case on the back seat, "What you doing down in the jungle anyway?"

Ray grumbled, "My probie got me a job interview down in Harlesden, I was just changing buses."

"Is he trying to get you killed?"

"It's she and yeah, probably. I figured if I showed up late and half-drunk, they'd never hire me."

"What's the job?"

"Butcher's shop."

Mitch chortled, "They're gonna let you handle a knife in public?"

"Apparently," Ray took a long swig of the beer.

"Don't know you very well, do they?"

"I guess not," he looked annoyed and changed the subject, "So where'd you get such a flash motor?"

"It was left out with no one to take care of it, so I figured it was my civic duty to give it a better home."

"D'you know what will happen to me if I'm caught in a stolen car? I'll be back inside before you can say shit."

"So, you should be too."

The two men burst out laughing, Mitch yanked the wheel to the right, and roared down a narrow side street, cars parked on both sides, barely a foot to spare on either side of the speeding car. Ray pointed out the sad truth to Mitch, "You know this thing's gonna stand out like a sore thumb at your place? Flash motor like this."

"Not in Chelsea it won't."

"You don't live in Chelsea."

"No, but I thought I'd head down there this aft and lift some car stereos. Maybe get a bit of posh tail while I'm at it."

"Yeah right, the car might fit in down there, but you? Not so much."

"You cheeky git, you coming?"

Ray stared at the car floor, "Can't, I've got an interview to fail."

"That should only take 5 minutes, I'll wait. Watch this!" Ray looked up to see an East Indian man exiting his car up ahead. Mitch accelerated and the car surged forward. "What are you doing!?" Ray exclaimed.

"I'm gonna scare the shit out of him!" Mitch laughed and gripped the steering wheel tight as he swerved the car at the man. The man looked up, opened his mouth to scream, but there was no time. The car hit him in the thigh, he rolled over the passenger side wing and disappeared from view, down beside the car. The impact caused Ray to drop his beer into his own lap and the contents spurted out all over him.

"Stupid Paki, I'll have to dump the car now, why didn't he move?"

Ray looks down into his soaking wet lap, "You stupid fuck, I spilt beer all over me."

"Oh well, you definitely won't get the job now then." The two men cracked up laughing, as the car sped away into the city, leaving the man lying injured in the street, his turban laying on the far side of the street where it had rolled to.

About five minutes later, they pulled up outside Cooper's Fine Olde Butchery Shoppe. Ray climbed out, slamming the door and went inside. Behind the counter stood an East Indian man who looked up at Ray, "Can I help you?"

"I was looking for Mr. Cooper, is he here?"

"I hope not."

"Why's that?"

The shopkeeper leaned against the till, "He's been dead for more than six years."

"Who are you then?"

"I am Abdijay Singh or Mr. Singh to you. This is my shop. And you are?"

"I'm Ray, I have a job interview, but I guess there's been some mistake."

"No, no mistake, I've been expecting you, you're late," he gestured at his watch.

"Something came up."

"So, I smell."

"If this is your shop, how come it still says Cooper's on the sign?"

Mr. Singh shrugged, "My people are big on tradition. I thought it a nice touch to keep Mr. Cooper's name on the sign."

"I thought you lot were vegetarians."

"Many of MY LOT, as you call us are, yes, but many of us aren't. We don't eat beef or pork, but chicken, turkey, duck, lamb, goat we do, but chicken mostly. That's where you come in."

"Me?" Ray followed the shopkeeper as he wandered through the store, "I don't get it."

"The job," Singh stopped and pointed toward a door in the back, "you will be in the back room preparing the birds for sale."

"I haven't said I'll take the job yet."

Singh chuckled, "No, but you will, your probation officer says you have no choice."

"Don't the animals have to be prepared a certain way, according to your beliefs and all that, I'd probably be doing it all wrong. You wouldn't want that would you?"

"Killed and cooked a certain way, yes, we really don't care who washes them." He leaned toward Ray, "Listen, in my culture we believe in rehabilitation, saving lost souls as it were, and I have a feeling your soul needs to be saved."

Ray let out a long sigh, "Fuck me."

The shopkeeper straightened up, "You start tomorrow morning at eight, don't be late and I'll thank you not to use that sort of language in my shop."

Ray turned and walked out the door, muttering under his breath, "I don't fucking believe it."

Dave woke up in his bedroom, to a soft repetitive clicking sound. He groaned, wiped his face with his hands, and surveyed the room. Terry was sprawled on the floor fast asleep. Dave climbed off his bed, stepped over Terry and lifted the arm of his record player that had become stuck in the final grooves of P.I.L's twelve-inch alternative version of Public Image. The instant the repetitive sound was broken Terry stirred awake, "You are not the first thing I want to see when I wake up, what time is it anyway?"

"Fucked if I know." Dave slammed out of his bedroom, into the living room, where his mum was sitting, watching Coronation Street, in an old cloth covered armchair that has certainly seen better days, the arms shiny, almost worn through, stains and a cigarette burn on the right-hand arm, where her ashtray had a permanent home. "What time is it mum?"

From the bedroom Terry shouted, "Hi Jean!"

"Evening Terry," she called back before regarding Dave, "it's about quarter after seven, there's plates in the oven for you both, shepherd's pie and baked beans, and you don't make a very good window."

Dave stepped aside from the tele and headed into the toilet, calling behind him, "Thanks mum."

Shortly after, Terry emerged from the bedroom, "Thanks Jean, you're the best."

"You're welcome, Terry love, just cause he's a waste of space doesn't mean you are, the hours you work you've gotta keep your strength up."

Dave was having a piss, the door half open, "Love you too mum."

"You're welcome too, and what you do in there is private, you could close the door, you know."

Dave walked out, zipping his fly. Terry took the plates from the oven, "Gotta love your shepherd's pie Jean, my favourite." Dave crossed the room, picked up the ketchup and poured it liberally over the entire meal. Terry shook his head, “Fucking Philistine, how you gonna taste anything but the ketchup?”

“That’s the point.”

The iconic closing music of Coronation Street starts to play, Jean pulled herself slowly up from her chair, “I don’t know why I bother, I really don’t.”

“Ignore him Jean, he don’t appreciate anything.”

“I swear, sometimes I think they gave me the wrong one at the hospital Terry, should’ve been you they sent me home with.” Jean winked at him heading toward her bedroom, “I’m turning in, I’m on earlies this week.”

“I know how that is.”

“D’you think you could get him a start down there, Terry?”

“I could, but the first time he screws up it’d be my head on the chopping block.”

“Best not then.”

Dave looked up from his plate, mouth full, “I’m in the room you know.”

Terry stared silently at Dave. Jean snorted, “Yeah, we know,” she laughed and headed into her bedroom, closing the door behind her.

Dave shook his head, “Thanks, I don’t think.”

“It’s true,” Terry took a bite of his food, “if I got you a start the first time you fucked up, I’d be hung out to dry.”

“Yeah?”

“Well then what’s the problem?”

“Why didn’t you just lie and say you couldn’t help me? Say they weren’t hiring, anything but the truth.”

“’Cause I like your mum, she always treats me real nice, I don’t like to lie to her.”

“I like her too,” Dave stammered, “but I don’t lose any sleep over telling her a porkie or two.”

“That’s different, she’s nice to you cause you’re her son, it’s s’posed to be that way, I’m not, so it’s different.” Terry said, between mouthfuls of potatoes. Dave leaned back and thought about it, he knew it was true, he also knew Jean had always had a soft spot for Terry. Terry's dad was, without a doubt, the hardest drinking man any of them had ever met, and that was saying something. His mum had left shortly after Terry's tenth birthday, after his father had battered her one too many times, and he had never seen her again. "I'm sorry son you'd better learn to duck."

Those had been her parting words to her crying son, and Terry learnt very quickly. He had pretty well raised himself from that day on, and Jean had pretty much adopted him. She was the only real mother he'd ever known. For that reason, Terry was fiercely protective of Dave, even if he didn't really understand him. That, and the fact he'd never forgiven himself for the day he'd left him behind on the grass, with his back burnt to a cinder, and condemned him to three months in juvenile hall. After the two young men had finished their meal, they left the flat and started the long descent down the stairs.

As they left the building, the kid, Sammy, the one who Dave had purloined the cigarettes from, shouted across the courtyard, "There they are, aren't you gonna do nothing?"

His older brother stepped forward, Bazza, a hulking muscular man, in his early twenties, arms, neck and face covered in tattoos, more than a match for Dave by far, but then again, most people were. "Hey, Terry, what's going on?"

"Not much Bazza, just heading home, you?"

"I need a word with Dave." Bazza stepped in front of them, his kid brother beside him, his chest puffed out. Dave and Terry stopped walking; a standoff seemed inevitable.

Sammy egged his brother on, "Sort him out, he stole my fags!"

"You know I can't leave it, Terry."

Terry asked Dave, his eyes never leaving Bazza's steady gaze, "How many fags left in the pack?"

Dave pulled the pack from his pocket, opened it, and counted, "Twelve."

Terry nodded thoughtfully, "You have one, give me one, give the rest back and apologise, we'll call it a compromise solution."

Dave put a cigarette in his mouth, handed one to Terry, and turned the rest of the pack over to Bazza. "Sorry about that Baz."

Bazza stared straight into Dave's eyes, "Not to me."

Dave looked at the kid reluctantly, "Sorry about that."

Sammy was none too happy, "What the fuck..." Bazza swatted him on the back of the head, "Sorry about that Terry, he's got a big mouth."

Dave blurted out, "That's what got him in this mess in the first place!" Terry swatted Dave on the back of the head. "What the fuck?"

"You've got a big mouth too."

Terry and Bazza stood facing each other, eye to eye. After what seemed to Terry to be an eternity, Bazza spoke, "I guess that's sorted then."

"I guess it is," Terry replied.

"See you around Terry," Bazza gripped his brother by the arm, and turned away, "C'mon you I'm sick of sorting out your problems."

Dave and Terry watched as the brothers left, the younger one twisting and protesting as they did. Terry turned to Dave, "Fucking problems you cause me, Dave."

"You should've told him to fuck off, you could've had him."

"Maybe, maybe not. Sometimes you gotta think, is there any gain before you act, you just don't get that do you?"

"Of course, there was some gain, now I have to buy smokes."

"Why don't you use the money you steal from your mum?"

"How'd you know about that?"

The pair began to walk away, "She told me, d'you think she doesn't notice? She always puts in extra to cover for it, so your dad doesn't find out. Poor Stan, he'd be mortified if he knew his son was a thief. And as for the fags next time you came through the estate without me, you'd have to deal with Bazza yourself, good luck with that."

4

Dave awoke to the sound of banging on his bedroom door, he begrudgingly lifted his head and shouted, “What?”

“I’m leaving for work, you’re already late, get up.” The front door to the flat slammed shut as Dave’s Dad, Stan, headed out to work. Stan worked on the building sites as an “inventory specialist” as he liked to put it. He’d been working as a crane gaffer, where he would direct the tower crane with a walkie talkie. A high paying job, until one windy day, two years back, an I-beam hanging from the crane, had spun out of control, hitting him in the back. His ribs had healed, but the muscle problems never would. To avoid any legal issues, the company had sent their foreman, Jack, around to visit him at the flat, whilst he was recuperating, with a bottle of Stan’s favourite whiskey in hand. Jack waited for the most opportune moment when Stan was suitably lubricated and offered him full time work, although, at a lower pay rate, to run the store sheds on their sites. Stan felt he had little choice. It was 1979, and the country was in recession, jobs were few and far between, and besides, it was very nice of the company to think of him and bring him the whiskey.

Jean had started to take extra shifts at the hospital to make up for the shortfall, and Stan felt they were getting back on their feet again. They could usually afford a couple of pints on a Friday or Sunday night, and takeout fish and chips on a Saturday. They were even managing to “salt away” a little bit, in a savings jar that Jean kept in the old freezer. Life was good. Stan now worked, sitting at the door of the store shed, and kept inventory, on a clipboard, of who took what and when, as he counted his blessings.

Tuesday morning already, Dave couldn’t believe it. He climbed out of his pit, pulled on some clothes, without bothering to wash or brush his teeth, left the flat and set off for work. As he headed out of the estate, a 52 bus passed him, Dave needed to catch it to get to work on time and ran for the stop.

Seeing the conductor on the back platform, Dave shouted, "Hey! Ring the bell, stop the bus." The bus sailed past the stop, and the conductor, the same conductor as on Friday night, gave Dave a wave and turned away. "Arsehole!" Dave shouted, "Fuck!"

He knew there was no way he was going to make it to work on time now, so he figured there was only one choice, Dave turned and walked back to Wordsworth. "I mean it's not my fault the bus didn't stop," Dave figured, "so how can it be my fault if I don't make it to work? That's only logical." Getting back to the flat, Dave reached under his bed, pulled out a dogeared old schoolbook, flopped on the bed and opened it. In the book were scribblings, notes, ideas and here and there, a completed poem. They represented everything he held dear, what was important in life. His job sweeping the floors in a sheet metal shop certainly wasn't. The floors were covered in so much machine oil, you could hardly move the piles of coagulated steel filings with the broom, and the shovel they gave you to pick them up with was bent on the front face and totally unsuited to its purpose. Served them right if he didn't show up, might teach them a lesson. He wrote in bold capital letters across the top of the page, "POSERS!"

Alex stood at the lathe, his head still a little foggy from the beers he'd drunk at the Laureate. He'd found his way home eventually, late in the afternoon, and passed out till the alarm had woken him for work the next morning. Now the lathe spun and squealed at a deafening pitch, and he held the handle, in a death grip, as if his life depended on it.

Mr. Tucker, the shop foreman, approached. Alex did his best to ignore him, but Tucker pushed the emergency stop button on the machine and it screeched to a halt, "Office! Now!" Alex didn't bother to ask why, he figured he was in shit for missing work the day before, yet again. It hadn't occurred to him that Dave was missing. Tucker opened the office door and waved him in, closed it behind him, and leaned against it, blocking Alex's exit, as if he was about to make a dash for freedom.

Mr. Thrift, the General Manager, sat on the desk waiting, all smiles, a glint in his eye like a fox eyeing a chicken, "Good morning, Alex, how are you? Nice of you to show up, hope we're not inconveniencing you at all."

"I had an upset stomach."

"That answers my next question, thank you."

"You're welcome."

Thrift lifted an envelope from the desk and handed it to Alex. "This is your last warning, if I had my way you'd be gone, but I don't, unfortunately."

"You what?"

"I'm quite sure you heard me, oh and as for your friend, what was his name?"

Tucker piped up, "David, David Simmons, sir."

"Tell him he's finished, we don't have to give him any notice, he's still on probation, it was you who recommended him for the position wasn't it?"

"Yeah, so?"

Mr. Thrift waved a dismissive hand, "You can thank him for the jam you find yourself in, that will be all." Alex turned and left the room, anger building in his throat, "Fucking Dave."

Ray jumped from the bus and stood outside Cooper's Fine Olde Butchery Shoppe, "I don't fucking believe this." Despite the desperate urge to turn and walk away, he headed into the store, if not his probation officer would have him back inside within the week.

Mr. Singh stood behind the counter waiting, "Raymond, good to see you, would you like some tea?"

"Nah, I'm good."

"Very well then."

The beaded curtains to the back of the store parted and in walked a middle aged East Indian woman, "This is my wife, Nadia. She will be running the front of the store while we work in the back. Nadia, this is Raymond, the gentleman I told you about last night."

"Good morning, Raymond, welcome to our store. Please help yourself to the tea, it is in the back room."

Ray stood towering over the two of them, looking from one to the other, "Where do I start?"

"I will show you," Abdijay kissed Nadia on the forehead, "if you need anything I will be in the back dear."

"I'm sure I can manage."

Ray followed Abdijay into the backroom and surveyed the scene. A concrete floored room with tiled walls, on two of the walls were long stainless-steel sinks with draining areas. Above one sink, a magnetic strip with a long row of different sized knives attached, and beside the other, a large mincing machine. To the left a heavy door into the walk-in fridge.

"I got you a nice new apron, didn't have much choice really, none of the ones we had here would have fit you. Hang your jacket up over there and put it on."

Ray begrudgingly did as he was told, Mr. Singh gripped the handle of the fridge door and pulled, the door swung open and cold air poured out, "Careful when you go in here, if you let the door close behind you there is no way out."

During the speech Mr. Singh pulled a heavy bag of bones out of the fridge and propped the door open, "There, now follow me." The interior shelves, lining the sides of the fridge, had rows of chickens hanging above them. "These chickens are ready to be sold. In these boxes are others, I will show you how to prepare for sale."

"It's fucking freezing in here," Ray rubbed his upper arms attempting to warm himself up.

"Hopefully, and I will not accept that sort of language, if you want to work here you must accept that," Mr. Singh quipped back.

"But I don't want to work here."

“Oh well, you are working here, like it or not,” Singh half ignored him and continued, “Now, please bring one of those boxes to the sink before we freeze to death.”

Ray lifted the box from the shelf and headed out the door. Mr. Singh pulled the bag of bones out of the way, letting the freezer door slam closed, “Now, take a paring knife from the rack and do as I do.” Ray pulled down the largest knife he could see, and turned towards Mr. Singh, “Not that one, here give me that.” He took the knife out of Ray's hand, “a paring knife is much smaller, see.” The shopkeeper handed him the smallest knife on the rack.

Ray stood, the smaller but extremely sharp knife in his hand, staring down at Mr. Singh. The shop owner continued, “Watch I will show you; you take the chicken and slide the knife in here and turn it and voila!” The chicken’s guts spilled out onto the drainage board and slithered into the sink with a loud splat, at the same moment the stench hit Ray’s nose, “Jesus Christ, that’s disgusting!” He gagged.

“You had better get used to it, I need you to clean at least fifty birds a day,” Mr. Singh continued his work, “plus I will teach you how to make the sausages. We make the best chicken sausage in all of London.”

“You have got to be kidding me.”

“No, it’s an honest day's work for an honest day's pay.”

“I’m not doing it.”

“I don’t see what choice you have.”

Ray glared at Mr. Singh and knife in hand lifted the next chicken, “Like this?” He slid the knife into the bird, twisted it and the bird’s guts slid into the sink.

“Very good, you’re a natural with a knife.”

“Just don’t ask me to clean out any cats for your dinner.”

Mr. Singh stared up at him for a long time in silence and then laughed and said, “Really Ray? What do you think I am? Chinese?”

Meanwhile, Donnie was at work, powering his way up a ladder, a hod, filled with bricks on his shoulder. He liked his job and was a natural at it. He figured it was like going to a gym, except, instead of you paying someone, someone paid you. The site he currently worked on was in Covent Garden, near the centre of London. The company he worked for was building a nine-story office, come flats, come boutique store development. As he turned to head back down the ladder, the buzzer sounded for tea break. Donnie was on the fourth floor, by the time he got down to the canteen, the lines would be so long the break would be over before he got a sandwich. He decided to stay up where he was and roll a cigarette instead. When he was finished, he leaned back against a cement mixer and took a long pull on the cigarette. From the corner of his eye, he saw a hunched figure walking across the room, "What are you doing Jimmy? You're missing tea break."

"No tea break for me Mr. Donnie, I've got work to do."

Jimmy was an old labourer who had worked every site Donnie had since Donnie had come down from Glasgow. The two men had everything and nothing in common. Jimmy was an immigrant from Grenada, he'd come to England after the revolution, referred to himself as a refugee and vowed to return, when what he referred to as true government was restored. Donnie was British but considered himself an economic refugee in his own land. That was where the similarity ended. Jimmy was devoutly religious, never missing Sunday services in a Baptist church in Bethnal Green. A two-hour train and bus journey for him, but a church with a mostly Caribbean congregation, and a Grenadian minister, where he felt closest to home. Donnie would only go to church if he thought it would get him laid. Donnie was white, Jimmy was Black. The two men got along well enough, mostly because Donnie found Jimmy's eccentricities highly amusing. "Let me help you search, you old fool."

Jimmy straightened up and looked at Donnie, "I may be old, young man, but I am not a fool, and for that you can give me one of those fags."

Donnie laughed, "Let me guess? I suppose you want me to roll it for you too."

"Uhuh, if I let you roll it, I get less tobacco, give me the fixings and I'll roll my own."

Donnie handed over the pouch with a smile and Jimmy set to rolling a cigarette. Most people Donnie would've told to take a hike, but he respected Jimmy. Jimmy never went to the canteen at break time, instead opting to scour the site for any discarded items he felt would be of use to him when he returned to Grenada, nails, screws, half empty paint cans, hinges etc. Jimmy had a small farm back home that he had lost in the revolution, and one day planned on returning with his treasure hoard to reclaim and rebuild it.

"Thank you, Mr. Donnie, very kind of you sir."

"Why don't you just face facts and settle down here, put down some roots, you're never going back."

"Never say never, you don't know what could be around the next corner."

"Be realistic..." Donnie stopped mid-sentence, interrupted by the strange wailing of an instrument he didn't recognise, "What the fuck?"

Jimmy ran across to the side of the site and peered out through a crack in the tarps that he had pulled open, "Quick Mr. Donnie, come see this."

Donnie joined him and looked through the same crack. He saw on the roof next door, the roof of The London School of Art, a young woman dancing in a white sari, a cameraman filming her, Indian music playing from a boom box beside him. She spun and twirled, and pulled more and more of the sari off, dropping it onto the roof, and now stood totally naked to a deafening roar of cheers and wolf whistles erupting from all over the building site. The poor girl looked up, embarrassed, and grabbed up the cloth, pulling it around herself, before running through the stairwell door.

"Now, Mr. Donnie, you see why I don't go down for tea break, you never know what's going to happen," Jimmy chuckled and continued, "So, are you going to accept my invitation and come with me to church this weekend?" Jimmy smiled, winked, and walked away, humming his appreciation as he took a long drag on the cigarette.

"Who knows Jimmy," Donnie called behind him, "you never know what's going to happen in this life."

The Royal Mail van screeched to a halt beside the curb. Terry, and his colleague Tim, jumped out, mail bags in hand. The third man, Ryan, sat behind the driver's seat and kept the engine running. The Stonebridge council estate communal mailboxes were outside of the estate but only just, Stonebridge estates made Chalkhill look upmarket, and the Post Office sent teams of three in to deliver the mail. In and out, as quickly as possible. Today was the worst day of the month for the mailmen. It was the last week of the month and, consequently, the mail bags were full of cheques: Unemployment cheques, pension cheques, welfare cheques, mothers allowance all came out at the same time. Terry and his colleagues had been carefully selected for the job. Tim was the fastest at sorting the mail and stuffing the boxes, Terry was big, tattooed, and frightening to look at, and Ryan drove like a maniac. Tim sorted the mail while Terry stood guard with a blackjack, a thick ebony coloured wooden truncheon, at the ready, tapping it rhythmically on the palm of his left hand while Ryan stayed behind the wheel, engine running, ready to get the hell out of there.

No sooner had Tim unlocked all the boxes and had begun to rapidly stuff the mail into the corresponding slots, when around the corner came two young, black boys. Terry looked them up and down, they were thirteen years old, at the most, he figured. Baseball caps worn backwards, baseball letter jackets, one red, one yellow with white leather sleeves, baggy jeans, skateboards under their arms. They approached laughing and giggling, pushing each other, "typical kids," Terry thought.

"Who are you, the local gangster rappers?" Terry laughed.

"That's right! Now why don't you give us the bags and piss off our estate."

Suddenly, Terry was staring straight down the barrel of the snub-nosed pistol Red Jacket was pointing at him. The kid had a huge toothy smile on his face, Terry stood mouth hanging wide open, stunned in shock, "You little fuckers..."

"Wha… wha… what do I do Tel?" Tim stuttered.

Red jacket laughed, "G-g-give me the bag, stupid!"

"Tel?"

"Give him the bag, stupid, I ain't getting shot for no welfare bums cheques."

Tim stared at Terry, "Some hard man you are."

Terry strode across to his colleague, grabbed the bag he was holding and shoved it into Yellow Jackets chest, "Here, help yourself." Red Jacket grabbed the other bag off the ground.

"You made the right choice," said Yellow Jacket, as they dropped their skateboards to the ground. The two kids, struggling from the weight of the mail, swung the bags over their shoulders and using their right feet to power themselves, pushed off on their skateboards into the estate.

Tim rose to his feet, a piece of mail still clutched tightly in his hand, and stared at their receding backs, "What do we do now?" Terry stared at him, baffled as to why he was even asking the question, "Deliver that last piece, lock the boxes and let's get the fuck out of here." The driver, Ryan, leaned out of the cab, "Let's get the fuck on the road before the next yardie shows up and puts a bullet in us this time!"

Carl finished installing a new chandelier and climbed down the step ladder, as the owner of the house stood watching him, arms folded across his chest. Carl crossed the room to the wall's switch and clicked it on. Light flooded the room. Carl nodded, smiling. The homeowner mimicked him, nodding, "Very nice job, sorry what was your name again?"

"Carl, sir."

"Do you have a work order for me to sign?"

"It's in the van, I'll go get it for you," Carl folded the step ladder and glanced around the room as he left, ten-foot ceilings, plaster cornices, solid oak doors. A world away, yet only a fifteen-minute drive, from the life he was used to. He retrieved the work order from the van and handed it to the customer, who signed it and handed it back.

"Thank you, Mr. Winstanley."

"Where do you live, Carl?"

"Kingsbury, in the Poets."

"Do you like it there?"

"Not really," Carl paused for a moment, "I shouldn't say that. It's the best my mum and dad could do for me, I don't want to sound ungrateful."

"You don't, you're entitled to your opinion," Mr. Winstanley handed Carl a five-pound note, "Here."

"You don't have to do that."

"I know, if I had to, I probably wouldn't."

"Well thanks then."

"If there's anything I can do to help you, just let me know."

"Sure thanks. If you don't mind me asking, what do you do?"

"I'm a lawyer."

Dave finished his poem, sat back and read it out loud,

POSERS
Vivien Westwood outfits,
Gotta look like truth,
Investment portfolios,
Price immaterial,
Gold plated safety pins,
Sex is a store,
Not an act,
Kings' road hairdos,
Twenty quid gel not Swarfega,
Tory mums and dads,
Black cabs not buses,
Ten-pound safety money in your purse,
University beckons and is heard,

Estates for tourism not living,
No parents on the dole,
In ten years, management,
Suburban reminiscing,
2 kids and a car,
Holidays in Portugal,
Trust fund careers,
Betraying as you pogo,
FUCK YOU!!!!!!

5

Dave opened the freezer door, took out the jam jar, stole another 10 quid, screwed the lid back on, replaced the jar, closed the freezer door, hesitated but then, despite feeling a deep sense of guilt, turned and walked away. He'd find some way to repay it soon, he was sure of it. He left the flat and started to jog down the stairs. One and a half flights down he found Queenie, struggling to pull her shopping trolley up the stairs.

"What's wrong with the lift Queenie?"

"That's Mrs. Bartrum to you and I've told you that before and the lifts are out of order. Again!"

"Tell you what, let me give you a hand by way of an apology." Dave grabbed the shopping trolley, threw it over his shoulder, turned, and ran up the stairs.

"Slow down you damn fool."

"Come on Queenie, hurry it up, I ain't got all day."

Queenie, already out of breath from the first seven and a half flights of stairs, wheezed at Dave, as she struggled to keep going, "Why aren't you at work anyway? D'you lose another job?"

"Employers today don't know quality when they see it. Their loss, not mine."

Queenie finally reached the ninth floor, clutching the railing tightly with one hand as she leaned on it, breathing in deep raspy breaths. Dave left the trolley outside her flat door, "There you go, Queen, saved you a bit of hard work."

"Thanks Dave, I do appreciate it, although you could've helped more if you'd took me by the arm and walked me up the stairs."

"What? No tip then?" Dave laughed and started to trot back down the stairs, "You can get me next time."

"Damn fool boy, you'll never come to no good."

Dave left the building and headed straight for The Laureate. You never know if there might be someone in who he could hustle at pool or cadge a drink off. As usual, on a Tuesday lunchtime, it was dead, his cohorts were at work. Lunch times were only busy with other punters, people starting their weekends early, on Thursdays and Fridays. Ray's sister Siobhan was working the bar.

"Hey Dave, what brings you in on a Tuesday?"

"Oh, you know, just looking for some stress relief, it's hard being young and upwardly mobile, always trying to keep up, there's a lot of stress involved."

"Yeah, I bet, don't know how you do it. Drink?"

"Nah, I'm a bit short this week."

"I'm buying."

"Oh, well in that case a bottle of white top would do nicely."

Siobhan smiled, she had always had a soft spot for Dave, he was cheeky, and she liked that, it made her smile. The fact he ordered white top, a premium beer, instead of a pint that contained more, and cost less was just typical. She poured him a pint of Skol, "Have a pint instead."

"Fair enough. Quiet in here today."

"Suits me, I'm pretty hungover from last night."

"Oh yeah, how come."

"I was bored, went round to Vickie's, got into a bottle of Southern Comfort."

"Vickie's?"

"Yeah."

"She say anything about me?"

"No, why? Should she have?"

"No reason, just asking, that's all."

"You and Vickie, eh?"

"What? Nah."

"You know if you're stuck for a little company, you could do worse than ask me out you know."

"You?"

“Yeah me, would that be so awful?”

“Not at all, don’t know how your brother would feel about it though.”

“You let me worry about Raymond, you hear?”

Dave was a little stunned, Siobhan was a good-looking young woman, it had never occurred to him she might fancy him. High self-esteem was one problem Dave definitely didn’t suffer from, quite the opposite in fact. “Like I said I’m a bit short right now, otherwise you know I would.”

“Tomorrow night we’ll go down the chippie, have a fish dinner, go for a walk, how’s that?”

“Sure, I could probably swing that.”

The door burst open, and Terry strode in and ignoring the conversation that was already in progress, “Give us a pint and a large voddie will yer Siobhan.”

“Sure thing Terry,”

“Hello mate, how come you’re not at work then?” Dave grinned as Terry plopped down on the stool next to him.

“Have I got a story for you...” Terry began.

By the end of the story, Dave and Siobhan stared at Terry in silence, after about ten seconds of their mouths hanging wordlessly open, Siobhan said, “Wow, glad you’re okay, that calls for a pint on the house.”

Dave added, “Fuck me! What now? You gonna quit? If they’re on the house I’ll have one too, cheers.”

“Fuck you? No thanks, I prefer my men with breasts and a vagina and are you fucking kidding me, me union rep figures this should be good for at least six months paid stress leave and when I do go back, I can refuse to work the estates ever again.”

“Bonus!” Dave burst into song, “Happy days are here again, the skies above are clear again...”

“Hang on to your day job Dave, that made my face hurt, never mind my ears.”

“I’m beginning to regret asking you out now.” Siobhan laughed, glancing at Dave.

“You asked Dave out? How desperate are you?” Terry couldn’t believe his ears.

“Why shouldn’t she, Siobhan knows quality when she sees it.”

“I’d shut up now if I was you or tomorrow night’s off,” Siobhan turned and headed into the Saloon bar to serve a waiting customer.

Terry stares at Dave in disbelief, “Are you fucking nuts? Ray’ll serve you your own nuts on toast when he finds out.”

“What was I supposed to say? No? If he heard she asked me out and I turned her down he’d kill me anyway, at least this way I might die with a smile on my face.”

“Wanna go over to Wobble’s place?” Terry changed the subject, “I bumped into him earlier, he said to come over, says he’s got a surprise for us.”

“Hope it’s not sexual.”

“You’ve got a sick mind Dave. Finish your pint and let’s head over there.” Dave and Terry poured the last of the beer down their throats, Dave slopping his on his chin and chest as he did. “You’re so fucking refined Dave, you know that? Always amazes me you’re still single.”

“I slipped alright. And maybe after tomorrow night I won’t be.”

“Amazing how you can miss that big mouth of yours. C'mon let’s go.” Without bothering to shout goodbye to Siobhan, they left, headed to Wobble’s place.

Wobble got his nickname back in junior school after his leg was broken by a bad-tempered janitor, in a school emergency exit door. Wobble, or Danny, as he was then known was inside the school during play time, strictly against school rules. It was rainy and cold outside, and Danny’s coat had been stolen the week before on a school field trip to the natural history museum. His mum couldn’t afford to buy him a new one. In fact, she had taken the missing one out of a lost and found bin at the local library, claiming Danny had left it there. To teach Danny a lesson, “It’ll make a man of yer," she had sent him to school in just a T-shirt and cardigan. Danny had got soaked on the way there, and come playtime was still shivering, so he had decided to remain inside, rules be damned. When Mr. Hannah, the janitor, found him in the corridor, there was only five minutes till the bell, and Danny thought he was going to get away with it when, "Oi, you, you're not allowed in here, scarper."

Danny felt a hand grab him by the back of the belt and felt a push. He crashed into the emergency push bar and tripped and fell. Mr. Hannah slammed the door shut and Danny's eight-year-old ankle, that was still in the doorway, shattered. Months later, when the final cast was removed, after multiple operations, Danny had a permanent and severe sideways limp. The kids in the school made fun of him and pushed him in the corridors and playground. Terry, being one of the few exceptions, as a lover of lost causes, had always protected him. The kids would sing, "Weebles wobble but they don't fall down." And for a while they taunted him by calling him Weeble, eventually this changed to Wobble, and he was Danny no longer.

By this time, even his own mother started to call him Wobble. Danny was determined not to fall, and the tears stung his eyes as his mother would taunt him, "Be a man, stand on your own two feet. Even if you are a gimp!"

Violet, Danny's mother, was one of two things when she was drunk: excessively maudlin and sentimental or excessively cruel and bitter. When she was the former, she called him, "My little Danny, my poor, poor little Danny boy." When she was the latter, "You little cripple, look at you, what use are you gimpy?"

Violet had been gone for two years now, choked to death on her own vomit one Friday night. Danny had been the only other person at home, and the rumour on the estate was that he had stood by and done nothing to help his mum. A rumour that he had never confirmed or denied. The police had done a brief perfunctory investigation, and that was that, Violet Cooper met her maker. Wobble was allowed to stay in the house, as he qualified for one of the townhouses on the estate by way of his disability. "Only good that came from it," he often thought. That and the cheques. Wobble received a monthly disability cheque, and shortly after the "accident" a lump sum payment from the school board.

Violet had squandered that money on nights out at The Laureate, cigarettes, drugs, her favourite being cocaine, and a week in Torremolinos on the Spanish Costa Brava. Really nothing more than a collection of British pubs selling Double Diamond, Watney's Red Barrel, and fish and chip shops in the sun, with a new boyfriend, who dumped her two days after they returned home. However, the court had decreed that, when Wobble turned twenty-one, they would review the effect his injury had on his adult life and reassess his compensation package. So, Wobble had held out hope to someday see more money.

Dave and Terry set off through the estate. It was rather predictably drizzling rain and Dave wrapped his arms around himself as he walked in a vain attempt to keep warm, "Gotta love the English summertime."

"Could be worse, I could be out delivering mail in it."

"Not everything's about you, you know."

"Yeah, it is."

They rounded the corner onto Acacia drive and headed to number 183, Wobble's house. Outside sat a car, a Ford Capri. Terry stopped and admired it, partly because, unlike a lot of cars on the estate, this one had only one paint colour, "Nice motor."

"Whatever, I'm getting wet." Dave rang the doorbell and then pounded on the door, "C'mon Wobble, you tosser. We're getting wet."

The door opened and Wobble stepped out, pulling on his Harrington jacket as he did, "Whaddya think?"

Dave stared at him, "Of what?"

"The car. Just got it yesterday," Wobble beamed proudly.

Dave was confused, "When d'you get a licence?"

"I didn't, you don't need one to buy a car just to drive one."

Terry nodded, "She's a beaut, how many miles?"

"Thirty thou."

"Nice, mind if I get in?"

"Course not, I was hoping you'd take her for a spin."

"Fuck yeah."

Wobble unlocked the passenger door and tossed Terry the keys. Terry let himself in the driver's door, Wobble tipped the passenger seat forwards for Dave to climb in the back of the two-door roadster. "How come I have to get in the back?" Dave complained.

"'Cause it's my fucking car you wanker."

Dave grudgingly climbed into the back, and Wobble got in the front, Terry turned the key, the engine roared to life with a deep throbbing growl. Terry turned to Wobble, a huge grin on his face, "Nice, three litre?"

"Fucking right, I call her The Throbber."

Dave leaned forward, "Are you fucking queer or what?"

"Fuck you Dave, you're just jealous."

Terry slipped the gear lever into first gear, slipped the clutch, the car roared forward, sending Dave flying backwards against the back seat. Terry screeched around the corner ignoring the "Give Way" sign and pulled onto the Kingsbury Road before changing up through second, then third, and fourth. The car rocketed past the park, devoid of any kids in the wet weather, and Terry yanked the steering wheel to the right into the car park. In the centre of the empty expanse of tarmac, Terry started to pull doughnuts, the tires screeching and smoking as the car spun in circles. Wobble screamed in delight! Terry clung to the wheel, a maniacal grin on his face, while Dave clung to the back seat with all his strength fighting the nausea building up in his throat. Wobble was having the time of his life, "Faster, Terry faster."

"I'm going as fast as I can."

"I'm going to be sick."

"Don't you dare Dave. I'll never get it off the leather." But it was too late, Dave hurled all over the back of Wobbles seat, vomit spraying inside the new car. Terry released the accelerator and the spinning nightmare stopped.

"MY LEATHER!" Wobble screamed over his shoulder at Dave.

"Jesus Dave that stinks," Terry and Wobble wound their windows down as fast as they could, arms spinning almost as fast as the car had been moments before,

"You arsehole! Look at my car!"

"I can't take you anywhere, can I?"

"Let's head back, I'll clean it up, sorry Wobbly."

"Fucking right you will, and don't call me that!"

As Terry drove slowly back to the estate the three of them sat in silence, the mood the complete opposite to the outward bound journey. Terry parked the car in the spot it had come out of and handed Wobble the keys, "Sweet ride! You might want to think about getting an air freshener though."

"You can say that again." Wobble grunted, anger and disgust building in his throat. Terry and Wobble climbed out, leaving Dave sitting in the back, "Wanna come in for a beer?"

"Is the pope Jewish?"

"Hey guys can you let me out of here, please."

Terry shook his head, "You'd better, he might take a piss next."

Wobble groaned and reluctantly opened the door tipping the seat forward as Dave stumbled out onto the pavement.

"Thanks for nothing."

"You're welcome, I'll get you a bucket of water and a rag," Wobble turned and limped into the house.

"Nice one, Dave."

"Fuck you, you know I don't go to the fair 'cause the rides make me sick, I can't even go on the teacup ride without getting dizzy," Dave leaned on the side of the car, his face pale, drained of all colour.

Wobble came back out with a bucket of soapy water and an old Led Zeppelin T-shirt, "Here, you can use this."

Dave was incredulous, "Led Zeppelin? What the fuck you doing with a Led Zeppelin T-shirt anyway?"

"It was my mums," Wobble replied, throwing the shirt at Dave.

The three of them fell into an awkward silence. After a while, Terry spoke, "Better get on with it, Dave, before it dries and gets even harder to clean up."

"Yeah right," Dave turned and started to wipe down the back of the passenger seat. Wobble shook his head, "Got a fag Tel?"

"Sure," he fished the pack from his pocket and handed one to Wobble, "How'd you afford such a nice motor anyway Danny?"

"Got my settlement review."

From inside the car Dave shouted, "No way! How much?"

"Enough, got the car and some more besides."

"Hope you put some aside for a rainy day."

Wobble winked at him, "Don't worry about me Tel, I'm set." Dave finished wiping up the mess and threw the bucket of dirty water out onto the road. Wobble took the bucket and rag and said, "Wanna shoot some pool?"

"Sure, me and Dave were at the pub earlier, there was no one on the table then."

Dave nodded in agreement, "Place was empty."

"You don't have to go to the pub, come see," Wobble turned and headed into his house. Terry and Dave exchanged a quizzical glance and followed Wobble into the house and up the stairs. Wobble opened the bedroom door out onto the landing, "Had to have the door rehung in reverse, couldn't get in the room otherwise."

Terry stepped forward, "Fuck me, you've gotta be kidding me."

Dave followed him in, "No fucking way!"

Wobble stood with a huge shit-eating grin spread across his face, "Isn't that the bollocks?" Inside the small, spare bedroom there was a regulation pub size pool table, four feet by eight feet, the room was twelve feet by eight feet in total. On the wall at one end a rack for the cues and balls and at the other end, a dart board and blackboard for scoring the games.

"Wanna play pool or darts? I got it set up for both." Wobble was as proud as a peacock.

Dave started to laugh, "I don't want to sound like a prick but..."

Terry shot him a look, "I think what Dave is trying to say is the room might be a touch small for the table, Danny."

Wobble looked annoyed, "What do you think I am, stupid?"

Dave smirked, "You said it..." Terry stabbed Dave sharply in the ribs with his elbow. "Ow."

"I know the rooms too small, but the council wouldn't let me knock the walls down to expand it, so I had the cues shortened to make up for it." Wobble held up a cue that was only three feet long, "See."

Terry took it, "Let's 'ave a go then!"

Dave grabbed another cue and broke the racked balls, "Now I know what a Thalidomide feels like." Terry stiffened and stared at him, then turned and looked at Wobble.

Wobble cracked up laughing, "Thalidomide babies, that's what we'll call the place." The three of them started to laugh. "I've got some white tops in the fridge, let's get pissed."

Terry laughed, "Good man Danny, we're both currently men of leisure, why not?"

"Fucking right, Wobbles, let the good times roll."

6

Dave, Terry and Wobble left number 183 just after seven that evening and headed over to The Laureate. Empty Whitetop bottles littered Wobble's games room. Terry and Dave told the reluctant Wobble, who had wanted to head to the off license, to replenish the in-house beer supply, they would treat him at the pub instead. Wobble wasn't, and never had been, much of a one for public places, mostly because of a natural shyness about his condition. But, with the other two by his side, literally giving him no choice, he figured, "What the fuck, might be fun."

Dave slammed through the door and into the bar, Terry and Wobble followed and headed straight for the Gents. "ALRIGHT THEN DAVE'S IN THE HOUSE!" he shouted.

Siobhan looked up from the bar, "You're in a fine state."

"'Allo sweetheart, 3 bottles of Whitetop lickety-split!"

"You got the money?"

"Course," Dave pulled out the stolen tenner and threw it on the bar.

Siobhan sighed, "Only if you quieten down."

"Look at the state of you, you near cost me my job, you wanker." Dave turned to see Alex standing beside him, Alex waved a handful of money in the air, "Another round please, Siobhan."

"Wasn't my fault, I ran for the bus, but he wouldn't stop, see."

"You're lucky me and Ray's got company or I'd give you a good hiding."

"What company?" Dave turned and looked around the bar. In the corner surrounding a small round table sat Ray, two older, early fortyish, short haired, big built men, a biker with an unmistakable tattoo of a hangman on his neck, and a young skinhead with a swastika tattooed on his cheek, "Who the fuck are they?"

"None of your business, just do your best not to embarrass yourself or us," Siobhan poured the last of the drinks, "Five quid even, please, Alex."

Alex threw a fiver and a single on the bar, "'Ave one for yourself later."

"Ta," she replied as Alex turned to head back to the table. Terry and Wobble emerged from the Gents, Ray looked up at them and called out, "Terry, I got someone you should meet!" Terry and Wobble stopped in their tracks, Ray glared at Wobble, who quickly took the hint and made haste to the bar. "I think you know Mr. Daniels," Ray began as Terry approached their table.

The bigger of the two men stood and stuck out his hand, "Long time Terry."

"You could say that" Terry took the man's hand and shook it.

Daniels turned to the group, "I knew Terry when he was knee high to a whippet, his dad was a good man, one of us."

Ray smiled proudly, "I thought Terry might be useful, in our endeavors, as it were. This is my friend Greg."

Terry looked slowly around the group, the strange mix of an outlaw biker, who stood and shook Terry's hand, a tattoo of a circle with a cross on it on the web of his hand, between the thumb and forefinger. The symbol of the far-right British Movement. Across the table, a fascist skinhead with the same tattoo on his hand, and the murky underworld figure of Daniels and his unnamed associate. Ray and Alex sit at the next table, as if on guard watching the room. There was nowhere that Terry could think of that would be worse than where he now stood, "What endeavors would that be then Ray?"

Daniels jumped in, "We were just discussing some fundraising opportunities."

"Fundraising?" Terry looked skeptical.

Daniels nodded, "For the cause Terry, I'm sure you understand, don't you?"

“Sure, of course, I’d better get back to my mates, don’t want the beer getting warm.”

“Of course, Terry, it was great to see you, we’ll be in touch.”

Dave leaned back on the bar sipping his beer watching as Terry shook Daniels’ hand and walked away.

Wobble approached, “Who the fuck are they Dave?”

“Fucked if I know.”

Siobhan leaned over the bar, “You don’t want to know, and you’d best stop staring.”

Dave turned to face the bar, “I’d rather stare at you any day.”

“For pity's sake Dave, you’d better not show up in this condition tomorrow night!”

Dave grinned slyly, “I’ve got way too much respect for you for that.”

Wobble looked back and forth, from one to the other, “Why what’s ‘appening tomorrow night?”

Both Dave and Siobhan replied at the same time, “Nothing!”

“I might’ve been born yesterday but I’m not a duck.”

Siobhan stared at him, “You don’t get out much, do you?”

By now, Terry had returned from the corner table and picked up his beer. Dave raised an eyebrow, “What’s that all about?”

“Nothing, one of them knew my dad that’s all, let’s go through to the other bar, shoot some pool.”

Dave turned to Siobhan, “You working the other bar?”

“Seen as how I’m the only barmaid on tonight, quite likely.”

“Good, I’ll see you over there then.”

Terry shook his head, resting his hand on Dave’s shoulder to steer him through the bar, “C’mon Casanova.”

Wobble followed behind, “Hey Terry, I think there’s something going on between those two.”

“No shit Sherlock, you figure?”

In the other bar, Ray, Alex, and their visitors stood and shook hands and the four men left. Ray and Alex crossed to the bar and through the open doorway behind the counter that joined the two bars. Ray shouted, "Oi Siobhan, leave your boyfriend alone and get us two more beers will ya."

Siobhan came through and poured the pints, "You need to learn some patience, you. Just 'cause you're me bruvver, don't mean you can talk to me 'ow you want. 'Ow would you feel if that was somebody else spoke to me like that?"

"I'd punch 'em straight in the teef!"

"Precisely, and what's this about a boyfriend anyway?"

Ray rolled his eyes, "I was kidding, you know you 'ave to ask my permission before you date anyone."

"Says who?" Siobhan's eyes narrow on his face.

"Says me that's who!"

Siobhan turned, hearing a voice from the other bar. It was Dave yelling, "Oi Siobhan we need some change for the pool table." Siobhan turned away from her brother, "Duty calls," she said and headed for the other bar.

Ray picked up his beer and strode through the door, into the other bar. He grabbed Dave by the lapels and stared down into his face, growling, "Listen here you Muppet, you don't talk to my sister like that, EVER!"

Dave stared back stunned into silence, Terry stepped forward, "For fuck sakes Ray, leave it out will ya?"

Siobhan rang a bar towel between her fingers, terrified of what she was about to witness, "Leave him be Ray, he didn't mean nuffin' he's just a bit pissed that's all!"

Ray loosened his grip, his face softened, and he tousled Dave's hair, "What are you all getting so upset about, I'm just kidding. Me and Dave are muckers, ain't we?"

Dave nearly collapsed as Ray let go, his legs buckling under him, "Course we are Ray."

"Give the man his change sis, I fancy a game of pool. Set 'em up Dave, there's a good lad," his voice was now overly cheery.

Wobble opened his mouth to object; he'd won the last game and therefore it was his table but seeing the look on Terry's face thought better of it. Dave racked the balls up wondering just how badly he'd have to play to let Ray win. Even as drunk as he was, he was a far better player than Ray, but didn't want to face the possible consequences of beating him, especially after what had just happened. Dave didn't believe all was forgiven. The evening progressed as Dave had expected, he let Ray win, then Terry beat Ray, then Wobble, Dave beat Terry, and then let Ray win again. The whole time Alex glared at Dave from the bar, still pissed about his drubbing from Mr. Thrift.

The door to the bar opened and in walked Carl. He put a ten pence piece on the side of the table ready to take his turn, "Evening lads."

Dave nodded, "What you doing out on a weeknight?"

"I went down the club but there's been a water main burst or somefin so I can't train. Was gonna do some sparring, but now I'll just hafta show you lot how to shoot pool instead," Carl stepped up to the bar, glancing at Siobhan, "Can I 'ave a Whitetop please darling?"

Ray dropped the cue down on the table, "You can 'ave the table Dave, I'm heading out, Alex you coming?"

"What? Oh sure," Alex downed the last of his pint and followed Ray out of the pub.

Carl watched them leave, "Something I said?"

Dave stepped forward, "Don't worry about it. I'll set up the table."

"Thanks Dave. I'm still gonna beat your arse though."

"You wish."

The door to the pub swung open again, and in walked Donnie, his eye had already started to swell from the encounter with the policeman. Dave eyed him curiously, "What happened to you? You get caught playing peeping Tom?"

“Fuck you Dave, you know even your policemen are wankers. I just saw Ray and Alex getting on the bus, where they off to?”

Terry shrugged, “They didn’t like the atmosphere, wasn’t to their current taste.”

Carl shrugged, “I don’t think I was welcome.”

Donnie shook his head, “Fuck ‘em if they can’t take a joke, you’re okay by me, Carl.”

“Well, now I’ve got the backing of the Scottish nation, let's shoot some pool.”

7

The door to Coopers Fine Olde Butchery Shoppe swung open and two plain clothes police officers entered. Mrs. Singh looked up from behind the counter, “Can I help you?”

“Is Mr. Cooper here?” The first officer spoke up, glancing around the shop.

“I’m afraid Mr. Cooper passed on some years back,” Mrs. Singh gestured up to a picture of a man hanging on the white wall near the cash register.

“Is the current owner here?” The second officer stepped forward.

Mrs. Singh glanced at the policeman and subconsciously pulled a towel from her apron in a nervous gesture, “That would be my husband, may I ask what this is about?”

“I’m Detective Sergeant Karen Miller, this is Detective Constable Eric Wainwright, we just have some inquiries we have to make.”

“I’ll get my husband,” Mrs. Singh headed through the curtains and into the back room. Abdijay and Ray were working at the sinks, side by side. Both men stopped and looked up as Mrs. Singh announced, “Abdijay the police are here.”

Mr. Singh shrugged, “Well tell them to come through.”

“Through to here?” Mrs. Singh looks somewhat confused.

“Yes, yes, through to here, I’m very busy and after all we have nothing to hide.” Having heard the conversation, the two officers entered the back room causing an awkward moment where they and Mrs. Singh tried to pass each other in the all too narrow doorway, the hanging plastic ribbon curtain slapping against their faces.

“Good morning I’m Detective Sergeant Karen Miller...”

"Yes, yes, I'm very busy. What can I do to help you, Detective Miller?"

"It's Sergeant... Never mind," the Detective shook her head, and continued, "I was wondering if you had seen anyone driving a grey 1979 Ford Capri in the area last Monday afternoon?" She held out a picture of the car with a badly dented right front wing. As she is speaking both she and Wainwright look at Ray, the square peg in the round hole.

"I'm not much of a car person I'm afraid. Maybe Ray did, he was here that day."

Almost too quickly Ray responded, "I take the bus everywhere I go."

Wainwright stares straight at him, "I didn't ask about your mode of transportation, I asked if you'd seen the car."

"Can't say I did, no."

Constable Wainwright was taking notes as they spoke. "What's your name?"

"Ray."

"Ray what?"

Ray snaps to attention, "Raymond Collins SIR! Prisoner number 5197623!"

Wainwright glanced around the room, "Unusual place for you to be working, isn't it? A Muslim butcher shop."

Mr. Singh takes umbrage to the question, "We are Hindus."

Wainwright shrugged, "I'm sorry?"

"You should be, we are not Muslim we are Hindu," the shop owner repeated, "totally different."

Sergeant Miller stepped back in, "My apologies Mr. Singh, it was a totally honest mistake I'm sure, but it's still a valid question."

"Raymond here was referred to us by his probation officer and has to this point been an exemplary employee."

Wainwright scoffed, "How long has he worked here?"

"Three days."

"Early days yet then."

"Perhaps. Might I ask why the interest in the car?"

Miller tried to regain control of the conversation, "It was used in a hit and run not far from here and then dumped on a back street behind Wembley Park station."

"Ah well, as I already said I know nothing about it."

"We have a witness who saw it parked outside your store on the afternoon of the crime."

"Lots of people park outside my store and visit other vendors on the High Road."

Constable Wainwright chimed back in, staring straight at Ray as he did. "I'm sure they do, Wembley Park is on the Bakerloo line same as Harlesden, probably just a coincidence but people who travel by bus are apt to take the tube as well."

"Again, as I said..."

Sergeant Miller cut Ray off, "Here's my card, if you hear anything let us know."

"Of course, I will, and I must say you are being very diligent in investigating this hit and run incident."

"If the victims condition deteriorates any further this might well be a murder investigation. As it is, it's a possible hate crime. Constable Wainwright and I are part of a new unit charged with investigating crimes of a racial nature. I'm sure you'll be pleased to know we take those very seriously. Good day Mr. Singh."

Mr. Singh shook his head, "Perhaps as part of this new unit you might do well to learn something of our culture,"

Miller nodded, "Indeed."

The two officers turned and headed back out of the curtain. Mrs. Singh headed into the back room, "Abdijay what is going on? I heard the word murder."

"Nothing to disturb yourself about my dear. Just a traffic accident. Okay, Ray let's get back to it, no time like the present." Mr. Singh and Ray turned back to the sinks and continued preparing the birds for sale.

Outside on the rain-soaked pavement Miller turned to Wainwright, "Muslims? You're an idiot."

"How am I supposed to tell them apart?" Wainwright uncaringly shrugged.

"Let me do the talking in future, tomorrow morning I want you to find out what we have on Raymond Collins."

Dave sat on his bed, Ian Drury and the Blockheads playing on the record player, his notebook sitting open on his lap. Several times he had started writing a new poem only to angrily scratch out the first line with a messy scrawl of pencil lines. He ripped the page out of the book, screwed it up and threw it away across the room into a steadily growing pile of discarded ideas. He laid back with his hands behind his head and stared at the ceiling. A thought clawed its way up from the deepest recesses of his brain, something one of his teachers, Mr. Anderson had once told him in English class. Apparently, Hemingway would stand at his typewriter typing page after page, rip them out of the machine, and throw them into the rubbish bin, without even glancing at them, he just knew they weren't good enough for anyone else to see.

Strangely this gave Dave some comfort, strangely because Dave had for a short time belonged to an after-school music appreciation club which Mr. Anderson had run. Dave had to leave the club after a bust up when Anderson, a World-renowned expert on Jazz, proclaimed that the marriage of punk and reggae was a commercial creation without any political or social merit. Dave felt very strongly about this and seeing as how it was an after-school club, had figured it was okay to call his teacher a stupid arsehole and a dumb fuck. This had not gone down well and earned him one of his many suspensions from school. Inspired by both the Hemingway story and the music club debacle, he picked up pencil and paper once more and went back to work.

NO WORDS
It doesn't matter what I write,
It isn't for you to be right,
It may flutter to the floor,
Or down 9 floors or more,

it might make sense,
there could be recompense,
it's whether I get it out or not,
whether or not it's got what it's got,
it's not for you to judge,
all judges have a grudge,
sat behind the bench up there,
or the editors chair,
thinking judging me is fair,
walk a mile in my shoes,
there's no way they could fit you,
fits are for the disturbed brain,
where all thoughts are technicolour rain,
Hendrix died and all his kind,
now we inherit and we're not kind,
smash hits? More like smash it!

He sat up smiling and went out into the kitchen to get a drink. Looking up at the clock, he suddenly realised he was supposed to meet Siobhan in thirty minutes, "Fuck," he muttered before running back into the bedroom. He rooted through the piles of clothes, finding a Joy Division T-shirt that didn't look too dirty, and didn't seem to smell, and a clean pair of socks and underwear. He made his way hastily into the bathroom and turned the shower on. Having stripped naked, he climbed into the shower and started to soap up. As he rubbed his dick he thought, "Why not?" Siobhan wasn't the sort of girl to put out on a first date and Dave figured a quick wank might calm him down. He was feeling nervous about his fish and chip date for some reason he couldn't quite figure out. Dried and dressed he headed for the door, as he put his hand on the handle he hesitated, turned, and crossed to the fridge. The jam jar twenty pounds lighter he hurried out the door and to the lifts, but in his hurry, he'd slammed the freezer door shut and, without him noticing, it had sprung back open.

Ray came out of Cooper's Fine Olde Butchery Shoppe and headed away to the right. As he passed an alley a few doors down a voice hissed at him, “Psst!”

He turned to find Mitch in the alley hidden in the shadows, “What the fuck do you want?”

“Come here quick!” Mitch waved him over frantically.

“Fuck you, you nearly got me in deep shit!”

Mitch stepped slightly out of the alley glancing from side to side, “Get the fuck in here!”

Ray allowed himself to be pulled into the alley and stood towering over his shorter, fatter cousin, “This better be fucking important.”

Mitch held his arm tightly, “It is.”

“Out with it then,” Ray growled, clearly in a hurry.

“I fucked up.”

“I know you did; the plod came to my work asking about that car you pinched,” Ray said, yanking his arm back out of his cousin’s grasp.

“Not that.”

“How precisely did you fuck up then, that causes me to be standing in an alley in Harlesden in the rain, when I should be heading to the pub for a pint?”

Mitch wrung his hands anxiously, “You know that smack I had last month?”

“Yeah?”

“And the month before that?” Mitch’s voice trailed off.

“What the fuck did you do Mitch?” The agitation rising in Ray’s voice.

“I didn’t exactly pay everything I owed on it!”

“How much?”

“All of it...” Mitch looked at the ground, too nervous to meet his cousin’s gaze.

Ray had nearly lost it at this point, “WHAT?” He shouted in a loud whisper, glaring at the man.

"I figured the first month wouldn't matter 'cause I'd make it back on the second."

"You stupid fuck, where's the money?"

"Gone," he shuffled his feet, his eyes locked on the ground.

"Gone? Gone where?" Ray was becoming more and more agitated.

"Ladbrokes mostly."

"You blew all the money you made on two weights of smack on the horses?"

"That and," Mitch cleared his throat nervously, "well... I took a little for personal use."

"A little? For personal use?"

"Yeah."

"Whose drugs were they exactly?" Ray already knew the answer to the question.

"The Hangmen."

Ray could no longer contain himself; he grabbed his cousin by the arms and kneed Mitch hard, in the balls. The short, fat man doubled over in agony before puking on Ray's boots.

"You fucking arsehole look at my boots!" Ray kicked the vomit at Mitch and attempted to wipe the top of his toecap on his cousin's pant leg.

"I'm sorry," Mitch looked up at Ray, begging him, "please you've got to help me."

"How am I supposed to do that?"

"You know people, you have dealings with them. I know you do," Mitch considered dropping to his knees to beg Ray in hopes of convincing him. Ray backhanded him, sending him sprawling down the alley. "What the fuck Ray, what's that for?" Mitch clambered to his feet, rubbing his cheek.

Ray pointed down angrily, "That's for my boots."

"You kneed me in the bollocks!"

"You should thank me," Ray glared at him, "when the Hangmen get you, they'll cut your bollocks off and feed them to you."

"Not if you help me."

Ray sighed, exasperated, "How am I supposed to do that?"

"That blag we've got lined up for next week we could move it forwards."

"You what?"

"I'd have the money then, you know to make it all good," Mitch's eyebrows raised, and he stared at Ray hopefully.

Ray lowered his voice, and glanced down the alley, "The robbery is planned for next Wednesday, and will only work next Wednesday."

"I don't see why," Mitch continued to prod him for answers.

"Did you not listen at any of the meetings?"

"Yeah, of course I did."

Ray threw his hands up in the air, "Then why is next Wednesday so important?"

"The Royal wedding," his cousin responded, the hope draining from his face.

"The Royal wedding that's right, while Chuck and Di have the whole nation riveted, and more importantly, our friends at the Metropolitan police force overwhelmed with all the revelers we take the opportunity to score big." During his speech Ray moved closer and closer to his cousin, and now loomed over him, "So we can't bring it forward, understood?"

"Yeah, yeah, but listen," Mitch continued, "if I tell them about it, they might give me some time. I can't go home. They trashed my flat last night. I don't know what to do."

Ray stared into Mitch's eyes and let what he'd just heard slowly absorb, "Go home, it'll be okay, I'll make a call."

"See I knew you'd know what to do, thanks Ray, I mean it!" Mitch felt like jumping for joy.

"Just fuck off will you."

Ray's cousin used his thumb to point behind him down the alley, "D'you want a lift? I've got mum's car."

Ray shook his head, "No it's all good I'll use that phone box and then get the bus."

"It'll all work out, I know it will, I knew you'd do alright by me," he beamed happily, relieved.

"Yeah, yeah," Ray rolled his eyes, "go on fuck off." Ray lit a cigarette, and Mitch hurried out of the alley across to his mum's Ford Escort, fumbled with the keys, opened the door, jumped in and drove off.

Ray walked across to the ubiquitous, red London phone box, stepped in, pulled out some change and dialed a number.

The phone rang in a rundown, smoke filled pub in Ladbroke Grove, The George and Dragon. The barman answered. "Is Greg there?" Ray's voice crackled across the shitty connection. The barman turned, nodding to a heavyset biker who was shooting pool. The same biker who had met with Ray, earlier, in the Laureate. He dropped the cue on the table and walked across to the phone and put it to his ear, "Yeah?"

"I have something you're looking for," the voice on the other end said.

The biker took a long drag from his cigarette, contemplating quietly before continuing, "I thought he was your cousin,"

"He is."

"Fair enough, where?"

"His place," Ray hung the phone up and stood staring thoughtfully at the receiver before hanging it up and leaving the phone box.

Dave and Siobhan sat in the park on a bench beside the rebuilt church hall finishing their last chips. Dave held out the bag with one malt vinegar-soaked soggy chip in the bottom, "You want it?"

"Nah you're good," Siobhan smiled at him.

He chucked the last chip in his mouth, talking as he chewed, "Fair enough," and then screwed up the bag and threw it in the rubbish bin at the end of the bench.

"I dunno how you can do that."

"What?" Dave licked his finger.

"There was nothing but vinegar with a soggy bit of potato left."

"Love it, that's the best bit!"

"Well, you'd better not try to kiss me then."

"You want me to!"

"Not with that breath!"

"Fair enough, what do you want to do then?" Dave moved his face closer to hers.

Siobhan stood up abruptly, "We could walk?"

"Walk where?"

"I dunno just walk,"

Dave rose, standing next to her, pointing down the path. "If we walk that way we could go to the pub."

"I work in the pub, why would I want to go there on my night off?"

"For a drink?"

"Do you always have to drink, I thought it was sweet you showed up sober."

"A man's got to show some respect!"

"Respect my arse, you must be broke."

"No, I've got a twenty in my pocket."

"That's all you need, isn't it?"

"What is?"

"Enough in your pocket for a laugh and a pint, no thought for the future."

"What future? There is no future," Dave shrugged.

"Oh, for Christ sakes Dave, this isn't nineteen seventy-seven, it's 1981, a whole new decade. It's time you got beyond all that!"

"Says who?"

The girl folded her arms, "Says me."

"Is that why you asked me out? Am I your new project?"

"Hardly, I've already got a job," Siobhan scoffed, "I don't need another."

"Then why?"

"Dunno really, guess I've always had a soft spot for strays, my mum says I should work for the social."

"Maybe you should, maybe you could get my benefits extended."

Siobhan suddenly grabbed him and kissed him long and hard. Dave was completely stunned, "What the fuck?"

"How's that for benefits?"

A wide grin spread over Dave's face, "Pretty good I'd say!"

She grabbed him again kissing him even longer this time. "That vinegar tastes disgusting," she stopped with a giggle.

"Sorry," Dave wiped his mouth with the back of his hand, sitting down on the bench again.

Siobhan stood up and looked down at him, "You'd better use some mouthwash when we get to my house."

"Your house?"

"Yeah, mum's at bingo and Rays going to be at the pub, so we'll have the place to ourselves."

"Oh. Right!"

"Come on then." Siobhan turned and walked away. Dave shook his head, stunned at this turn of events, jumped up and ran after her. When he caught up, she reached out to take his hand. Dave glanced around to make sure no one was watching. As they approached Siobhan's house, Dave's head was swiveling nervously like a weathervane panicked about someone seeing them and telling Ray. "Your necks going to get stuck if you're not careful."

"I'm just checking..."

"I know what you're doing."

"D'you blame me?"

"No. He's a murderous lunatic."

"Well then?"

"If you want to go, go, but you'll never know what you're missing!"

"If we could just maybe walk a little faster?"

Siobhan laughed as she turned into her front garden. Her house was the centre one in a row of seven. Dave nervously glanced at the curtains, in the front bay windows, of the two next doors, identical, pebble dashed houses, wary of any movement. Siobhan chuckled.

"Come into my web."

"You're evil."

Dave smiled and followed her through the front door. As soon as they were inside, he grabbed her and started to kiss her hard and passionately. She playfully pushed him away, "Slow down Casanova, mouthwash, remember?"

"Yeah, yeah, right of course!"

Siobhan started up the stairs, Dave followed at her heel. "Get your boots off, were you born in a barn?" Dave stopped and bent down, rushing to loosen and untie the laces on his twelve-hole Dr. Marten boots. He couldn't remember ever having so much trouble, it seemed as if he was all thumbs. Finally, he got it done and threw the second one down on the mat, before turning to run up the stairs. He stopped on the landing, staring at the four doors, his head rotating from one to another. The bathroom door was open, so he walked in to grab a bottle of mouthwash off the sink, quickly swilling his mouth out. Heading back out to the landing he again surveyed the doors. Noticing one of them was slightly ajar, he pushed the door open. There, sitting on the edge of the bed was Siobhan, wearing only her knickers. Dave's mouth hung open as he stared, stunned by her beauty. Her full, heavy breasts on display. Despite the nearly naked girl in front of him Dave couldn't help but be slightly distracted by the David Bowie Aladdin Sane mural that took up the whole wall above the bed.

"I thought you got lost," Siobhan teased, patting the bed next to her.

"No, I, I er..." Dave stood there, still at a loss for words.

"Don't just stand there staring with your mouth hanging open, shut the door and come here!"

Later, as they lay together, Siobhan's head on Dave's chest, Dave stared up at the ceiling with a grin on his face. Siobhan teased him, "Look at you looking like the cat that got the cream."

"What?" Dave dragged his fingers through her hair, "I'm just happy that's all."

"Good."

"Did you paint that?"

"Bowie?"

"Yeah."

She smiled, "I did yeah."

"Wow you're talented, I love Bowie."

"Thanks."

They lay quiet for a couple of minutes. And then Dave slowly and awkwardly said, "It was alright, wasn't it?"

"Couldn't you tell?"

"Yeah, I just, you know, wanted to make sure that's all."

"That's not sexy."

"What isn't?"

"Self-doubt," she said, kissing his chest, "especially not right after what we just did."

"Sorry."

"Neither's that."

"I just wanted to make sure you were happy that's all, I mean otherwise I guess we'd have to go again; you know to make sure."

"It was fine, besides Vickie told me what to expect."

"I thought you said..." Dave could feel his cheeks redden.

"Girls tell each other everything."

"That ain't right."

"Like you lot don't! I'm a bar maid remember?"

"Oh yeah right, it's still..." The front door slammed open cutting Dave off, the sound of heavy footsteps thudding up the stairs and into one of the other bedrooms. He watched her door anxiously, holding in his breath as he heard another door slam shut, "What the fuck? Is that..."

Siobhan quickly slapped her hand over Dave's mouth, "SSShhh, yeah that's Ray!" They lay there silently in her bed as Ray thumped and banged around in his room. To Dave it felt like ages before the door down the hall opened, and Ray's footsteps headed down the landing. The bathroom door slammed shut, the distinct sound of the shower starting came through the thin walls. Dave realized that this was his chance.

"Quick get dressed and get out of here he never takes long," Siobhan stood, throwing his clothes at him. Dave sat up and pulled on his jeans, socks, and T-shirt, before heading for the bedroom door. "Here!" He turned and Siobhan threw his underwear at him hitting him in the face. Dave started to laugh, grabbed them and shoved them in his back pocket. "Go on," she urged.

He waved at her and turned and ran down the stairs. Sitting on the second to bottom step, he pulled on his right boot and, as he lifted the left one, the bathroom door burst open. Ray came out, drying his head with a towel as he walked past the top of the stairs and went into his room. Dave let out the deep breath he'd sucked in, pulled his other boot on quickly, stood up and bolted out the door.

8

Detective Sergeant Miller sat at her desk in a squad room cubicle reading that day's copy of the Guardian. Detective Constable Wainwright approached, stopping at the cubicle entrance. He cleared his throat to announce his presence. She glanced up, "You know I watched you coming from the far end of the room, this is a frosted glass cubicle not an office."

"Yes ma'am."

"And don't call me that, I'm not your mother, I'm six years younger than you for Christ sakes!"

Wainwright dropped a thick file on the desk. "Raymond Collins in all his glory."

"What's the Coles notes?"

"Lots of juvenile, shoplifting, joy riding, vandalism, expelled from school for assaulting a teacher!"

"Busy boy!"

"The vandalism was a cause for some concern."

"Oh?" Miller thumbed through the file.

"Spray painted the windows of a corner store."

"Go on?"

"Pakis out, NF, England for the English and so on."

"Bigoted little shit then?"

"Three weeks later the store was burnt to the ground, Molotov cocktail through the window, no arrests."

The female officer interjected, "Did they bring him in?"

"He had an alibi."

"And as an adult?"

"Just did two years for armed robbery."

Miller slowly folded the paper and put it down on the desk, "Go on."

"Kebab joint on the Edgware Road, Colindale. Seems Mr. Collins was drunk and didn't think the proprietor was cutting the donair kebab meat thick enough. Took the knife and threatened to cut his throat, emptied the till, shouted some nasty racial epithets and scarpered."

"Really?"

Wainwright nodded, "Yep, seems he's got quite the history."

"I meant really, epithets?"

"Yes ma'am, epithets, an adjective used as a term of abuse."

"I know what it means," she tsked, "I'm just surprised you do that's all."

"The Daily Mail has a word of the day Ma'am and that was one of last weeks."

"Fascinating."

"Along with dolor," Wainwright stood straighter, proud of himself.

"Dolor?"

"It means sorrow."

"Does it?"

"According to the Daily Mail, yes."

Miller chuckled, "My ex-mother-in-law was named Dolores, maybe that's why she was such a miserable cow, doomed at birth."

Wainwright picks the file back off the desk. "One thing of note, there was a second arrest at the kebab shop, a Mitchell Collins."

"Same last name?"

"Cousins," the officer added quickly.

"Was he convicted?"

"Released without charge, the shop owner says he and Raymond were together, he claimed coincidence."

"Coincidence?" Miller's eyes narrowed, "There are no coincidences."

"I couldn't agree more, apparently when he was arrested, Mitchell was eating a kebab and claimed that as proof of his innocence."

"The kebab alibi defence, I believe Ronnie Biggs tried that one."

"Really?"

"No," she stated blandly in response, "That Colindale kebab shop, what was it called?"

"Andy's."

"Same place that got shut down in the heroin bust?"

"Previous owner. Although his cousin runs it now."

"More coincidences," Miller added slowly, the wheels turning in her head.

"The drug squad keeps a tab on the place, squeaky clean apparently."

"If you say so."

"One other thing," Wainwright continued, "when young Raymond was arrested for joyriding Mitchell was driving the car. They spent some time in juvie together for that one and he was the alibi for the corner store arson."

"Apparently the short sharp shock didn't stun them back to the straight and narrow."

"Apparently not, no."

Miller closed the file and sat it on her desk, "Check Mitchell's prints against the Ford Capri they used to run Mr. Patel over."

"You think they did it?"

"There are no coincidences."

"Right ma'am," as he turned to leave her office she called out behind him, "And get me a cuppa, will you? I'm parched."

Carl drove past Brent town hall on his way to visit his aunt, Marvin Gaye was playing on the cassette deck as he sang along, "Tell me, what's going on..." He pulled the work van into a parking spot on the Chalkhill estate, climbed out, locking the driver's door as he did, and then walked around the van checking all the other doors. He turned slowly in a circle and stared up at the blocks of flats. Not one face visible on the drab concrete walkways, but he knew without a doubt that someone was up there watching. No one came on the estate without word spreading like wildfire. Grey, concrete, drab, six-storey monolithic monuments to the state of the country and the government's lack of forethought as far as housing it's poor. "Shove them away into the countless estates nationwide and let them rot," Carl shook his head in disgust. The Poets wasn't exactly luxury but compared to this place he felt like his family had won the pools.

He surveyed the walkways that ran along the third and fifth floors, the flats were two-storey units and entered one of the blocks, through one of the frosted glass doors. After jogging up four flights of stairs, he turned onto one of the walkways and walked to the third door on the left. The door was painted pink, fuchsia; his aunt, Beatrice, who lived there, had informed him on the day he had helped move them in. Every fourth door was fuchsia, there were blue, yellow, green and fuchsia doors in every block always in that order, in a council mandated attempt to brighten the place up and make it more palatable. The council had an employee, Harry Green, whose sole job was scraping down and repainting the doors as they faded and cracked or as was more often the case, became vandalized. He compared himself to the crews of painters who spent their entire careers painting and repainting the Forth bridge. There were 1900 front doors on the estate.

"Keep me going 'til the pension cheques roll in."

Carl knocked on the fuchsia door and, through the frosted glass, saw his aunt shuffling slowly down the hallway. He stood and waited patiently as she drew back the top bolt, the bottom bolt, the centre bolt, unlocked the deadbolt and finally turned the door handle. The door opened inward, and his aunt looked up at Carl, who towered above her.

"Carl, what you doing here?" She stared up at his face and reached up and held it in her hands, he was a good foot taller than she was.

"Mum sent me over, she made up a poultice for your ankle."

"Oh, she didn't have to do that, and you certainly didn't have to come all the way over here with it."

"It's no problem auntie" The kettle started to whistle in the kitchen. She let go of his face and turned and shuffled into the flat.

"You're just on time, come in, have a cup of tea."

"I should be getting back to work."

"Nonsense, nonsense, we never see you, a cup of tea won't kill you."

"Just a quick one then, I don't like to leave the van unattended." Carl walked through into the open plan kitchen come living room, where he found his cousin, Dejean, laying on the sofa smoking a joint. A set of headphones from his Walkman plugged in his ears barely muffling the sounds of Steel Pulse playing as loud as the device would allow, distorting the bass and treble lines that escaped into the room as if fleeing the abuse being afflicted upon them. "You're up early," Carl wasn't even sure his cousin could hear him over the music.

Beatrice snorted, "He hasn't gone to bed yet."

"Must be nice."

Dejean pulled one of the headphones loose from his ear, his only token politeness to Carl's presence, "What you worried? Think just cause you're on the Hill we gonna rip off your van?"

"Like it doesn't happen!"

"Think just cause you got a job, got a nice fat pay cheque from your honky white boss that we've all got to capitulate?"

"Oh, it's a political stance, is it?"

"Every ting's political!"

"Bullshit, you should meet my mate Dave he'd lap all this up."

"I've met him, saw him at Linton, does he know he's not black?"

"Think I'll skip the tea auntie, got work to do."

Dejean smirked, "Run along, make sure you jump when your Master calls!"

"Fuck off Mustard!"

"Carl!"

"Sorry auntie, gotta go." Carl turned and headed away down the hall.

"Thanks for that Dejean. He hardly ever come around and you drive him away when him does."

Dejean made a clucking sound, like a chicken, and took a big, smoky drag on the joint, "The boys a coconut."

"A what?" Beatrice gives him a questioning look.

He snorted, "Brown on the outside, white on the inside."

Dave lay on his bed staring at the ceiling. Suddenly, there was a loud knocking at the front door, he wasn't expecting anyone, so he ignored it. The knocking started again louder and more urgent this time.

"For fuck sakes." Dave rolled out of the bed and pulled on some jeans, his foot caught in the bar mat that was pinned on either side on the back of them and when he gets the jeans pulled up the bar mat is wrapped around his crotch, like a nappy. "Jesus fuck" he muttered but didn't bother to correct or straighten it up, he's only going to tell the unwanted door knocker to sling their hook when he gets there anyway. The knocking starts once more, even louder, and even more urgent. "I'm coming, hold yer horses." When he reached the door, he undid the three bolts and yanked it open, "WHAT!?"

Siobhan was standing there, "Morning." She had a grin as big as a Cheshire cat on her face.

"What are you doing here?"

"That's charming!"

"Just didn't expect to see you here, that's all."

"Thought I'd come and see where you live." She leans from side to side trying to see over Dave's shoulder into the flat.

"Really?"

"You gonna invite me in?"

"Yeah, yeah of course." Dave stepped back and held the door open. Siobhan stepped in looking around as she did. He began to feel a little embarrassed, "It's nothing special,"

Siobhan looked around the sparsely furnished flat, a dresser on one wall with family photographs, a vase devoid of flowers with a brown stain partway up the inside indicating that it had been some time since there had been any. Above the dresser, on the wall, on one side hung the wall phone and on the other a faux velvet picture of dogs playing poker. An old wood cabinet television sat in the centre of the room, Jean and Stan's matching worn and stained armchairs facing it, and on top of it, old framed black and white photos of Dave's grandparents. On the opposite wall to the dresser a faux velvet picture of dogs shooting pool, and on the wall beside the front door, one of the same canines betting on a horse race to complete the set. "Nice art."

"Fuck off." They both start to laugh.

"Come here," Dave grabs Siobhan around the waist and kisses her on the lips.

"Gonna dump me now?"

"No, why would I?"

"Cause you've seen the way I live."

She fluffed her hair with her hand, and playfully asked, "Where's your room?"

"Why would you need to know that?"

She grinned, "Why do you think?" Dave turned, pulling her by the hand, and led her into his room. Siobhan stood in the door of the room and took it all in. The piles of clothes, the clean indistinguishable from the dirty, the stacks of records, most of which aren't even in their sleeves. The newspapers on the windows, empty beer cans and cider bottles, several empty Actifed cough medicine bottles. Empty popper bottles scattered on the windowsill with an overflowing ashtray. Yellow cigarette smoke stains on the ceiling. "Had a cold did you Dave?"

"Not for a long time, no, why?" He replied cautiously as Siobhan picks up an Actifed bottle.

"Oh That?"

She turned the bottle over in her hand, examining it, "Quick high for losers, Ray says."

“They’re old,” Dave defended himself, “I haven’t done that in a long time.”

“How’s it go? Open the cider, drink enough so that you can pour the cough medicine in, close the cap, shake it up and shoot the lot while it’s still frothing and get a quick blast.” She tosses the empty bottle back onto a messy table, “Lasts for what? Ten minutes tops and then do another?”

He defensively repeated, “Like I said I haven’t done that in a while.”

She smirks at him, “Maybe I should dump you.”

“What? Why?”

“Cause now I’ve seen the way you live. Not your family.”

Dave laughed nervously, “Gave you a shock, did it?”

“It’s exactly what I thought I’d find.”

“Had low expectations, did you?”

“I’m a realist,” she shrugged, eyeing the room.

He watched her, surprised at her words, “You’re not gonna dump me then?”

“Depends?”

“On what?”

“Why are you wearing a diaper?”

Dave looks down at the bar mat wrapped around his groin and laughed, “It’s a new fashion fad.”

“Sexy... Not!”

“Maybe you should do me a mural?”

“Bowie?”

“No, me, imagine it we’re doing it and everywhere you look there I am?”

Siobhan rolled her eyes dramatically, “If you think I’m ever doing anything in here you’ve got a heck of a lot of cleaning up to do first.”

“So, we’re not...” Dave felt his heart sink.

“No, we’re not. Let’s put this place in order.”

“Can’t!” He looked relived, “I’ve got things to do.”

“Like what?”

"First, go down the cafe and get a bacon and mushroom sandwich," he stated, urging her back toward the front door.

"A bacon and mushroom sandwich?" She was clearly interested.

He continued to encourage her, glad her mind was on something else beside the state of his room, "Breakfast is the most important meal of the day."

"Then what?"

Dave closed and locked the door, "Gotta go down the social and reopen my claim."

"Okay then that should only take an hour, we'll clean this pigsty up after, besides I've never had a bacon and mushroom sandwich."

"It's the bollocks," they laughed together and walked off.

In Abdul's Sunshine Cafe, a typical London greasy spoon, there were twelve tables with salt, pepper, ketchup, and H.P Sauce Dispensers on them, a vinyl tiled floor with a checkered black and white pattern with one row of five white tiles in front of the counter where the original ones had worn out and no black tiles had been available to replace them with. Behind the stainless-steel counter, a tea urn and a griddle where Abdul, the Turkish proprietor, was frying bubble and squeak. Dave crossed the room and nodded. Abdul grinned at him, "Dave, my friend. Bacon and mushroom sandwich on white?"

Dave held up two fingers proudly as Siobhan followed close behind him, "Two of 'em."

"You must be hungry."

"Only one's for me," the boy grinned at him.

Abdul finally spotted the lovely young lady close at Dave's heel, "And who is this beautiful young woman?"

"This is my friend, Siobhan."

"Your friend?" The shop owner nodded slowly, knowingly.

"Yeah, that's right."

Abdul winked at Dave, "Methinks she must be more than that."

"Oh, and why's that?"

"Because other than you no one has ever ordered a bacon and mushroom sandwich in my establishment." Abdul laughed and Siobhan echoed his laughter.

"Thought I'd give it a go. Dave says it's the bollocks."

"Does he? Well, if you ever get tired of Dave's eloquence, I am Abdul and I will cook you all the bacon and mushroom sandwiches you desire."

Dave feigned insult, "You keep your eyes in your head you cheeky bastard."

Siobhan smiled, "Maybe I should try this famous sandwich first before I base my entire future on an unending supply of them."

"As you wish. Would you and your friend like some tea Dave."

"Yeah, I'll have...."

Abdul cut him off, "Three sugars and double milk, I should know that by now. And you my dear?" He asked turning to the young woman.

She smiled politely, "Just black thanks."

"Very well, go and sit and I will bring them over."

"Stick them on my tab Abdul there's a good man," Dave piped up hopefully. Abdul hesitated, Dave's tab is a long way over what he would normally allow but due to Siobhan's presence he nodded and gave Dave a tight-lipped smile. Dave and Siobhan sat at the table nearest the window and stared out at the grey sky. "Think it's going to rain?" he asked her.

"You don't have any money Dave?"

"It's all good. There's a temporary lack of funds that's all."

"You should have said," Siobhan looked disappointed, "I could have paid for the sandwiches."

"That ain't gonna happen!"

"Why not?"

"I'm the man, how would that look?"

"What do you think this is 1958?" Abdul approached the table with the cups of tea. Siobhan pulled a ten-pound note from her jeans pocket. "How much for the sandwiches?" She asked him with a smile.

Abdul hesitated, tempted by the proffered money, "I can't possibly accept your money Dave is a trusted friend and customer, he will pay me as it suits him. But thank you, I will finish your sandwiches" Abdul turned to head back to the counter and Siobhan shoved the money back in her pocket.

"See I told you, it's all good." They now sat in awkward silence until the sandwiches arrived, Dave stared out of the window and sulked.

"Let's see then," Siobhan ignored him and picked up the sandwich to take a bite; the grease from the butter running on her hand as she did.

Dave looked askance, watching her, "You're doing it wrong."

"I'm eating a sandwich wrong?"

"Yeah, there's a method."

She set the sandwich gently back on the plate, and slid it toward him, "Go on then, show me." Dave took the top off both his and her sandwich and poured a healthy, thick, dollop of ketchup in each followed by the same amount of H.P Sauce. Then replaced the top slices of bread. Siobhan wrinkled her nose, "That's disgusting."

"Try it," Dave laughed and pushed the plate closer towards her.

She lifted half the sandwich, the butter, ketchup and H.P flowing through her fingers like an oily tidal slick, "Gross!"

"Bite into it," Dave encouraged her.

She timidly bit into the sandwich, not knowing what to expect, and her eyes rose above her hands even as she was still tearing a mouthful off. Dave started howling, laughing as she chewed. "Oh my God! This is freaking delicious!" Siobhan exclaimed, plunking the sandwich back onto the plate before wiping her hands on a napkin.

"Didn't I tell you?!"

Behind the counter Abdul started to laugh, "I guess it's a match made in heaven, praise the Lord!"

After their breakfast, Dave and Siobhan leave Abdul's Sunshine Cafe and head across the small park on the corner. There is a pathway that runs diagonally across the grass to the bus stop at the top of Church Lane. At the far end of the path there is a small, shed no more than a six-by-six-foot square, with a broken wooden door that hasn't been used for any official purpose for as long as Dave can remember. The door creaked open as they passed, and a disheveled man, of around 25, who looked more like he's forty stepped out. Dave regarded him, "How's it going, Gimpish?"

"Good Dave you?"

"Alright."

Gimpish scratched a scab on his arm and wiped a dirty hand across his nose."Got a fag?"

"Sure." Dave pulled a crumpled packet of Rothmans from the chest pocket of his denim jacket, took out three cigarettes and gave one each to Gimpish, Siobhan, and himself. He lit his cheap plastic BIC lighter, before holding it out to the other two who lit their cigarettes.

"Fanks, Dave," Gimpish unzipped his trousers and pulled out his dick and took a piss on the corner of the building. Siobhan looked away, completely baffled and disgusted, by what was unfolding in front of her.

"'Ow's Sally Gimp?" Dave asked. At this point, a woman emerged from the shed. She was wearing a T-shirt with a picture of Janis Joplin on the front, obviously no bra as evidenced by her prominent nipples. The track marks on her arms and neck making obvious her affliction. Sally snorted and stood next to Gimp, scratching under her arm, the daylight causing her to squint bloodshot eyes in greeting to Dave. "I'm fine, you got another one of those?"

"For you of course I do," Dave once more pulled the cigarette packet back out of his pocket and gave one to Sally.

"And for later," Sally held her hand out to him.

Dave simply handed her the rest of the pack, "Here."

"Got any dosh?" Sally looked the couple up and down as Siobhan reached for her pocket where Dave knew she had the ten-pound note.

Dave grabbed Siobhan's arm quickly, "Nah sorry Sally we're both skint."

Sally stared intently into Siobhan's eyes, "Is that right?"

Siobhan didn't miss a beat, "Yeah, we're on the way to the social." A 79 bus pulls up at the stop opposite as she spoke.

Sally sneered, showing empty spaces where her teeth used to be, "Better get your bus then."

Siobhan turned and watched people get on and off the bus. "We're walking, like I said, skint."

The entire time Sally's eyes were boring a hole through to the back of Siobhan's head. Dave pulls on Siobhan's arm. "We'd best get going," he turned her away and they walked down Church Lane towards Wembley. Sally snarled, looked away without a word and disappeared back into the shed.

Siobhan looked at Dave confused with what had happened, "Who the fuck were they?"

"That's Gimpish and Sally, local smack heads."

She looked over in disgust, "They live in that shed?"

"Sometimes yeah, depends on how busy Sally's been."

"Busy?" Siobhan's eyebrows raised curiously.

Uncaringly, Dave answered, "Yeah busy, she gets enough cocks to suck they'll get a room in that doss house down in the Welsh Harp."

"How do you know these people?" Siobhan was silently questioning her current friendship with Dave.

"Gimpish used to drink in the Laureate."

"I've never seen him."

"Long time back, before your time."

"What happened?"

"Sally," he shrugged, "Sally happened, she used to be half decent, when he took up with her, he lived in my building with his mum."

"Now he lives in a shed?" A wave of pity crossed her face.

"Unless she's busy, like I said, yeah, his mum kicked them out after they sold her fridge."

"Christ!" They walked along in silence for a few minutes."Have you ever?"

Innocently he asked, "Ever what?"

"With Sally."

Dave burst out laughing, "Fuck off. Not enough whiskey in Scotland!"

She linked her arm in his, "Good." Dave sighed quietly, relieved that she had believed his lie.

At the bottom of Church Lane, they turned right, at The Blackbirds and headed towards Wembley Park. However, Dave had a better idea, he knew of a shortcut. "C'mon, this way," he pulled her by the arm and started to head across the busy four lane road.

Siobhan looked surprised, "What are you doing? You'll get us killed!"

"It's quicker." They were now in the centre of the four lanes, waiting to get across the next two. Dave saw his chance and ran out, leaving Siobhan behind, but he misjudged and the driver of a Mercedes, coming off the roundabout, had to slam on the brakes so as to not run him over. The driver screeched to a halt, wound down the driver's side window and shouted at Dave, "Get out of the road you moron!"

At this point, Siobhan had caught up to Dave in the centre of the road. Dave swung his foot hard, his steel toe capped boot putting a dent in the centre of the driver's door. "Fuck you, you rich fuck!"

The driver, a man in his mid-fifties, looked totally stunned, and screamed, "You arsehole!" Before driving away as fast as he could.

Siobhan grabbed Dave by the wrist, "C'mon you lunatic, you'll get us both arrested!" They sprinted across the road, through the corner gate, and into the Chalkhill Estate.

"Why are we going through the estate, Dave?" Siobhan was getting nervous.

Dave shrugged, "'Cause it's quicker."

Siobhan hesitated, "Ray told me to never come in here, says he wouldn't."

"Ray's a pussy."

She looked at him with surprise knowing her brother's reputation, "You gonna tell him that?"

Dave stood up straighter, "Of course," he bragged.

Siobhan chuckled, "Sure, you will."

"It's the middle of the day," Dave groaned walking in front of her toward their destination, "nothing's going to happen."

"You'd better be right!"

At this end of the estate the units were all three-storey townhouses, arranged in square blocks. The bottom floor with a brick exterior, the top two with a fake plaster finish coloured somewhere between grey or mauve. The front gardens consisted of concrete to park cars on, the doors were blue, yellow, green, and fuchsia, just like in the blocks they were heading toward. The houses and the blocks were divided by a small area of woodland no more than fifty feet across and running down to the back fence of the estate. The Copse, a sign grandiloquently announcing its name, had been designed to add a park-like atmosphere to the area, but, it had long been used as a rubbish tip. There were old prams, sinks, bags of rubbish scattered around, used needles and syringes spread all over, old mattresses, tyres, and even a car door. As Dave and Siobhan walked past, a group of kids were running through the rubbish, shouting and yelling, playing without a care in the world, on an old tyre swing someone had hung, at some point, in an attempt at making the area more park-like. Past the Copse, were the blocks, and, as they turned the corner, the blocks loomed ominously above them. Siobhan gripped Dave's elbow with both hands. She had ridden past on the bus, during shopping trips with the girls to Wembley High Street, Marks and Sparks, HMV, Cromwell's Bazaar cut price fashion boutique, however, being on the bus and walking through here, were two totally different things. "Scared?" Dave asked, noticing the death grip on his arm.

"A little yeah," Siobhan huddled closer to him.

"Don't be. I told you it's the middle of the day, it's quicker going this way," Dave ducked into a passage between two of the blocks. In here, they were momentarily obscured from view from the street and walkways. At that moment, two Black teenagers stepped in front of them. Dave and Siobhan froze. One of them, Samson, was holding a machete. Dave's mouth felt suddenly as dry as sandpaper, Siobhan was gripping his arm so tightly it hurt. The two boys stared silently at them; Samson didn't take his eyes from Dave's face. The other boy's eyes were running all over Siobhan's body. Dave could feel his heart beating so hard he felt like his chest would certainly explode and blow blood all over the walls.

From behind Dave a voice suddenly spoke, "Leave them be, him going to the dole, he got nothing."

Dave turned to find Dejean, Carl's cousin. The two of them had nodded recognition to each other at the Linton Kwezi Johnson concert but that had been their total contact, before now. When Dave turned back to his two assailants they had already faded into a corridor. He turned back to Dejean, to thank him but the man had already walked away, he and Siobhan already forgotten and irrelevant. She pulled his arm, gasping out a sigh of relief, "Let's go!" They hurried through the rest of the estate in silence. When they emerged on the road at the station, she turned to him, tears running down her cheeks, "You fucking arsehole! You could've got us killed!"

"It was the middle of the day though!"

A 79 bus came past heading back to Kingsbury. "Fuck you, Dave!" Siobhan turned away from him and hopped on the bus, leaving Dave standing alone on the pavement.

Samson had moved to Chalkhill with his mum two years earlier, they had been living in Linwood, Scotland, where he was born. But, after his father had been laid off, yet again, from the Chrysler plant in the latest round of cutbacks, the strain on his family had become intolerable. Samson came home from school one day to find his mother packing their bags, her fresh black eye evidence of what had transpired whilst he was out learning long multiplication. Being from Harlesden originally, his mother moved them back to Brent, and they settled into a new life on the Chalkhill Estate.

Samson's heavy Scottish brogue did not go unnoticed at either the school or on the estate. The bullying made his life hell, until one day, he was coming home from school wearing a Bob Marley T-shirt and sporting a fresh black eye of his own when Dejean came out of his flat and saw him. Samson looked down sheepishly and attempted to walk past. Dejean placed his hand on Samson's chest, kindly but firmly, and stopped him in his tracks, "What 'appen to your eye?"

"Nuffin'," Samson looked down at the pavement and turned slightly attempting to hide his face.

Dejean grabbed Samson's face looking over his injury carefully, "Don't look like nuffin', so I ask again, whappen?"

Samson pulled away from him and bashfully looked at the ground, "Kids at school."

"'Cause you talk like dat?"

"I reckon," he replied with his thick accent.

"You stand up for yourself?"

"I try."

Dejean noticed his shirt, "Bob Marley huh."

"My ma's favourite."

"What about you?"

Samson really had no opinion on the subject, "He's alright I guess."

"You wanna listen to Reggae," Dejean attempted to educate the younger boy, "you should be listening to Linton or Steel Pulse, British reggae, reggae that says something 'bout us."

He looked up at Dejean with a shrug, "Don't know them."

"What do you know?"

"Nuffin' I guess."

"Well, it's time you did."

"Like what?"

"You gonna grow up weak?" Dejean began his lecture, "Or you gonna grow up strong? In this country a Black man ain't got nuffin' unless he takes it, they won't let us be anything more than they want us to be."

"Who?"

"The politicians, the Government, they keep us down, they talk about rivers of blood if we live here, I say we give them rivers of their own blood."

Samson nodded along in agreement, "My ma says we need to follow what Martin Luther King had to say."

"That right, that how you come get that black eye, you wanna listen to some dead politician, listen to Malcolm X, listen to the Black Panthers, to Marcus Garvey. The politicians force us to live in Ghettoes, we're not slaves, we stand up!" From that day on the bullying stopped, Dejean took Samson under his wing, preached violent revolution to the boy, taught him self-reliance, and sowed the seeds of what would eventually unfold.

9

Dave stood in a long line of bored, glassy-eyed claimants. They had all been here before, most of them multiple times. There were no surprises, you were either eligible for more dole money, or you weren't. There was no point in wasting your time coming down here if your claim had expired. If that was the case, then you had to either find a job, and good luck with that, or head down to the social office in Hendon where you would plead your case for welfare. Single young males, like Dave, who weren't physically handicapped, as was the case with Wobble, had slim to no chance of scoring enough points on the council rotor system to qualify for those benefits.

There were about six people in front of him, he figured, it was hard to be certain because so many people brought company: girlfriends, boyfriends, mates, mothers, someone to pass the time with. Dave was bored and fidgety, he wished Siobhan was here to keep him company. He had an uneasy feeling and wasn't sure if it was because he was worried about her telling Ray about the insanity of taking her through the estate, or, and this was more disturbing to him, because he didn't want her to dump him.

The queue shuffled slowly forward, and for want of something better to do, Dave read the multitude of warning posters, warning of the consequences of attempting to defraud Her Majesty's Government out of her coffers by making fraudulent statements on your claim forms. Including the possibility of jail time, three square meals, and a cot, Dave thought to himself, not that he'd ever been to prison. At least, not beyond a couple of nights in the local police cells for drunk and disorderly and that didn't count because you needed three in a twelve-month span for it to go on your record permanently or for you to see the inside of a courtroom.

Dave had reached the front of the line and was becoming more impatient by the minute. A young man in front of him, an East Indian, as was the clerk, were having a heated argument, but it wasn't in English, so Dave had no idea what they were arguing about. Not to mention, it seemed to be going on for an inordinately long time. The people in the lines to his left and his right were being seen, signing the necessary forms and leaving, as was the norm. The "in and out shop" was one of the many nicknames for the place, the dole office, the pogey amongst the others. Finally, the man ahead of him left, still shouting in his, to Dave, incomprehensible language. Dave walked up to the counter and presented his UB40 form, "I want to reopen my claim, it still has six weeks to run."

The clerk didn't look up from his paperwork, "Does it?"

"Yep."

"You were employed where?" He continued shuffling papers at his station, clearly uninterested.

"A machine shop," Dave answered quickly and then added, "down in Hendon."

The employee picked up a pen and began to write on a paper, "And what happened?"

"I guess we didn't hit it off."

"You didn't hit it off?" The clerk finally looked up at Dave over the brim of glasses perched on the tip of his nose.

"No."

The clerk stopped writing, set his pen on the desk and regarded Dave, "You need a much better reason than that to reopen your claim."

"Why?" Dave looked confused and the argument he had witnessed earlier in another language finally started to make sense, "It's still got six weeks to run."

"Yes, but you secured employment thereby suspending your benefits."

"That don't matter," Dave insisted.

"Oh, but it does," the clerk began to look past Dave's shoulder at the line forming behind him.

"No, no, no."

"Oh yes, yes, yes," the administrator quipped back as if he was a pro at arguing with people.

"Nah, see I've done this before," Dave continued to plead his case, "if you've got time left the claim is still open and you just refile see?"

The clerk pulled out a fresh form and stacked some papers on his desk, "Once upon a time that was true, yes, but now you must prove bona fide reasons for leaving your employment in order to reopen your claim. NEXT!"

"Wait a minute, I'm not done here." But he was, as the next claimant, a short, stocky Black man, had slipped in front of Dave and started to engage the clerk in conversation about his claim. Dave turned and trudged slowly back through the crowded office and out of the door.

A voice called out, "Oi, Dave." He turned to see Andy the Weasel. Andy was a short, skinny, middle-aged man, who lived on The Poets and drank in The Laureate. He had a skinny face with a long skinny nose, and sported a thin weak looking moustache, that and his general proclivity for dishonesty had earned him the moniker, "Weasel."

"Andy? 'Ow's, it going?"

"Any better there'd be six of me," Dave smiled, Andy had an irritatingly ingratiating way of speaking that never ceased to rub Dave the wrong way.

"Signing on then?"

"Captain fucking obvious," Dave thought silently then stated, "Apparently not."

"Wanna earn some quick cash?" Andy hissed.

"Doing what?" Andy was always hatching some scheme or other and Dave knew not to go along without checking just how much trouble he could be getting himself into.

"Got two lines of income currently, you could be useful in either," Andy responded, curling his lip to pick his teeth with a toothpick, a motion that Dave felt furthered his weasel-like features.

"Which one won't get me arrested?"

Andy thought for a moment, "Got some manual labour over in Greenbush. Or I could let you in on an opportunity in the insulation field?"

"Manual labour it is then," Dave knew exactly what the "opportunity in the insulation field" was. It was a scam being perpetrated all over the country. Door to door sales of pumped in spray insulation. Andy's partner Lionel did the sales. Lionel could do a posh accent that would convince the bluest of blue toff that he was from Knightsbridge, not from the council estates in Burnt Oak where he was really born and bred. He'd go from door to door and hope for an elderly gullible mark. Prewar houses were the target, cold, draughty and with failing damp proof courses.

The scam was simple, Andy and a helper would show up at the house on the appointed day with a lorry. In the back of the lorry were large, pressurised gas tanks and lengths of hose. Holes were drilled around the bottom of the house and the hoses were attached. The compressor in the back of the lorry was turned on and there would be loud hissing and banging noises for an hour or so. The hoses get removed from the house and bundled back in the lorry, the holes in the house get filled with cement and the job is complete and payment collected. The only problem is the tanks in the lorry contain nothing except air and the house is as draughty and cold as when the workmen arrived.

"Shall we?" Andy waved his arm expansively as if proffering a ride in a Rolls Royce. Instead, Dave turned to find Andy's beat up multi coloured Ford Anglia parked at the curb.

"You just hanging out at the pogey trolling for a date?"

"Me?" Andy chuckled, "Nah, I've still got three weeks on my claim, I'm on weekly sign though so I come down on my lunch, then head back to work."

Dave got in the Anglia and Andy pulled out from the curb, as they continued their previous conversation, "What's the pay?"

"Twenty quid cash per day paid daily, we leave the estate at seven and 'ave you back at the Laureate by five thirty for opening time. Plus, there's always a case of beer on hand in case any of you get the DTs and can't cope"

Siobhan had got off the bus two stops up from the stadium and had walked back. She was mad, yes, and she felt she had a right to be, but she liked Dave and didn't want it, whatever it was, to end like this. She walked past the stop where she had jumped on the bus just as Andy's Anglia pulled around the corner with Dave in it and drove away. She raised her hand to wave at them to stop but they were gone without either of them noticing her. "Fuckin' charmin'," she rolled her eyes and turned back to the bus stop, slumped against the shelter and waited for a number 79.

Andy pulled the Anglia to a stop outside a row of terraced houses with their windows and doors boarded up, Dave looked around curiously, "Demolition?"

"What's that?"

"The job? We knocking this lot?"

"Nah. The job's out back. C'mon." Andy led Dave down an alley, between the two houses to the back gardens. In one garden were piles of metal, military style, ammunition cases, heaped two stories high. Across the alley, in the next-door backyard, was a huge pile of what appeared to be large, black, plastic, coffee cups with no handles. There were two young men, leaning on the brick wall that separated the alley from the coffee cups, smoking cigarettes. Dave knew them both, one was Bazza, and Dave was instantly relieved the cigarette incident with his brother had been resolved. The other was Andy's son, Andy junior. Dave couldn't stand Andy junior, no one he knew could, he made his dad look like an upstanding pillar of the community. Dave had no problem with a bit of graft and ingenuity, you had to get by as best you could, anyway you could, he figured. But Andy Junior was in a class of his own, he'd steal the last penny from his best friend's pocket and there were rumours about him being with young girls and boys, as young as twelve, on the estate. Andy had greasy hair and his dad's weasel-like features had twisted more to rat, hence his derogatory nickname, The Rat. Andy shuffled up to the pair, “Alright boys.”

“Daaaave,” Andy junior hissed as much as spoke Dave's name.

Dave sighed, “You haven’t got a spare fag, I don’t suppose?”

“Wheeere’s yours?”

“Ran into Gimpish and Sally.”

Andy Junior sneered, “I’ll sell you one.”

At this point, Bazza spoke up, “Here you go, Dave.” He handed Dave a cigarette. Bazza was no fonder of the younger Andy than anyone else was and although the irony of him giving Dave a cigarette didn’t escape him, he wasn’t about to put up with Andy's bullshit. Dave took the cigarette and leaned in for a light. Bazza smirked, “Who’d’ve thought, eh?”

“I know,” Dave agreed, “Cheers, Baz.”

The Weasel clapped his hands together, “Alright then, if we’ve finished with the mutual lovefest, do you think we could get down to some work?”

The three took long, last puffs on their cigarettes, and because he’d hardly started his, Dave scraped it out on the wall and put what was left of the butt behind his ear. Andy Junior waved at him to follow, “I climb up the top and drop a case down to you, don’t drop it, they're valuable, you pass it to Bazza who empties it and starts a new pile.”

“Ok I guess.”

And so it began, one of the strangest days of work that Dave had ever done. Andy passed one of the brown, metal, military grade ammunition cases down from the top of the pile to Dave who balanced halfway down the pile. Dave handed it to Bazza who opened it and removed a cylindrical black tube that was hinged in the middle. He threw the tube into the alley and carefully stacked the metal case. Stacking them neatly so that they formed a staircase that allowed him to climb up higher than he would otherwise be able to reach.

The work was repetitive and fast. Dave was certain that Andy Junior was pushing the pace to try and force him to screw up, but he kept up. Both he and Bazza worked, grim-faced and determined, not to give their nemesis any satisfaction. The whole time Bowie's "Aladdin Sane" played on a cassette player, each time it ended Dave would run to the deck, press the eject button, flip the tape over and run back in time to catch the next case Andy dropped. Eventually the alley was so full of the cylinders that they had to stop. Dave gasped for breath; he wasn't used to such hard physical work, "What now?"

"Dunno 'bout you but I'm gonna 'ave a fag." Bazza was wheezing; he might be big, he might be tough, but he certainly wasn't fit. It gave Dave a whole new perspective on him, perhaps he wasn't indestructible after all. Andy Junior joined them and took a beer from the case of Red Stripe.

"Gimme one of those," Bazza wheezed. Andy handed Bazza the beer. "And one for Dave, you cheap cunt. It ain't like you pay for 'em." Andy muttered under his breathe and handed Dave a lukewarm beer.

Dave opened it and took a sip, grimacing as he did, "It's warm!"

The Rat hissed, "It's free, stop your bitching or I'll take it back."

Dave sized him up. He wasn't much for direct confrontation, he only weighed nine stone two soaking wet, but he figured he had a good chance against The Rat. "Fuck you, Rat!"

"Don't call me that."

"Why not?"

"Cause I'll fire you that's why!"

"You?"

"Yeah me, I get paid a tenner more than you two do per day to be foreman."

Bazza choked on his beer. "Like fuck you do!"

"Do too!" Andy Junior was whining like a small child now, much to the other's amusement.

"And if you're firing Dave for calling you 'Rat,' not that you really 'ave the power to fire him 'cept in your own 'ead, then you'll 'ave ta fire me or anyone else your old man hires from the estate to replace me. Fucking foreman my arse!" Bazza let out a bellowing guffaw.

The driver's door of the Anglia opened, and Andy emerged, carrying a copy of that day's Sun. The front page was a reprint of an older photograph of Diana Spencer backlit and showing her long legs through her dress. The headline read *"FUTURE ROYAL SHOWS HER FORM BEFORE BIG DAY."* Andy rolled his eyes and grumbled at them, "What the fuck are you three doing lollygagging, the lorries'll be 'ere in an hour, get back to work!"

"What do we do now?" Dave looked at Bazza and The Rat for an answer.

Andy Junior picked up a pair of pliers and two rusty old Stanley knives from the ground, "I'll show you." He handed Dave and Bazza a knife each and kept the pliers for himself. Lifting one of the tubes, he popped it open in the centre and used the pliers to pull the hinge and the locking pin off before tossing one end to Bazza and one to Dave. Dave watched as Bazza scraped a sticker reading "High Explosive" off his end. Bazza looked at Dave and nodded at the end Dave was holding. Catching on, Dave scraped the serial number decal off his end. Bazza threw his into the pile in the next-door back garden and Dave followed suit. And so, it went on. As they were near to finishing there was the sound of H.G.V engines from out in the road followed by reverse gear beepers. "Hurry up! Dad gets furious if we don't get them all done."

The three men go into a frenzy of opening, scraping, piling and, just as the lorry had finished backing into the alley, Dave threw the last canister into the pile. Andy whooped and they all high fived each other, celebrating their small inconsequential victory. Bazza started to laugh, "You'd think Chelsea won the cup!"

“Arsenal more like!” Dave piped in, Bazza tilted his head and stared at Dave. “Or… Chelsea if you’d prefer. Why not?”

“That’s better Dave, much better!”

“Come ooon, you two, let’s get on with it,” The Rat hissed, seeing his father’s disapproving stare at the lack of activity.

Dave shrugged, “What do we do now?”

The lorry that had backed in had a large machine on it’s flatbed. The machine had an even bigger hopper on the top and a chute at the bottom. The driver started the machine up, and it emitted a deafening roar that made Dave recoil in shock. The driver put on a pair of ear protectors, and Dave looked at the others wondering where theirs were. Bazza just shrugged, obviously they didn’t count. Andy Junior had climbed to the top of the pile of plastic containers, scrabbling and sliding as he did, the driver climbed onto the truck bed. As Andy threw him the plastic cups, he threw them into the hopper and the roar became ever more deafening.

Bazza tapped Dave on the shoulder and signaled for him to follow. Around the side of the lorry, where the chute jutted out of the machine, the driver had previously dropped a pile of feed sacks. Bazza held one up, chest high, and down the chute poured black granulated powder. The machine was milling the cups down into the powder. As the sack filled, growing heavier and heavier Bazza’s sizable biceps began to bulge. He nodded for Dave to get a sack and get ready. Once the sack was almost totally full, Bazza threw it over his shoulder and took it to the box van that had backed into the alley in front of the milling lorry.

Dave put the sack in place as the ever-flowing river of black powder continued, but it wasn’t quite in the right position, so the plastic overflowed the edge of the sack, and spilled over, onto the ground. The Weasel started shouting at him to get it fixed, but Dave couldn’t hear a word he was saying over the deafening roar of the machine. He finally wrestled the sack back into place. By the time Bazza returned the sack was a little over half full and already Dave was struggling to hold it up. Bazza saw him struggling and grabbed the sack, nodding for Dave to get the next one ready, as he took over. This continued for the next hour. Dave's arms were burning in pain, and he thought he was going to go deaf from the machine. The plastic continued to pour, and pour, and pour out of its mouth in a never-ending stream of black powder. Finally, the machine was turned off. The driver waited for Andy to hand him a wad of cash and the two lorries left.

"Thank fuck for that. I need a beer!" Dave wiped his brow and grabbed a beer before sitting on the step mountain of metal boxes.

The Weasel started to laugh, "You're a long way from done yet, son." The intermittent beeping sound of a lorry backing up began again and another box van backed into the alley.

"What the fuck now?" Dave felt like he could cry.

The elder Andy slapped his hand down on one of the metal boxes, "Now you load this lot."

By the time the empty cases were all loaded, and the lorry was gone, Dave was exhausted. The four of them piled into the Anglia and set off. All four of them were smoking, so Andy opened the driver's window. As they headed off, the smoke poured from the open window, as if the car had an electrical fire in the dash. After a while, Dave realised that he had no idea where they were. "This ain't the way to Kingsbury?"

The Weasel grinned, "I gotta make a little stop first."

The car pulled off the North Circular Road, behind the Guinness brewery in Park Royal, and into the car park of a large factory that according to the worn out, painted sign on the brickwork above the entrance door was "HE DER ON MANF." The letters "N" and "S," that would have completed the name HENDERSON, had been replaced with bricks that almost matched the yellow-beige colour of the rest of the building.

At one of the loading doors, the box van with the bags of plastic was parked, beside it, the box van with the metal boxes. Andy pulled into a parking spot, turned the car off, and headed across to the main entrance doors. The heat in the car was stifling and the other three climbed out, leaving the doors open, in the vain hope that the car would cool down, and leaned on the bonnet. Bazza took out his fags, and held the pack out to Dave, "Now you owe me."

"No problem. Soon as I get paid."

"Where's miiine?" The Rat whined, holding out his hand.

Bazza shoved the smokes back in his pocket, "Fuck you. You get a tenner a day more than we do for the same work remember?" Andy pulled out his own packet and sulkily lit one up.

Dave pointed at the factory, "What do they do here anyway?"

Bazza laughed, "This is where it gets precious."

"How's that?" Dave was dying to know.

"They manufacture mortar bomb cases." Bazza helpfully informed him.

Andy Junior laughed, eager to get in on the joke; the joke that he and Bazza shared, and Dave didn't. "Then they put them in ammunition caaaaases."

"Then his dad buys them cut price."

"Then we unpackage them."

"Then we break them."

"Then we mill them down."

"Then they buy them back and make more."

"Then we destroy them..."

"Get the fuck out of here!" Dave couldn't believe what he was hearing.

Bazza shrugged, "No seriously, that's the whole thing."

"But why?" Dave was totally incredulous.

"'Cause the military don't use that style of mortar anymore."

"The shells don't even get made, don't exist."

"Then why don't they stop making the cases?" Dave thought he was onto something now.

Andy Junior announced, "They, 'He-der-on manufacturing,' that is, got a contract to make X amount of them."

Bazza finished the statement, “And they’re gonna keep making ‘em until the contract runs out.”

Dave is totally flummoxed, “It doesn’t make any sense though!”

Bazza put Dave straight, “If you was in government would you want to go on the nine o’clock news and announce the closure of ‘Hederon manufacturing,’ throwing more people out of work?”

“Especially round here?” The Rat finished Bazza’s sentence.

“I guess not no, but still. How long have you been doing this?”

“Nine months, me and dad,” Andy Junior puffed his chest out proudly. Although Dave thought it was a strange thing to be proud of.

“I’ve been there for the last five weeks,” Bazza continued, “I was hod carrying on a site in Hounslow but when that finished this was all I could find.”

Dave shook his head, trying to get it around the twisted logic of what he’d just been told. It was so absurd it gave him a headache. Finally, he started to laugh, “Do we have any idea how many more they’re going to make?”

“Dad told me to save some money for gloves and winter boots, so I figure we’ll be at it for a while yet.”

“Unfucking believable,” Dave shook his head and laughed at how ludicrous the whole situation was.

The Weasel pulled up outside the Laureate after collecting an envelope stuffed full of cash, he pulled some notes from his trouser pocket and handed Bazza and Andy a twenty each and held out a tenner to Dave, half as much as the others, as he’d only worked half a day. “You back tomorrow?” The Weasel held tightly onto the note until he got the answer he was looking for.

“Sure, why not?” Dave shrugged, “I’ve got nothing better to do, do I?”

“Seven on the dot we leave, don't be late,” Andy finally released the money, “We stop for sandwiches at Abdul’s and then on to work.”

“Fine, see you then.”

Andy drove off, leaving the other three standing on the pavement outside the pub. Bazza turned to Andy Junior, “Looks like you got the same twenty as me.”

“Eh? Oh, yeah, well dad keeps my other ten, says he’s saving it for me.”

“Bullshit, you ‘earing this, Dave?”

“I hear it, I don’t believe it.”

“It’s true!”

Bazza leans into Andy’s ear, “You’re a liar, wanna know how I know you’re a liar?”

“How?”

“’Cause your dads too cheap to pay you it, and he’s a thief, and even you would know better than to trust him.”

Andy flushed red, more embarrassed than mad, “You don’t know nuffin’ and you better be careful case I tell ‘im what you’re saying!”

“Go ahead,” Bazza grinned at him.

“Beer Baz?” Dave interrupted.

“Can’t Dave, told the missus we’d go bingo later, ‘nother time though?”

“Course.”

Andy stood as if waiting for an invite, an invite that would never come. Dave turned and headed towards the pub, and Bazza headed off home, leaving Andy standing awkwardly where they’d left him. Dave walked into the public bar, there were no other customers in yet, and Siobhan was wiping down the bar. “Hey!” Dave was almost whispering. She stared at him in stony silence. “I didn’t know that would happen!” He tried desperately to explain.

“I hope not!”

“You alright?”

“I guess.”

"Good"

"What were you and the Weasel up to?"

"'Ow'd you know about that?"

"Never mind." She turned to walk away into the other bar.

"You came back!"

"Who says?"

"You must've!" Dave is incredulous now.

"Yeah, alright I came back to give you a bollocking and you were leaving with Andy." Tears began to well up in her eyes, she waswringing a bar mat out in between her fingers, trying to stop it from happening.

Dave is still totally stunned, and oblivious to her reaction, "You came back?"

"So what? What were you up to Dave?"

"I got a job."

She looks at him, surprised, "With the Weasel?"

"Yeah!"

"You're not doing the insulation are you?"

"No, no way, he offered me that, but I turned him down."

"Good," Dave can hear the relief in her voice. "What are you doing then?"

"It's complicated, any chance of a Whitetop?"

"Not 'til you go home and shower, look at you, you're filthy and you don't smell too good neither."

Dave looked down at himself and realised, for the first time, that the black powder and sweat had ground into his shirt and jeans and left him with a black stain from his chest to his knees. "Right, yeah, I'll be back! Don't go anywhere." He turned and quickly walked out of the bar with a grin, like a Cheshire cat, plastered across his face. "She came back," ran through his mind repeatedly. Now, nothing could go wrong with his day.

10

Dave took the lift to the ninth floor, crossed the landing to his flat, unlocked the door and walked inside. In the centre of the living room sat an old suitcase, the one his mum and dad had used when they'd gone to Margate for a week a couple of years back. They had picked it up, used, at a stall, at the Wembley Sunday Market. The market was held every Sunday morning in the car park of the stadium. You could buy almost anything there, whether it was knock-off high fashion clothes and bags, vegetables, fresh from the farm, supposedly, and china sold by barkers, who would toss the pieces from hand to hand, whilst barking the ever-lowering prices. The locals would sometimes go down just for the entertainment factor: "ALL THIS, ALL TWENTY-FOUR PIECES AND DO I WANT TWENTY QUID? NO! DO I WANT FIFTEEN QUID, I WOULDN'T INSULT YA. FOURTEEN EVEN? DON'T BE A PLANK! ALL THIS FOR THE UNBELIEVABLY, LOW PRICE OF TWELVE KNICKER. THAT'S RIGHT, TWELVE QUID, 'OW DOES HE STAY IN BIZNESS YOU MIGHT FINK, WELL THAT'S NOT YOUR PROBLEM IS IT, WHAT'S THAT DARLING? TWO SETS FOR TWENTY? WHY NOT? LET'S DO IT SHALL WE? SORRY MATE DIDN'T KNOW SHE WAS MARRIED!"

Dave's dad sat in his armchair filling out his weekly pools draw sheet, his mum in hers. "Evening," Dave said, as cheery as could be.

His mum got up, she went to speak, but the words caught in her throat. Instead, she went into the kitchen and fiddled with dirty pots and pans at the sink, not actually washing them, just trying to keep occupied. "You and I have to talk!" His dad stated coldly, unmoving, he wouldn't even turn to face his son.

“Sure dad, what’s up?” Dave’s mind was racing, trying to figure out what this could be about, why his mum wouldn’t talk to him.

His dad spoke again, still slow and deliberate, but with a definite edge to his voice, “I think you know.”

“No,” Dave hesitated, “I don’t.”

“Well, you should.” His dad said, not bothering to look up from the draw sheets. Dave stood, wondering where this was going. He and his dad rarely spoke, hadn’t since the first time Dave had come home with his hair dyed bright pink. Although since, it had been through the spectrum in between, blue, red, black, green and for quite a while, bleached blonde. “Petulia!” his dad had called him that first day. Stan had always figured it would pass, that his son was going through a phase, but it hadn’t, and they had grown apart, slowly and gradually, until here they were at the inevitable moment. “We’ve put up with a lot from you, your mother and I, but enough is enough.”

“What are you on about, dad?”

“You seem incapable of holding down a job, you drink too much, and God knows what else you’re taking. I always wondered how you could afford it. But, now I know, don't I?” Stan's voice had started to rise, not just in volume, but in intensity as well. Dave stepped forward, noticing on top of the small Formica coffee table, in front of Stan, was the jam jar from the fridge freezer, the contents stacked beside it, in piles of five-, ten- and twenty-pound notes. “You’re a thief. A petty, nasty, backstabbing thief and your mother tells me this isn’t the first time. You turned your mother into a liar. Your own mother put in a position where she had to choose between ‘er husband and ‘er son, ‘Ow could you?” Stan stood up abruptly and was now bellowing at his son.

Dave stammered at him, unsure what to say, “I was just borrowing it till I got a steady job...”

“AND JUST WHEN WOULD THAT BE? HUH? NEVER WITH YOUR RECORD!” Stan was beside himself with rage.

“I got a job today!”

“Doing what?” His father’s eyes narrowed.

“Working for The Weasel,” Dave thought this would go some way towards placating his father.

Stan was outraged at this point, he stood, stooped but indignant, in front of his son, “YOU WHAT? FIRST YOU STEAL FROM US AND NOW YOU’RE ON THE GRAFT!”

“IT’S NOT LIKE THAT!” Dave was desperate to get his point across, to explain that he isn’t who his father obviously thinks he is.

Stan had heard enough, he lifted the suitcase and threw it at Dave, it landed at his feet, “GET OUT!” He bellowed.

Dave didn’t move. Stan stared at him, his voice now barely a whisper, “Get out, your stuff’s in there. Everything what you’re entitled to that is.”

Dave slowly picked up the suitcase and walked to the door. He opened it slightly, and before he left, he turned back, “Bye mum.” Jean gasped and sobbed in the kitchen but kept her back to him, unable to watch as her son left. Dave stepped out of the flat and closed the door behind him.

In the Laureate, Donny stood at the bar chugging his first beer back like it was a shot of whiskey, as was his habit after a day at work. Terry pushed the bar door open and walked in, nodding to Siobhan, who opened him a Whitetop.

“One for Donnie too please, sweetheart,” Terry smiled at her.

Donnie was taken aback, “What’s that in aid of?”

“Keep it under your hat, but I hit on a long shot at Doncaster today.”

“Get the fuck out, how much?”

“Put on a fiver at thirty to one, so you figure it out.”

Donny looked aghast, “You jammy fucker!”

Terry chuckled, “Skill mate, all skill.”

“Right, that’s why you deliver the mail is it? Cause you’re a professional fucking gambler?”

“Put that beer on Donnie’s bill, Siobhan,” Terry called out to the bartender, Siobhan laughed and continued washing glasses.

“Fuck you will she!” The two men laughed and chinked their beers together.

The door swung open and in walked Alex, hair freshly cropped to a number one, a new white Fred Perry tennis shirt with red collar and sleeve trim stitching, twelve-hole Dr. Martens and red tag Levi’s. He puffed his chest out proudly, “Evening boys.”

Terry and Donnie stared at him, the newly minted skinhead. Donnie spoke first, “What the fuck?”

“What? You’ve both been skins for years,”

Donnie is flummoxed, “Aye I know we have; I’m just wondering what suddenly brought this on with you?”

“Gotta fly the flag boys!” Alex reached up with his left hand, and slowly rolled up his right sleeve. On the top of his bicep was a circle with a cross in it, the British Movement logo.

Donny shook his head in resignation, “Ah for fuck sakes Alex, you fucking numpty, why?”

“Because it’s time we made a stand, that's why,” Alex proclaimed, reciting what he’d been taught in backroom meetings, in grimy pubs and clubs with Ray and the other right-wing extremists. Terry leaned back against the bar and watched silently, knowing that whatever he said would fall on deaf ears. Alex had no idea what skins like he and Donnie stood for, skins from before the taint of fascism. “Tell the Scottish git will ya?” Alex turned to Terry, mistakenly believing that he would get some support.

Terry threw his arms up in the air, wanting nothing to do with the conversation, “Don’t bring me into this.”

The bar door opened again, and Dave walked in, head hung low, suitcase and all. The other three turned and stared, bemused at this new development, forgetting their previous discussion. Terry spoke first, “Please tell me that you’re about to thump that down on the table, throw it open and try to sell us silk scarves and watches, Dave.”

"I wish." Dave replied, his voice hardly more than a whisper.

Alex laughed cruelly, "Stan and Jean finally got you sussed and turfed you out!"

Dave snapped back at him, focusing all his hurt and confusion on Alex. "Fuck you, Captain Skinhead!"

Alex lunged at him, Terry and Donnie sprang into action cutting him off. Terry drew himself up to his full height, puffed out his chest and put his hand on Alex's chest, "Steady, Alex."

"He's got it coming!" Alex glared at him as the two young men faced-off, chest to chest, staring into each other's eyes.

Siobhan spoke up, "Not in here you don't. You two want to kill each other, do it somewhere I don't have to clear the mess up."

Alex turned back to the bar and Terry glanced at Dave, "So?"

Dave shrugged, "Alex got it right, he just didn't have to be such a dick about it did he?"

Without turning back from the bar, Alex smirked, "Didn't I?"

Terry put his hand on Dave's shoulder and leaned into his ear, "Does this involve a jam jar?"

"Yeah," Dave sighed.

Terry sighed and leaned back out, "You fucking idiot, I tried to warn you, didn't I?"

Donnie called out to Siobhan, and turned a stool towards Dave, "Give Dave a beer on me darling, I've a feeling he needs one."

Siobhan handed Donnie the beer and he turned to Dave. "Where you gonna kip?"

"Dunno, don't spose..."

Donnie nearly spat out his sip of beer, "Nay fucking way, where? I've got a cot, a hot plate and a shelf and no room to swing a cat, not that I like cats. Where d'you spose you'd fit?"

The newly homeless man looked longingly at Siobhan, a look of desperation in his eyes. Her mouth dropped open at his incredulity, “No, are you nuts?”

Donnie, Terry and Alex watched with wide eyes. Alex was the first to speak, “What the fuck’s going on here then?”

In a panic, Siobhan quickly responded, “Nothing. Are you nuts? Me and Dave? He wishes!”

Terry added, “Could you imagine? In his wildest dreams!”

Alex looked thoughtfully between Dave and Siobhan, slowly turning a fifty pence coin over and over in his fingers. Feeling the intensity of his stare, she turned and headed into the other bar to avoid the conversation. “Does seem somewhat ridiculous.” Alex laughed, kicking the leg of a chair as he began to walk towards the Gents, “I’ve gotta piss.”

He headed away to the Gents, Donnie’s turned head followed him for a moment before he addressed Dave, “I never thought you had it in ya, well done, my son!”

Dave grinned, “I’ve got no idea what you’re on about.”

Donnie burst out laughing in response, “Fuck you, you’re doing ‘er, it’s written all over your boat.”

“We’re keeping it shtum,” Terry gave Dave a wink.

“Nay fucking wonder, Ray’ll ‘ave ‘is guts for garters when he finds out.”

At this point, Dave was beginning to feel desperate. With everything that had happened that day, he had moved the thought of Ray finding out, about Siobhan and him, into the far reaches of his mind. “IF he finds out, you mean?”

“Oh Davey,” Donnie faked a laugh, “he’s gonna find out at some point and it’ll’ve been good to know ya. Can’t say I blame ya though she’s got quite the bottle.”

“Fuck you, sweaty!”

Donnie grabbed Dave playfully around the neck, “Your secret’s safe with me! In fact, I commend you for going out in a blaze of passion, but you might want to tone it down when her brother gets here.”

Terry laughed, "Put him down, Samson, we've still gotta figure out where Goldilocks is puttin' 'er 'ead down for the night"

Donnie still held Dave around the neck, taunting him, "But he's so cute when he's annoyed."

Dave gasped for air, attempting to pry the fingers from around his throat, "You're choking me!"

Finally, Donnie relaxed his grip on his red-faced victim with a smirk, and Dave fell back against his stool, rubbed his neck and gave an exaggerated cough.

Terry pondered thoughtfully, "I've got an idea!" He used his elbows to push himself from the countertop, "Finish your beer and come with me." Dave tipped the bottle up to the ceiling, swigging his beer quickly before plopping it down on the bar. He moved to follow Terry to the door. Terry turned back towards him and added, "You might want your toothbrush."

"What?"

"Presuming you packed one that is?" Terry nodded at the suitcase Dave had left sitting on a table.

"Oh right!" Dave hurried to retrieve the case, calling back over his shoulder, "I'm not really sure what's in it, never looked inside."

Donnie guffawed, "You never want to say that at an airport."

Dave, having never travelled, is confused, "What?"

Terry rolled his eyes, "Never mind, let's go." They walked down the empty pavement, crossed the street, and continued their journey towards the townhouses that comprise the outer edges of the estate.

Dave was getting curious, "Where we going?"

"You'll see," Terry gave him a dismissive wave of his hand.

A few minutes later, Terry stopped outside number 183, Wobble's house. "Wobbles?" Dave asked curiously.

"Why not?"

Dave was stunned, he would never have thought of it, "Good fucking idea, Tel. Nice one."

"Let's see if he thinks so," Terry shrugged and stepped forward to knock on the front door. He peered through the frosted glass window as Wobble limped down the hall. Wobble unlocked the standard three locks and pulled the door open. First, he looked at Terry, before noticing Dave standing there with the suitcase. "No!" He stated matter-of-factly and shut the door in their faces.

Dave shrugged, "Well, that went well."

"I was afraid of that," Terry sighed, bending down to open the letter slot on the front door.

"What now?"

"Calm down David, all is not lost," Terry leaned forward and pushed the letter slot open. "Oi! Danny, don't be like that mate, come back and let me plead his case for him."

"Sod it, Tel," Dave sighed, "he don't want me I'm not gonna beg!"

"Oh yeah? Spoilt for choice are you Dave, your mum 'n dad don't want you, your girlfriend can't admit you exist, where else you going to go? Down Euston station and suck some cock for a couple of quid?"

Dave grinned like a buffoon, "Got a nice ring, doesn't it? My girlfriend."

"You're an idiot!"

"Maybe, but I'm an idiot with a girlfriend."

Terry returned his attention back to the letter slot, "Oi! Wobble, I know you can 'ear me!" Inside the house music starts to blare, "Heaven Up Here" by Echo and the Bunnymen.

Dave smiled and nodded, swaying side to side with the beat, "I like the Bunnymen, good taste in music Wobble. I'll like living here."

"We've got to get you in the door first," Terry banged on the door and leaned back to the letter slot, "Come on Danny don't be like that, he's, my mucker. I know he's a bit of a dick sometimes, but he needs a solid." The music stopped suddenly, and Danny returned, limping back down the hall, and opened the door. Terry stood up and smiled at him, "That's better."

Dave stepped through the door, nearly knocking Wobble to the side with his suitcase, "Hey Wobs!"

Terry reached in, and grabbed Wobble's arm to stop him from falling, "His name's Danny, you ingrate."

Danny muttered under his breath, closing the door behind them, "Don't bother Terry, he's a lost cause."

Terry and Danny followed Dave down the hall and into the back room. Dave immediately threw his suitcase on the floor and sprawled out on the couch, making himself at home. He looked up at the other guys, "Got any Whitetop, Wobs?"

Terry glared at him, "His name's Danny, you twat! Try and remember that."

Dave corrected himself, "Got any Whitetop, Danny?" He propped himself up on the arm of the old couch.

Wobble folded his arms across his chest, "We have to agree terms first."

Dave looked confused, "Terms?"

At this point, Terry was getting exasperated, "Yeah, terms, it's his house, so his terms."

"Yeah of course," Dave sat up on the couch now, trying to look genuinely interested.

Wobble began, "You get the couch, it pulls out into a bed, but it gets made. I don't want it left like that all day."

"I can do that," Dave looked hopeful at the easy request.

"I'm not finished."

"You're not?"

Danny was getting testy, "No I'm not."

"Sorry Wobs," Dave made a half attempt to help arrange the suitcase against the arm of the couch.

Terry was growing thoroughly irritated with Dave by this point. "His name's..."

"Don't bother Tel," Danny interrupted, "I'm used to it."

Dave finally started to catch on, "Sorry Wobs... Danny, I mean."

"Rents twenty-five quid a week and if you don't 'ave a job..."

"Oh, but I do!" Dave looked as proud as a peacock.

Wobble ignored him and continued with his thoughts, "As I was saying if you don't 'ave a job you're not 'anging around 'ere in my way all day."

Dave crossed his arms, "I've got a job so stop blathering on."

Terry stared at him intently, "Doing what?"

"I'm working for the Weasel."

Both Terry and Danny blinked, stunned by this revelation. Terry sputtered, "You didn't tell me that!"

"You hear that Tel, he's a scam artist!" Wobble reached forward to take the suitcase ready to show Dave the front door.

"I ain't!" Dave attempted to grab his suitcase from Danny's hand.

Danny wouldn't drop it, despite his natural inclination to ignore any of his friends putting one over on the Social or their employers, which he was all for. However, scamming other working-class people was below the belt, and he wasn't having any of it, "He ain't staying!"

"You said I could."

"That was before."

"You've got it wrong, I'm not on the insulation or nuffin!'"

"What are you doing then?"

Dave explained his new, strange job to them. The other two listened intently as the bizarre story unfolded then stared at each other nonplussed. Danny broke the silence, "So it goes round and round in circles?"

"Yeah!"

Danny was incredulous, "Absolutely, pointlessly?"

"Yeah!"

"Fuck me, Dave, if that isn't the definition of punk then I don't know what is."

Dave could see Wobbles point, he didn't totally agree but gift horses and mouths and all that, "Yeah! That's right Wob... Danny, I mean."

Terry saw an opportunity, "Can he stay now then, Dan?"

"Fucking right he can, that's the dog's bollocks that is!"

Dave's living arrangements were settled, with the unlikely help of The Weasel. Danny pulled three Whitetops from the fridge, "No helping yourself, this ain't part of your room and board. In fact, you don't get a room 'cause you're on the couch and as for board there's always Tesco's or Abdul's." The friends sat around chatting together for some time.

After they had each finished another three beers, and the fridge was empty, the boys decided to head for the Laureate. They wandered down Acacia Drive before running into Ray, Alex, and Donnie. Ray nodded, "The pubs shut."

Dave looked at him, confused, "Can't be, 'ow late is it?"

Ray leaned back and looked him up and down, "It's not closing time you nonce, there's a burst pipe under the bar. They had to close it off at the main."

Dave still wouldn't let it go, "Beer taps still work, don't they?"

Ray's voice was getting louder as he got more annoyed at the questions, "Some department of health rule, Gerry says they gotta close."

Dave had now become curious, "Where you lot going then?" He inquired nosily.

Alex begrudgingly answered, "There's a new club down in Willesden, thought we'd check it out, you coming Tel?"

Terry shrugged, "Why not?"

Ray stared disdainfully at Wobble, eliciting the response, "I'm heading back in. You coming Dave?"

Alex laughed, "You married to the gimp now?"

Dave took a small step away from Danny, "No."

Wobble turned back in the direction of his house and added, "I'll leave the door open till midnight."

Alex, Ray, and Donnie cracked up and Alex couldn't let it go, "'Ow come we weren't invited to the ceremony then? Was he dressed in white? Who was the best man? You or..."

Terry was not amused, "Dave needed somewhere to stay, Danny helped out, it's just that, nuffin' more. I'd say it was mighty white of him."

Ray could sense how annoyed Terry was getting, and attempted to lighten the mood, "Alex was just 'aving a laugh, Terry, no need to get cross. Weren't you Al?"

Alex shook his head, "Of course I was. It was just a crack."

Ray held out his hands to make sure everyone was placated, "See, now let's get going."

They walked as far as Kingsbury underground and waited on the pavement outside. Donnie made his way into the alley, between the station entrance building and Lyons's stationers, and waited. Not long after, he heard the rumbling sound of an approaching train. "Alright lads we're off." As one group, the five of them ran into the station, jumped the ticket turnstiles and ran down the stairs to the platform just as the train arrived. The doors opened and they stepped into the tube car. There were few other passengers at this time of day, and those there were glanced up and immediately back down when they saw who was getting on the train. Eyes fixed on their magazine, book, the floor, or listen intently to their Walkman, anything but catch the eye of their new travel companions. Making eye contact meant there was an inherent danger, an invitation for who knows what to happen.

Alex stared at the other passengers, relishing the fear that he and his kind caused, enjoying their discomfort. The others slouched into the seats. A voice called over the intercom, "MIND THE GAP!" The doors slid closed, and the tube moved away,

Dave cracked, "Mind the gap? Why did it fart or something?"

Donnie groaned and rolled his eyes, "Jesus Dave, do you have to make that same lame joke every time?"

"I've never been on the tube with Al or Ray before, they might've appreciated it," he chuckled, an attempt to show the others how funny he was.

Always looking for a reason to dig at Dave, Alex replied, "We didn't."

They sat in silence. When the train arrived at Wembley Park station, a man sitting opposite Dave, stood up to get off the train, dropping the Evening Standard on the seat as he did. Dave leaned forward, picked it up, and glanced at the front page, noticing an article about the fast-approaching royal wedding with a map of the route, "Fucking bullshit this is. 'Ow much is it gonna cost us, the tax paying working-class men and women of this country, for Charlie to get his rocks off?"

Donnie was first to respond, "You've nay paid any taxes as long as I've known ye."

Then Alex piped in, "What are you a fucking Socialist?"

Dave was never one to avoid poking the bear, in fact he quite enjoyed it, "Maybe I am."

Then Ray added, "So am I. A fucking National Socialist!" A silence fell over the entire car. A young, East Indian man, of about twenty years old, sitting four seats along from Ray, tried to physically shrink into the back of his seat. The train pulled into the next stop, Neasden, and he jumped to his feet, hopped off the train, and turned to wait on the platform for the next one. It wasn't his stop, but there was no way he was going to stay in the atmosphere of escalating violence that was looking for an escape that could well have been him.

The train travelled on, the next stop Dollis Hill. When nobody got off, Dave tried to remember if he had ever seen anyone get on or off at Dollis Hill. Finally, Willesden Green, the five men hurried to their feet and ran from the train car and up the stairs, almost as quickly as they had entered the train. The ticket collector, a Sikh man in a turban, stood at the top, waiting to collect their overdue fares or tickets. The usual trick was to claim that you'd got on one stop before, that way the cost of the ticket was greatly reduced, but, with Ray at the head, the five of them bowled straight through at full speed. Ray, followed by Terry, Donnie, Dave, and lastly Alex.

Alex had hung back deliberately, and as he ran through, he swung his arm and punched the man's turban, sending it falling from his head and partially unravelling on the dirty cement. The five hooligans turned right, sprinting, shouting and yelling down the street. The ticket collector and one of his colleagues darted out onto the pavement. The enraged victim shouted behind them, "COME BACK YOU COWARDS!" They weren't listening, in fact only Alex knew what had happened with the man and his turban, the rest of them trotted away, happily oblivious, thinking that they had simply scammed The London Underground, yet again.

Alex laughed, feeling clever and righteous, "You see Dave that's why your Mrs. the Gimp can't come with us. He'd have us all getting caught."

With Ray in the lead, they turned a corner and there in front of them was a door, a large, flat metal door in a brick wall. Ray balled up his fist ready to knock, "This is it."

Dave looked at him, confused, "I thought you said it was a club?"

Ray shook his head, "It is. A very exclusive club!" He pounded on the door and a peephole slid open.

Dave smirked, "It's a speakeasy."

Ray scoffed and questioned Terry, "Why do you bring him anywhere?"

The door opened inward, revealing two huge skinheads, big enough to even make Ray look small. One of them nodded, "Evening Ray, they with you?"

"Yeah," Ray said, unsure if he wanted to admit to being with Dave.

The two giants stepped aside, allowing Ray to enter. Dave began to follow, but as soon as Ray had passed, the doormen had closed together again like a massive wall of muscle. "Raise your arms," the one on the right stated, blocking Dave's view of Ray. Dave did as he was told, and the other bouncer patted him down.

"Shouldn't you take me on a date first?" Dave tried to sound funny.

"We don't know you, so you get frisked." As soon as he finished, he bellowed, "Next!" And they parted, like huge opening doors, allowing Dave to walk between them, and enter the hallway. There was a flight of stairs leading up to the club and he could hear the muffled sounds of loud punk music playing. He waited in the semi-dark hallway, until the other three had been frisked and then the four of them headed up the stairs together and through the door at the top.

The room they entered was dimly lit and smoky, a bar to the left, to the right a stage, where a DJ was set up. Above his station a banner hung, crudely spray painted with the words THE BLITZKRIEG. On the floor, nearly a hundred young men, almost all skinheads, milled around in small groups. Groups determined mostly by where they were from. In a city as tribalistic as London, where exactly you were from mattered. Here, South London, Southwest London, North London, and Northwest London were all represented. The four newcomers awkwardly stood just beyond the doorway and surveyed the room. Dave didn't recognise anyone except those he had arrived with, Donnie was in the same boat. Both Terry and Alex spotted some familiar faces from football, some friendly, some not so much.

Dave strained his eyes, squinting as he tried to see Ray through the smoke. He noticed Ray at the back of the stage, behind the DJ, shaking hands with a man Dave recognised from the pub a few nights earlier, the mysterious Mr. Daniels. "Isn't that...?" Dave whispered loudly to his friends.

Alex took him by the arm. "Never mind, let's get a drink." They zig-zagged their way through the crowd, to the bar. "Liddle Towers" the punk anthem by The Angelic Upstarts was blaring out of the sound system. Menzie, the lead singer, was screaming,

“WHY DID HE DIE? IT WAS JUST A LIE, POLICE KILLED LIDDLE TOWERS.”

“At least they’re playing good music,” Dave thought, although a Socialist anthem was not what he would have expected given the crowd. Hatred of the police being the common theme across most youth subcultures of the time, it wasn’t totally surprising a choice of song. If you viewed the far-right youth subculture in England at the time, as against the far-left, on a circular line, other than race and immigration, they wouldn’t be at opposite sides of the circle's circumference but rather touching at the apex.

They waited at the bar, the next song to come on gave Dave a complete shock. “Young Gifted and Black,” by Bob and Marcia. It was incongruous and totally unexpected, the skinhead throng started to dance the shuffle. Dave felt like he might have had a stroke or that someone had put LSD in his Whitetop earlier. He then heard them singing as one, more a chant than a song, “YOUNG GIFTED AND WHITE THAT’S ALRIGHT!” They threw their right arms high in the air on “that’s alright” in a Nazi salute and as the song finished, they screamed in unison, repeating over and over, “SEIG HEIL! SEIG HEIL! SEIG HEIL!” At this point, Dave knew for certain where he was, and couldn’t wait to escape. Terry put his hand on Dave’s shoulder and nodded to the door, where Donnie was already waiting, and they headed out the exit door. Once on the pavement past doormen and eavesdropping ears, Dave breathed out in relief, “It’s Nazi central in there.”

Terry grabbed him by the elbow, quickening their step down the sidewalk, “Keep your voice down, we’re not safe yet.” Eventually, they approached the tube station, they stopped dead in their tracks. A panda car with the lights flashing and an unmarked police car were parked at the entrance to the station. The three friends weren’t at all sure what to do, and they were ignorant of Alex’s assault on the ticket collector, but they shared a natural distrust of the police, of authority in general.

As usual, Dave deferred to Terry, “What do we do Tel?”

"We catch the train home, we done nuffin' wrong."

As they neared the station, the ticket collector pointed at them and shouted, "THEM! THEY WERE WITH HIM!" Without the slightest hesitation, the three innocent men turned tail and broke into a run down a side road on the right. Two uniformed police and Constable Wainwright, immediately set off after them. The street was a dead end, and the three fugitives stopped and desperately tried to figure a way out. They turned and saw the three officers in hot pursuit.

Once again, as usual, Terry took charge, "This way!" He pointed as he headed down a driveway between two of the houses. The other two followed closely behind, but at the end they found they were now facing three brick walls, one to the left, one to the right and one straight ahead, all of them at least six feet high. The only way out was back towards their pursuers.

Donnie was fed up, "Fuck this, what are we running for anyway? Back in Glasgow we'd've just taken them on."

Terry realised what Donnie had proposed and couldn't disagree more, "Good luck with that, come on Dave!" He held his hands out waist high, cupped together, waiting to boost someone over. Dave knew what to do, he put his heavily booted foot into Terry's hand and his friend pushed him up onto the top of the wall. Dave landed chest first on the top, immediately crying out in pain.

Donnie looked confused, and attempted to jump up to get a better look at Dave, "Wassat, what's goin' on up there?"

Dave groaned, trying to move as delicately as possible, "Glass, the top of the wall is covered in fuckin' glass."

Terry turned to Donnie, holding out his hands, "You next."

"Fuck you, Terry! I'd rather take my chance with the cops," Donnie crazily laughed and turned to leg it out of the alley.

Terry hesitated for a moment, looking up at Dave, "You're on your own mate, good luck." He shrugged and ran off down the alley after Donnie.

Dave, having little or no choice, dragged himself over to the other side of the wall, cutting his chest further, tearing open his hands and his legs. When he landed on the far side, he found himself in a small back garden surrounded by three glass topped walls one of which had a gate. There was no grass, just patio stones, a few plants in pots, a small outdoor table, two chairs and a shed. He opened the door to the shed and crawled in. He sat quietly on some bags of potting soil, waiting for the ruckus outside to subside.

Donnie found his escape route blocked by one of the policemen and ran straight up the boot of a parked Ford Escort, as the uniform dove at him but narrowly missed. He clambered up the car's roof and down over the bonnet before jumping to the ground. Wainwright and the other uniform were on the far side of the street watching as Donnie ran. Shooting them a two finger "fuck off" sign as he did, far outpacing the pursuing policeman as he made his escape.

Meanwhile, Terry had crawled under a parked car, jamming himself as far under as he could possibly get. He desperately tried not to breathe too deeply in order to not give himself away, despite the stench of petrol leaking slowly from the petrol tank his chest was jammed tightly against. Wainwright walked to the end of the dead-end street and stood not more than five feet away from the hidden youth, who was staring straight at the policeman's black Dr. Marten brogues. "Nice shoes," Terry thought to himself, "other than the colour identical to my cherry red pair."

The uniform with Wainwright shook his head, "They vanished into thin air the bastards, fucking Houdinis." Slowly, the three officers turned and headed back to the tube station.

In the club, Ray emerged from the office and headed across the dance floor to Alex, "Where's the others?" he asked, looking around the smoky room.

Alex shrugged, "Took off I guess."

Ray looked disgusted by his response, "Bunch of wankers."

Alex pointed at the bar, "Want a beer?"

At this point, the lights of the club come on, startling everyone. One of the hulking skinhead bouncers from earlier, approached the DJ and shouted something in his ear. The music immediately stopped, and the bouncer walked to the front of the stage, addressing the group. "Sorry lads, the evening is being cut short at the request of the local Constabulary. We would ask that you file out in a nice, orderly fashion, so that we can reopen next week without any problems with our license." There was a deafening silence followed by the clanking and thudding sound of multiple knives and knuckle dusters being dropped to the floor. The crowd began to thin out, drinks were hurriedly swigged so as not to waste them.

Ray looked confused, "Let's go." He and Alex joined the crowd pushing and jostling its way down the stairs and out the door. As they emerged onto the street, there was a heavy police presence, the officers had lined up along the edge of the pavement in order to force the crowd to head for the tube station, and nowhere but the station.

The ticket collector, who Alex had earlier assaulted, sat in the front seat of Wainwright's police car, both watching intently. "I can't believe you went to all this trouble because of a simple assault, I wasn't even really hurt," he said, pushing the glasses up his nose as he peered out the windshield.

Wainwright smirked, "We didn't, we've been looking for an excuse to get in there and see what's going on since they applied for a license, and now we get photographs of all of them and get to go inside. You, my friend, are a gift that just keeps on giving!"

The ticket collector spotted Alex in the crowd, he pointed frantically at the tall, hard to miss, young skinhead, "There! There he is, that one!"

Wainwright saw Ray walking next to him and scoffed, "Interesting, I know his friend." The officer climbed out of the car and approached a burly Sergeant and spoke into his ear. The Sergeant then nodded to four equally large uniforms, who were waiting to one side. The five of them immediately moved through the police cordon, grabbing Alex and Ray, pinning their arms behind their backs, and flattened their faces against a white-washed shop window. The Sergeant leaned in, “You boys are coming with us.”

11

Dave waited in the shed for what seemed like an eternity, although it was probably only an hour, and then, figuring the coast would be clear, slipped out. He painfully limped into the yard, opened the gate, and headed away down the back alley. Turning right at the next junction in the maze of high, glass topped, brick walls, he stopped and debated which way to go, every direction looked the same. He headed straight on and turned the next right where he bumped chest first, straight into Terry, coming the other way around the corner. They both jumped and at the same time shouted, "FUCK!"

Dave held his side, panting heavily, "Jesus, Terry, you scared the shit outta me!"

"I scared you?" Terry scanned the alleyway behind Dave, looking for anyone that might have followed him, "My hearts doing a tango now you little prick."

Having no appreciation for dance, except perhaps the pogo, Dave had no idea what exactly that meant, but figured he had the gist of it anyway. "Where'd you come from?" Dave glanced over his shoulder trying to see what Terry might be looking at.

"Never mind."

Dave wrinkled his nose, "And why do you stink of petrol?"

"Again, never mind," Terry took a step away from Dave, "you nearly got blood all over me, be more careful next time." Terry glanced nervously up and down the alleys, then turned in the direction that Dave had originally been heading, "This way."

Dave looked down at his tattered clothes and still bleeding cuts, somewhat amazed that with the adrenaline rushing through him, from the chase, he had somehow forgotten about them. Terry steered Dave back into the maze, and they came out in another dead-end street and hiked down to the main road. However, as they turned the corner they froze. The street to their right was lit up by flashing lights on the top of police cars. In the centre of the road a plainclothes policeman, Constable Wainwright, stood talking to a large burly uniformed officer, the officer signaled some others and they moved through the phalanx of police lining the opposite pavement. Dave and Terry watched them enter the crowd and grab Alex and Ray. Terry took a step back, partially hiding behind the corner of a brick garden wall, similar to the one that Dave had sustained his injuries on earlier. "Fuck this we're out of here," He sighed, and grabbed Dave by the elbow, turning to head down the street to his left, toward they knew not where, anywhere but here.

"Why d'you think they pinched Alex, Tel?" Dave did his best to keep in step with Terry, but could feel the pain of his injuries creeping in.

The stronger man shrugged, still pulling Dave along by his arm, as if he was a child, "Who knows, serves him right for thinking he's Joe Hawkins." Dave smirked at the reference to the ultra-tough literary skinhead character of their youth.

Mitch came out of the public bar of The Blackbird Inn and leaned against a concrete streetlight and lit a cigarette. As he drew in his first deep breath of smoke, a rusty Ford Cortina pulled up at the curb in front of him. Not recognising the car, and with a feeling of trepidation rising in his throat he turned to walk away, but standing directly behind him was Greg, the biker. Greg put his large hand on Mitch's shoulder to stop him, "Get in the car Mitch, we need to talk."

"Greg," Mitch tried his best to pretend that he was relieved to see him, "I was just going to call you!"

Greg steered him towards the Ford, nudging him forward, "Good, let's chat in the car."

"Of course, Ray said he was gonna straighten the whole thing out. He did, right?" The short fat man looked at Greg hopefully.

"Course he did, it's Ray we're going to see. Get in." Greg opened the front door of the car and gestured for Mitch to get in. Mitch obliged peacefully, ducking his head as he slid into the passenger seat. Greg slammed the door shut before climbing into the back behind him. The car pulled away from the curb and took a sharp left into Chalkhill.

Mitch watched out the window, confused and somewhat frightened, “What are we going in here for?”

Greg reassured him, “It’s all good, I’ve got to do a pickup.”

Mitch wasn’t placated, and began surveying the car looking for an escape route, “At this time of night?”

Greg shrugged, leaning forward, “My business doesn’t work nine to five, Mitch.”

Mitch began to stammer, “But still, in here? at night......?”

Mitch didn’t hear the gunshot, didn’t feel a thing. Greg had put the barrel of a snub-nosed pistol behind the back of his head, pulled the trigger and the front of Mitch's skull exploded into the windshield, shattering it. The car pulled to a stop beside The Copse, the driver and Greg climbed out and walked to the boot, where they retrieved a petrol can and poured the entire contents over the car. Greg offered the driver a cigarette, which he took. He struck a match, lit the two cigarettes and then stared thoughtfully at the match before throwing it on the car. The petrol immediately ignited in a huge conflagration, lighting up The Copse, the tower blocks, and the two bikers who stood impassively watching smoking their cigarettes.

From a nearby fifth floor walkway, Samson, Dejean’s runner, watched as a second car pulled up, the two bikers got in and were driven away. As the car pulled away, Greg looked out the window watching the car, enveloped in flames, warmly lighting the cold grey tower blocks. He smirked at the driver, “If this doesn’t start the war, I don’t know what will, fucking Black bastards.”

12

As the first dull grey morning light crept through the barred windows, Alex and Ray awoke in separate cells. This bothered Ray, as they hadn't been charged when they were brought to the station. They didn't have to be under the S.U.S laws that Margaret Thatcher's government relied on so heavily. The only thing they needed to have done was to have acted suspiciously and apparently intended to commit a crime. They then could be held for forty-eight hours without charge merely on suspicion of their having planned to commit a crime. The irony was not lost on Ray, the laws had been dredged up from antiquity to help the authorities quell anti-social behaviour without the victims or perpetrators having any legal recompense or rights. This led to the Brixton and Handsworth riots against them in April of that year.

Yet here he was, a white nationalist skinhead, being held under the same legislation that was in his, and most other people's opinions, enacted solely to keep the predominantly Black populations of those areas under control. What bothered him was that if they were just being held overnight on a minor charge such as drunk and disorderly, or disturbing the peace, they would have been thrown into the group cells with the other drunks, vandals, and troublemakers. Instead, they'd been separated and given their own cells, and this gave Ray pause for thought. As he sat there, trying to wrap his head around just what it could mean, the eye hole in the cell door slid back with a scraping sound, the door locks opened with a loud clank, and the heavy, metal door opened. A police constable stood in the doorway

"Raymond Collins?" He boomed in an overly loud voice.

"Who else?" Ray looked up at him from the metal cot, trying to sound completely uninterested. The constable repeated, his voice now bland and flat, "Are you Raymond Collins?"

Ray shrugged, "Maybe."

"Let's go," The officer wasn't even slightly fazed by Ray's flippant remarks, he just appeared bored with the whole thing. He stepped back as the prisoner exited the cell. Ray glanced at the officer's chest as he passed, "Officer Windsor?" He paused, standing next to his jailer for a moment, "Looking forward to the big wedding next week?"

The officer shrugged, still uncaring, "As much as the next man I suppose."

"Going to watch the celebrations somewhere nice, are you?"

"Down the corridor, third door on the right," Windsor gestured for Ray to move down the hall, "and no, I'll be on duty."

"Shame," Ray stated dryly, as he trudged down the corridor, Officer Windsor following closely behind him. He glanced over his shoulder, "Got a first name?"

"Yes. In here." Officer "In Here" Windsor opened a door and Ray entered a small room with a table, three chairs, and a camera mounted on the wall high up in the corner of the room. Windsor pointed to the single chair on the far side of the table, "Sit there."

Ray shuffled over to the chair and slouched down into it, and the officer left, the lock clanking shut on the opposite side of the door. Ray smirked, thinking "it wasn't as if I could get anywhere if the door was left wide open."

Alex sat perched on the side of his metal cot, staring at the cement floor. Unlike Ray, he was nervous. This was the first time he had ever seen the inside of a cell. He looked up as the eye hole opened, then the lock, then the door. Officer Windsor stood in the doorway, "Alexander Higgins?"

"Yes sir," Alex swallowed anxiously.

"Follow me."

Alex did as he was told, and the officer led him down the corridor to the next room, past the room Ray was in, and was shown into an identically furnished and laid out room. The rooms were interchangeable with one exception, in the room with Alex, were Detective Sergeant Miller and Detective Constable Wainwright, waiting for him. Windsor gripped Alex by the arm and led him to the empty chair across the table from the two detectives, "Sit down." He again did as he was told and sat nervously awaiting his fate. Miller and Wainwright were seated directly across from him, staring at him in silence. The young man felt his mouth go dry. This wasn't how he had imagined he would feel. He had always pictured himself defiant, a truly hard man he'd thought he'd be when he'd imagined these exact circumstances. However, now, his heart was racing fast, faster even than his mind, which was doing gymnastics. D.S. Miller finally spoke, "Alex Higgins?"

"Yes. Er yes sir, ma'am I mean, yes ma'am," Alex's brain and tongue stumbled over each other.

"I hate that word," the detective responded as she sorted a stack of papers in front of her.

He looked confused, "Sorry?"

"Ma'am. You tuppenny ha'penny hoods come in here and all of a sudden that word comes spilling from your mouths like we're in some Dickensian novel or a Play for Today. Ma'am? Do I look sixty to you?"

"No ma'am, shit, no, no you don't..." he paused, wondering how to address her, "officer?"

The detective sat back comfortably in her metal chair, enjoying the look of panic in Alex's eyes, "I am Detective Sergeant Miller, this is Detective Constable Wainwright. You can call me Sergeant and him Constable. Does that help?"

"Yes ma'am…" Alex cleared his throat, "Sergeant."

"Good," Miller responded blandly, before the two officers began to barrage Alex with speech to the point that there might as well have been three or four not two of them. Alex's head swiveled, looking constantly from one to the other, unable to take it all in, piecing it together as he went.

"You've been a very bad boy..."

"Really stupid…"

"Did you think no one would care..."

"Hard to believe how dumb…"

"We have been appointed to deal with..."

"Idiots like you..."

"Racial crimes…"

"No respect..."

"Fellow human beings..."

"This is a serious offence..."

"People have rights..."

"You could lose your job..."

"Never mind your freedom..."

"Sickening..."

"Is this how your parents taught you to behave..."

"You won't last five minutes behind bars..."

"Do you know what they'll do to you in there...."

"We could help you…"

"But why would we..."

"Throw the book at you..."

"Tell me about your friend Ray," the woman blurted out, the comment hitting Alex in the face, like a wet towel.

"You… what?" Alex swallowed.

"Your friend Raymond Collins, the man you were arrested with," the Detective questioned again, slower.

Alex stared straight at Miller as she repeated the question, not at her eyes though, nor even at her face in general. He was staring straight at her mouth, at her lips, as if he could hear the words better that way, and make sure he was understanding exactly what he was being asked to do: Potentially betray his friend and mentor. "What about him?"

Wainwright picked up and opened a file from the table, "You were arrested with him last night."

Alex stared thoughtfully at him and then answered very slowly, "Yes."

Wainwright continued, scanning the text, "After the pair of you assaulted the ticket collector at Willesden Green tube station."

"No."

"No, what?" the Constable peered up over the top of the folder.

"That isn't what happened."

Wainwright looked doubtful, "You didn't assault the ticket collector at Willesden Green tube station?"

"Yeah, I did," he quickly responded.

"You admit to it?"

"Well yeah I guess, I dunno about assault though, it wasn't no GBH or nothing."

Wainwright laid the folder down, pen tip resting on the first page, preparing to take notes, "You didn't punch the turban from his head?"

Alex shrugged, looking between them, "Well, yeah, but that's not really an assault, is it?"

Miller spoke up, "It's very much an assault. The turban is a symbol of that man's religion, a symbol that he is obliged to wear, and you violently removed it."

"Hold on a minute," Alex interrupted, correcting her, "it's a hat."

"A hat?"

"Yeah, suppose I walk in the pub one night," Alex was desperately trying to get his thoughts in order, ready to prove his innocence.

"Which pub?"

"Eh?"

Miller pressed him again, "Which pub?"

"I dunno, say... The Laureate." It was the first pub he could think of.

The Sergeant nodded slowly, the Constable took notes, "Okay, you walk into the Laureate, the one on the estate?"

"Yeah, I mean that's the only one I know of."

"And?"

"My china Dave, is shooting pool wearing a trilby..."

"Dave who?"

Alex replied without hesitation, "Dave Simmons."

The entire time Wainwright is taking notes. Miller continued the interrogation, "Go on."

Alex continued with his example, "Dave's shooting pool and I walk in and wanna put him off a shot. So, I knock 'is trilby off his loaf! That's not exactly an assault, is it?"

Miller quickly corrected him, "If your 'china,' as you put it, chose to press charges, then yes, it most definitely is."

Alex laughed, "He wouldn't though, would he?"

Miller smiled as she posed the question, "Who knows what Dave Simmons would or wouldn't do."

Alex was getting flustered, "So the Paki at the tube, he's pressing charges, is he?"

Wainwright chimed in, "He most definitely is yes!"

Miller shot Wainwright a dirty look and then continued in a calm, official sounding tone, "He's not, as you so succinctly put it, a Paki, he's from Uganda, not that I expect you to know the difference. But he most definitely is, yes."

Alex was baffled, "That's not right!"

Miller continued to patiently push him, "Isn't it?"

"No."

"How?"

"How what?" Alex asked confused.

"How is that not right?"

Alex thought for a moment, "It just isn't, maybe it's a cultural thing."

"A cultural thing?"

"Yeah, you know, they're different to us ain't they!"

Miller changed the subject as she had clearly had enough of the circuitous nature of the conversation, "How long have you been an associate of Mr. Collins?"

"I dunno, about six months."

She scribbled something on a notepad, "How did you meet him?"

"His mum and sister live in Kingsbury."

"You know everyone who lives there?"

"No, but when he got out on parole, he had to move in with them, my auntie lives next door. I was visiting her one day and we got to talking about Siobhan..."

Miller interrupted him, "Who's Siobhan?"

"Ray's sister," Alex answered quickly.

"Friend of yours?"

Alex leaned back in his chair, "I wish!"

"Good looker, is she?" Again she wrote something on her small notepad.

"You could say that."

"I did. Ever dated her?"

"Nah, she's out of my league," Alex knew his place amongst the women in the local area, "I'd be punching well above my weight with that one."

"So, you met Ray how exactly?"

"My auntie had a flat tire, that's why I was there," he began to ramble on nervously, "to change the tire and Ray comes out to have a fag, his mum won't let him smoke in the house. He offered me one and we got to talking."

Miller continued to scribble in her book, never looking up, "About?"

"You know, the usual stuff, Arsenal, whether Terry Neill would ever get them out of fifth, stuff like that."

"Coincidence," Wainwright piped in, "you both being Arsenal supporters."

"Ray's a casual supporter," Alex paused momentarily, wishing they would stop firing questions at him and hoping, if he's honest, this would end soon, "not like me and Terry."

Miller glanced over the top of the leather notebook with sudden interest, "Terry who?"

"Davis, Terry Davis," Wainwright responded.

The policewoman nodded at her partner, and returned her attention to her notebook before continuing, "What else did you and Ray talk about?"

"Nothing much," Alex swallowed nervously, "I told him he should come down to The Laureate and meet the boys."

"Did he?"

"Oh yeah, he's a regular now, he even got Siobhan a job there."

"Handy that, for you I mean."

"I guess," Alex shrugged trying to keep his cool.

Miller continued to fire off the questions, "Did you talk about tattoos?"

"No, why would we?"

"You both have the same tattoo," she pointed to his arm, "in the same place."

"I didn't have mine then, it's new." Alex rolled his sleeve up proudly to show off his new tattoo.

Miller sneered, "I've seen the photographs."

"Oh right."

"Gang and hate symbols are always catalogued."

Alex regarded her with surprise at the comment. "I'm not in a gang," he defended his character.

"You're a skinhead," she added bluntly.

Alex nodded and ran the palm of his hand over the top of his head, "It's more of a movement."

"More frightening still."

Alex proudly supported his new ink, "And the tattoo represents love not hate."

Wainwright looked confused, "Love?"

The proud youngAryan stood up self-importantly, "Love of my country."

"The British Movement," Miller began, "which that represents are a violent, fascist, Neo Nazi group, dedicated to the subjugation of everyone who isn't white or even Protestant." She paused and took a deep breath to keep herself calm, "They hate the Catholics as much as they do the Blacks."

"D'you blame them, look at what's 'appening in Belfast!" Alex fired right back, intent to teach them 'the truth' about the situation, “Innocent babies being blown to smithereens, Tommies being gunned down for trying to keep the country safe from the IRA bastards. You should be with us. We’re on the side of law and order!”

Alex was growing more and more agitated as he spoke, and Miller watched him with detached curiosity, “Did Ray teach you all this?”

“Some of it, I heard some of it at meetings, most of it’s just common sense.”

“Meetings?”

“Yeah,” Alex rolled his eyes wondering when they’d stop questioning him, “Ray takes me.”

Miller held her pen poised to write once more, “Where are these meetings held?”

“There’s a pub in Camden Town, The Golden Archer, in the back room there mostly.” He paused, thinking, “Sometimes down east, Bethnal Green way, sometimes in The Bald-Faced Stag in Burnt Oak.”

Miller was incredulous, “You go in The Stag?”

“Only if I’m with Ray.”

“I don’t blame you,” she chuckled.

“I’m not crazy or suicidal.”

“And does Ray speak at these meetings?”

Alex felt he had the upper hand now, that he knew something they didn’t, “No, no they bring in guest speakers, political experts.”

“Different political experts at every meeting?”

“Yeah, Mr. Daniels always does the introductions and then the experts speak.”

Miller nodded to Wainwright who pulled a photograph from a manila envelope and dropped it on the table, in front of Alex. In the photograph Alex saw Daniels shaking another man's hand. “Two middle aged white men shaking hands, under any other circumstances what could be more innocuous,” Miller thought to herself. She watched Alex's face intently as Wainwright started to question him, "This Mr. Daniels?"

Alex was keen to explain, clear the whole matter up, after all he couldn't understand what he had done wrong, "Yeah that's him."

Wainwright pointed to the second man in the picture, "And the other man?"

"McCaffrey, I think," Alex paused for a moment to think, "yeah. Seamus McCaffrey."

"He was at the meetings?"

"Just one."

"Just one that you know of?" Wainwright stared directly at Alex, watching his facial features for any hint of a lie.

"Yeah," he responded bluntly.

"And he spoke at the meeting?"

Alex repeated himself, "Yeah."

"About?"

"Northern Ireland and the struggle."

The detective looked surprised at the comment, "The struggle?"

"Yeah, he was from there, he talked about how the war was real, how the British government called it 'The Troubles' cause they're cowards but to the Protestants in the North it's a war." Alex leaned forward, resting his elbows on the table, shocked that the cops didn't already know this history, "A war for their country, for our country. It's part of England you know?"

Wainwright rolled his eyes, "It's part of the U.K. Not England"

"Whatever!" Alex flicked his hands dismissively and flopped back abruptly against the back of the chair, "same difference!"

"What did he want?" Miller pressed for more information, "From the people at the meeting?"

"Money."

"For?"

Alex grew tired and realised he was probably saying too much, "He didn't say."

"For the struggle?"

"Yeah," he looked nervously around the room, his thoughts racing.

"I see," Miller stood up, the chair made a loud scrape against the concrete floor and Alex looked hopeful. Wainwright put the photograph back in the envelope and followed suit, standing next to his partner.

A look of relief crossed Alex's face. It was finally over, "Can I go now?"

Wainwright laughed at the question, "No," he said dryly, "we have some colleagues who are going to want to talk to you, probably at a different division."

Alex glowered at him, "You can't do this!"

"Oh, but we can," Miller chuckled as she gathered the remaining papers, "under the prevention of terrorism act we can do all sorts of things."

"Terrorism?" the suspect was confused, in his heart he was innocent, "I'm English," he attempted to reason with them, "I'm not a terrorist!"

"Then you'll be happy to cooperate with them, I'm sure."

The door opened from outside in and Windsor stepped into the room. Miller nodded to him, "He's all theirs."

"Yes ma'am."

She grumbled, "I hate that word."

"There's something you might want to know before you see the other one."

Windsor pulled Alex out of his chair, standing him to his feet abruptly. Miller and Wainwright exited into the corridor where a large, plainclothes officer, Sergeant Tate, stood and waited. He looked at Miller, theoretically his equal in rank, but because of the Division Tate worked in, she would never question his commands, "When you're done with Collins let him go."

Miller demurred, "Of course."

Windsor brought Alex out into the hall. Tate grabbed him by the arm, spun him around and pressed his face against the cold, hard concrete block wall. "You're all mine now laddy," Tate snarled in his ear as he pinned the young man's arms behind him, handcuffing him tightly.

"But I ain't done nothing," Alex struggled, his efforts only constricting the handcuffs.

"We'll soon find that out," Tate clenched Alex's arm tightly and led him away, down the corridor, twisting his arm upwards to keep him off balance.

Wainwright opened the next door, the door to the room containing Ray. Miller entered followed by Wainwright. "Mr. Collins," she began, "I'm D.S Miller, this is D.C Wainwright,"

Ray rolled his eyes, "I want a lawyer."

She faked a smile, looking as pleasant as she possibly could, "No need for that Mr. Collins, we just want to chat."

"I want a lawyer!" Ray repeated, setting his elbows on the table, looking defiantly at her.

Wainwright leaned on the table, "You can want."

Ray folded his arms, leaning back against the metal chair, "I know my rights..."

"This isn't Z cars, you're not on the tele. You can have a little chat with us, or we can send you off to remand prison for a while whilst we sort out your request."

Ray leaned against the back of the chair and looked from one implacable face to the other. "What do you want then?"

Wainwright shifted in his seat and Miller took over, "Why were you at The Blitzkrieg club last night?"

"There was a burst water main at the pub, so they closed, and I was still thirsty."

"By the pub you mean The Laureate?" she inquired.

Ray attempted to change the subject, "How is Alex?"

Wainwright sat on the end of the desk and leaned in towards Ray, "Again, why were you at the club? Why slake your thirst at that particular club?"

Ray clearly didn't give two shits about these cops, "They play my kinda music, my friends go there," he lied.

Wainwright looked through some notes and continued, "Is Eric Daniels a friend of yours?"

"He's an acquaintance," Ray shrugged, "yeah."

"Was he there last night?"

Ray is determined not to give them any information, "I wouldn't know."

"What about Seamus McCaffrey?"

"Who?" he rolled his eyes and tipped backwards in the chair, "Never heard of him!"

Miller ignored his demeanour, "Your friend, Alex, says you have."

Ray shrugged uncaringly and continued to stare at the ceiling, "He's mistaken, and 'ow is he anyhow?"

"Says he spoke at a British Movement meeting you attended."

"Oh him," Ray pretends to have a sudden revelation, "the Paddy. I didn't pay much attention."

"Then why were you there?"

He sat the front legs of the chair down again with a loud thump, "See some old friends."

Miller's eyes narrowed on his face, "Nothing more?"

"Nope," he yawned a wide, open mouth at the pair.

The detectives had seen this act too many times in the past and carried on as normal, "It's a pretty serious crime, assault, with your record you could be looking at a nice long stretch."

A look of surprise crossed Ray's face, "What assault?"

"You and your friend Alex attacked the ticket collector at Willesden Green underground station last night."

"I never attacked anybody," Ray hated being wrongly accused, "and whoever says I did is a liar."

Wainwright leaned in, "Your friend Alex says you did, the ticket collector says you did."

"Bollocks. I didn't do it and there's no way Alex said I did. He knows better. Now unless there's something else, I'm going!" Ray started to stand up. However, what Miller said next, stopped him short.

"Your prints are all over the stolen Ford Capri, the one that was used in the hit and run in Harlesden." Ray sank slowly back into his seat. "How do you explain that?"

"I was in it."

Miller tilted her head to the side quizzically, "You told us you weren't."

"And?" Ray rolled his eyes.

"And now you say you were."

"Mitch picked me up from my job interview at the butcher shop."

"So, Mitch was driving?"

Ray shrugged, "Yeah."

"And when Mr. Patel was run over, who was driving then?"

"Dunno, weren't there."

Wainwright added in, "So, you admit to being in a stolen car, enough in itself to put you back inside, but not to being present when the hit and run occurred?"

"You got it. Ask Mitch if you don't believe me."

"That could be a little difficult."

"'Ow's that?"

"Your cousin Mitch turned up dead last night."

This time, Ray was totally shocked and rose to get up out of his seat, "What?"

Wainwright placed a warning finger up to his chest, and he sat down again. "His body was found on The Chalkhill Estate, looks like a drug deal gone wrong."

"Fucking swartzas?"

Miller grunted and smirked. Ray jumped out of his seat and leaned against the table, towering over her. Wainwright quickly moved to stand next to him and the table. "What's so fucking funny? My cousin is dead and you're doing fuck all about it, go arrest the Black bastards who did it!"

Wainwright put his hand on Ray's chest, attempting to push him back into the chair, "Sit down."

Ray stared straight into his eyes, full of contempt and hatred, but begrudgingly sat back down. Miller was unfazed by the outburst, "What's so funny? You sit there covered in white nationalist Nazi tattoos and use a Yiddish term to denigrate Black people, you don't see the irony?" Ray didn't respond as he glared ahead.

At this point, Miller started to really push him, "Why did you lie to us about being in the car if you did nothing wrong?"

Ray stated what he thought was obvious, "Force of habit. I always lie to the police. Besides you said it yourself I could go back inside just for being in that car."

"So, you knew it was stolen?"

"No!"

"Then you had no reason to worry."

"Mitch couldn't afford that car so there was a good chance it might have been stolen."

Miller looked across at Wainwright, "We're done here, let him go."

Ray glared at her, "You going to do anything about Mitch?"

Miller shrugged, "That's our job."

Ray growled from deep in the pit of his stomach, "Black bastards!"

"What makes you so sure his killers are Black?"

"He was found in the jungle, wasn't he?"

"We'll look into it."

Ray fumed, "Don't strain yourselves." Miller stood up, pushing in the sturdy chair, the sound of metal scraping across the cement floor. She gestured to Wainwright, and they stepped out of the room, closing the door behind them. Ray shouted after them as the door slammed shut, "If you don't do something about it I will!"

13

Carl pulled on his jacket and opened the front door of the flat ready to head out for work. Queenie came out of the kitchen, and into the hallway to speak to him, "You sure you're okay?"

"Yeah, I'm fine mum," Carl shrugged, zipping up his jacket, "I took some Alka Seltzer, I'm sure it'll settle me down in no time."

"Well, if you're sure," she looked at him hesitantly.

Noticing her worry, Carl repeated, "I'm fine."

Queenie sighed and rested her hands on her hips, "I need half a pound of hamburger, and a pint of milk don't forget."

"I won't," Carl rolled his eyes as he hurried through the front door.

His mother called after him, "And pick up the herbs from your Auntie Beatrice!" Carl nodded and closed the door to the flat, stepped out onto the landing, and waited for the lift. One of the disadvantages of living in the blocks was there was no milk delivery. The milkmen delivered to the townhouses on the periphery of the estate, but not to the flats in the blocks. It wasn't the end of the world, but it did mean that Carl always had to come home after work, with whatever small grocery shopping list his mum had given him before he could go to the gym, or to his girlfriend Sherry's house. It was a bit of a pain, but Carl knew it was his mum's way of checking up on him, and he found it kind of cute, so he went along with it by pretending not to know Queenie's real motives.

Climbing into the company van, he glanced up and saw Dave limping past the Laureate in his disheveled state. Finally getting home after hobbling from Willesden Green. Carl leaned out the open window calling to him, "Oi Dave what're ya doin'?"

"'Eading 'ome," Dave didn't even bother to look up as he trudged on.

Carl snickered, “Hope she was worth it.”

“I wish,” Dave turned and headed towards Wobble’s house.

“Where you going?” Carl jabbed his thumb at the Wordsworth building, but Dave was walking away and didn't notice. “You live in here, and what happened to your clobber?” he sighed, seeing that Dave had continued to walk away, shrugged, started up the van and drove off, mumbling, “I was gonna buy him breakfast at Abdul’s too.”

Dave turned the front door key and fell more than walked into Wobble’s place. The kettle whistled as he walked down the hall and into the kitchen. Danny stood, his back to him, pouring water into a teapot. “You’re like an old granny Wobs, you and your teapot and cozy.”

“It’s the only way to make a decent cuppa,” Wobble replied as he covered the teapot with an old, stained, knitted cozy.

“Pour me one, I’d love some Rosie right now”

“I’m not your grannie, pour your…” Danny’s voice trailed off as he turned and saw Dave for the first time. Stopping, mid-sentence, he stared at him, teacup in one hand, teaspoon in the other, mouth hanging open. Dave’s jacket and jeans had multiple blood-stained rips on the front, the gashes on his right thigh were still oozing blood, and the right leg of his jeans was soaked with blood. “What the fuck ‘appened to you?” Wobble finally found his words.

Dave looked down at his mess of clothes, “Got in a bit of a ruck with a brick wall.”

Danny set the teacup down on the counter, “Jesus fucking Christ, sit down!” Dave moved to sit in a chair at the kitchen table, but he abruptly stopped him, “Whoa, whoa, ‘old up, just a minute!” Wobble looked around for something to lay on the chair, to protect it from the blood, and settled on a tea towel. One with pictures of the sights of London: Big Ben, Tower Bridge, The Tower of London. It had belonged to his mother, and he had always wondered why a Londoner owned a souvenir of their own city. It didn't make sense to him, but in Violet's life, what did? He carefully spread it over the chair seat and helped slowly lower Dave down onto it, "There take a weight off, Dave."

"Thanks Dan, good job you didn't go last night we had to do a runner," Dave groaned, leaning to the side to examine his stomach.

"How come?" Wobble asked as he poured the tea. His hands were shaking so badly from the shock of Dave's state that the tea was slopping over the side of the cups and onto the counter.

"Cops were everywhere, Alex got nicked."

"For what?"

Dave pondered the question and after a brief pause. "No fuckin' idea, me, Tel, and Donnie did a runner, but I got impaled on some glass."

"We'd best 'ave a butchers at that," Danny handed Dave a cup of tea.

"Thanks Dan." Dave took a quick sip and then set the cup down on the table, "It don't half fuckin' 'urt,"

Danny pulled the gash in the jeans on Dave's right thigh open, and Dave cried out in pain, "Jaysus do you 'ave to?"

The cuts in his thigh were about four inches long and deep. Wobble looked concerned, "We've gotta get you to the hospital."

Dave gingerly sat up straighter in the chair, "Not 'appening."

Wobble knelt next to him, still looking over his wounds, "You're bleeding like a stuck pig!"

Dave put his hand on Danny's shoulder, "You're gonna have to do something about it."

"What exactly?"

"I dunno, something."

Wobble leaned slightly back from him, holding his hands up in amazement that Dave expected him to help when he was so badly injured, "I'm not a doctor, Dave."

"No, but you have spent a lot of time in hospitals," Dave looked at him hopefully.

"So what? You've spent a lot of time in the pub d'you know how to brew beer?"

Dave reached out to grab Wobble's face, but Wobble grabbed him by the wrists to stop him. "Look at your hands!" he said in shock as he glanced over his friend's palms. Dave winced, they were almost black from the amount of dried blood, both gashed along the side of his palms, up to the base of his little fingers. "They're gonna need stitching too," Wobble gently let his hands go.

Dave sighed, "Well I'm not going to the hospital. I already told you that!"

"Let me think..." Danny started to look around the kitchen for a solution. He pulled open the cabinet door, under the sink, and retrieved an old shoe box and began to rifle through the contents: an old dish cloth, some batteries, a bobbin of thread, half a can of Swarfega, and a roll of duct tape. Grabbing the roll of tape, he opened a kitchen drawer and pulled out a pair of kitchen scissors. Placing the tape and scissors down on the kitchen table he left the room. Dave heard his boots hobbling up the stairs and then, moments later, back down again. He reappeared in the doorway, holding a bath towel, and a small, glass bottle. The bottle was placed on the table next to the earlier items, and the towel was laid out on the floor. "Lay down," Wobble gestured to the towel on the floor.

"What for?"

"'Cause I told you to, that's why!"

Dave moved from his chair, cringing as he laid down on the towel. Wobble approached him, with the scissors in his hand. "What the fuck are you doing with those?" Dave's voice rose, showing a slight panic.

Wobble snipped the scissors open and closed, "I'm gonna cut your Levi's off like on the telly shows."

"Sod that!" As quickly as he could, Dave lifted himself to his feet, undid his jeans, and pulled them off with a loud groan, "Isn't that easier?"

"Yeah, I guess," Danny looked disappointed as he laid the scissors back on the table.

"What now?"

Wobble pointed to the towel, "Lay down again."

Dave followed directions, holding his stomach delicately with his arms, in a fruitless attempt to help the pain.

"This is gonna hurt you more than me," Wobble picked up the glass bottle and twisted the lid off. He knelt beside Dave and started to pour the brown, oily contents into Dave's cuts.

"OW!" Dave cried out, his face twisting in pain, "What the 'ell is that?"

Wobble turned the bottle towards him, showing him the label, "Iodine."

"It 'urts!"

"No shit Sherlock!" Wobble said as he continued to pour the iodine over Dave's wounds, "I told you it would."

"Then why d'you do it?"

"'Cause it was fun," Wobble laughed.

Dave lifted himself up slightly, totally bemused, "FUN?"

"It'll kill the infection,"

The "patient" laid back again, resting on the scratchy material, "I didn't know I had one."

Wobble placed the cap back on the bottle, "You won't now!"

"Just as bleeding well," Dave stated, staring up at the ceiling. Wobble reached for the roll of duct tape on the table and Dave choked slightly in disbelief, "You are joking?"

The "doctor" shrugged, picking the end of the silver tape that had long been stuck to itself, "You won't go and get stitches." He picked at the end of the tape that has long been stuck down to itself and finally having got the end started pulled a long strip out with a loud ripping sound, "Lift your leg up."

Dave stuck his right leg up in the air, blood and iodine running freely into his crotch soaking his Y-fronts as he did. Danny started at his knee working his way up his leg, wrapping the tape round and round. Dave clenched his jaw tightly shut, grimacing through the pain. Eventually, when Danny reached the top of his leg, he began to cut the tape with the scissors, and Dave broke the silence, joking with him, "Careful there Danny, don't slip, I've got a lot of use for that." Danny chuckled and began to wrap his other leg before moving on to his forearms. Next, he helped Dave to a sitting position and began to wrap his chest and then the hands. Dave looked his body over, and chuckled, "I look like Bela Lugosi from 'The Mummy.'"

"Boris Karloff," Wobble corrected him.

"What?"

"Boris Karloff was the original Mummy," Danny said as he wiped the scissors clean.

Dave tilted his head, glancing curiously at Danny, "Why would you know that?"

"Came out in 1932, co-starred Zita Johann. Interesting fact Leonard Mudie had his feature film debut in it, the first of almost a hundred and fifty films."

"Now I'm worried about you Wobs."

Danny shrugged and slowly looked at the strangely wrapped Dave, his eyes traveling up and down. Dressed only in his underwear and socks, both now stained a strange sepia colour from the mixture of blood and iodine and wrapped in grey tape almost from head to foot he was quite the apparition. Wobble rose to his feet, placing the instruments back on the table, "You're worried about me?"

Dave was truly curious, "Seriously though, why would you know that?"

"When I was stuck in the hospital 'aving my operations I asked mum to get me some comic books. She showed up with a classic film encyclopedia, turns out it was left at the end of a jumble sale the Scouts were having. She asked if she could have it, and they gave it to her. Cheaper than comics, all I deserved, she said."

Dave looked stunned, "For Christ sakes, I'm sorry Wobs."

"That's alright," Wobble leaned over Dave and grinned, "I'm quite an encyclopedia on the subject now. You ever need to know anything about the golden age of Hollywood, I'm your man."

"Good to know, now how about helping me to the sofa?" The tape made it nearly impossible for him to stand.

"Oh right!" Danny slipped his arm around Dave, helping him across the room, and lowered him down onto the settee. The blood was starting to seep through the tape where the cuts were at their worst, on his right thigh, "We're going to have to keep an eye on that."

"It don't 'alf hurt," Dave protested.

"I bet. 'Ow you going to work in that state?"

Dave sighed, "Don't worry, I'll figure it out."

Wobble looked doubtful, "I hope so, you promised."

"Yes mum." Danny moved towards the front door, "I'm going to head down the shops get some more tape and some aspirin."

Meanwhile, Carl sat at a table in The Sunshine Cafe reading that morning's Sun, and its dire predictions regarding the Arsenal match at Sunderland later that afternoon. He took a sip from his coffee as Abdul's wife, Louella, crossed the room with his breakfast. Just as she reached the table, Carl's stomach let out a long, deep growl. Louella stopped and looked at him, "You sound like you haven't eaten for a week." She set the greasy looking food in front of him.

"Sorry Lou, dunno what's going on, don't feel Tom but I did have a two-day old Ruby after the gym last night."

"No need to apologise, just eat up, you'll feel so much better," she smiled at him and turned to leave, "Cheers!"

Carl tucked into his breakfast, fried eggs, beans, tomatoes, mushrooms, bacon, and fried bread. When he didn't have a fight coming up, he allowed himself a good breakfast on Saturday mornings before heading out to make some quick cash. The door to the cafe swung open and Ray walked in, the other customers taking no notice, no real reason for them to, but Carl watched as Louella visibly stiffened at the skinhead's presence. Abdul closed the cash drawer tightly, "Can I help you?"

"Yeah, coffee black," Ray replied as he approached the counter.

Abdul fixed the coffee as Ray fished through his jean pockets for some change but came up empty. He pulled out a twenty, "Don't wanna break this, I'll get you next time."

Abdul's eyes narrowed, and he stated firmly, "No credit."

Ray stood holding the money out in front of him. "Sorry?" he replied equally defiantly.

Abdul folded his arms across his chest and nodded at the sign on the till, which read, "IF YOU WANT CREDIT DON'T ASK."

Ray glanced at the sign briefly and sneered, "It's a coffee."

"It's the principal," Abdul tried to remain calm.

Ray's temper was visibly rising, "You've got to be kidding me!"

"If I give you credit, I will have to give it to every Tom, Dick, and Harry," Abdul held tightly to the coffee cup.

"Tom, Dick, and Amrit you mean!" Ray mocked him.

Abdul continued trying to hide any sign of emotion, especially fear, "I can break the twenty."

"I don't want to break a twenty for a lousy coffee," Rays temper was beginning to get the better of him now.

"Then you can't need the coffee too badly, can you?"

Ray glared at Abdul, his nostrils flared, his eyes wide open and glaring. He leaned forward, both hands gripping the edge of the counter, his knuckles white. Louella nervously broke the silence, "Perhaps just this once?"

However, Abdul was determined, "No."

Ray was now even more enraged. "Maybe you should listen to your pretty little wife," he growled through clenched teeth.

Abdul didn't blink, he stared straight back into Ray's eyes, the silence seemed eternal, the whole room had fallen silent.

Finally, from his seat, Carl broke the silence, "Put his coffee on my bill."

The entire room including Ray swiveled to see who had spoken. Abdul protested, "You don't have to do that, Carl."

"Yeah, I do, you didn't bring my toast and now my beans are getting cold."

Ray glared at Carl, but even he had to think twice about provoking a confrontation with the fit, agile, and capable boxer. "Keep your coffee," Ray spat as he turned and strode out of the cafe, slamming the door shut behind him, the dangling bell dinging and clanging loudly as he did. The customers sat in silence; the gurgling coffee machine suddenly seemed deafeningly loud.

Louella picked up the Styrofoam, to-go, coffee cup that contained Ray's now unwanted coffee and walked across to Carl's table, holding it out, "Refill, on the house?"

The room reverted to normal, although the subjects of conversation from before Ray's entrance have been forgotten and replaced with debate over what he might have done had Carl not been there to intervene and why was he like that anyway. Carl pushed his plate back, "Thanks Lou, I'll take it to go."

"And next week's breakfast is on the house," Lou said with a relieved smile replacing the look of fear and panic that had previously painted her face.

The boxer laid his napkin on the top of his plate, "There's no need for that."

"Yes, there is and baklava whenever your mum wants some," she reached forward picking up his cutlery.

"We'll see." He nodded to Abdul, took his to go coffee and left.

While he sipped his coffee from inside his van, he opened the glove box and pulled out a clipboard. On the front was a work order with an address for one of Mr. Whittaker's friends who needed some new light fixtures hung. It was in the nicer part of Wembley, over where Vickie lived. As he drove away, Carl smiled and hoped he might bump into her.

He pulled up to the curb outside the house, and rechecked the address, 20 Acacia Avenue. He was in the right spot. Gathering his belongings, he climbed out of the van, walked up to the front door, and pushed the doorbell. Instead of a "ding-dong" or a loud grating buzz, the sound of opera filled the air. Carl was taken aback from the unexpected turn of events and looked around to see if anyone had noticed. The door opened and there stood a middle-aged white man, in John Lennon glasses, white pressed pants, a white shirt with a pink bow tie, and a pink cardigan. He smiled at Carl, "Yes?"

"Mr. Devine?" Carl looked at his clipboard, hoping he was pronouncing his name correctly.

"That's me, you must be Carl."

"Yeah, that's me."

"Well do come in, I'll show you what we need and then I have an errand to run, you come highly recommended."

Carl was a touch surprised, "I do?"

"Yes, you do," Mr. Devine eyed Carl up and down as he spoke.

"I aim to please, as they say," Carl immediately regretted saying it, it just seemed too familiar to him.

"I do hope so," Mr. Devine stepped back, holding the door, allowing Carl to enter. The young Black man stepped into the front hall and glanced around the large foyer. The homeowner closed the door behind Carl, noticed him looking around curiously, and continued, "We need a new light hung here in the foyer, and one above the mirror here in the toilet." He pointed out the locations, the round marble floored foyer had a small toilet off to one side with an old slightly tacky brass light hung above it, and finished with, "The new fixtures are over here on the console."

Carl turned his attention towards Mr. Devine once again, "Sorry?"

"The entrance table," he gestured towards a small, ornate table near the front door.

"Oh right," Carl stepped across the tile floor and picked up the fixtures from the table, watching as Mr. Devine grabbed an expensive looking coat from the nearby closet.

"If there's nothing else, I have to dash."

"No, no nothing, I've got it, two lights, I'll get my stuff and be done in a jiffy!"

"Good, I'll be back in about an hour," Mr. Devine said as he slipped into his jacket before heading out the front door.

Carl turned and started to follow when his stomach let out an enormous growl and a pain shot through his guts. His eyes bulged wide open, and he clamped his arse cheeks as tight as he possibly could before rushing into the handily adjacent toilet. Wrenching his jeans and underwear down around his ankles, he plopped down just in time as his bowels emptied themselves into the toilet loudly, repetitively, and with an unnaturally disgusting stink. "JESUS CHRIST!" Carl couldn't believe what was happening to him. His uncle had told him once about how "they" had given him a "purge," as he called it, to drink in the army to clean him out and how unpleasant and effective it had been. As the fourth wave of the shit tsunami gushed out of him, he could only think that this must have been what it was like. After the fifth and final wave had finally petered out, and Carl lifted his head from the doubled over fetal position, he had found the only comfort in, to notice in his hurry, he didn't shut the toilet door and now Mr. Devine was standing, in the foyer, staring at him, holding a hankie tightly to his nose.

"I forgot my wallet. I don't think we'll be needing your services after all. You can let yourself out," Mr. Devine tried to keep himself from gagging.

Carl couldn't believe what was happening to him, "It's not my fault I think the Paki I had last night was off!"

"Really Carl? As if what you did wasn't bad enough, now racism?" He shivered, stepping back from the entire scene to open the front door for Carl, to show him out, "I have to go and call a plumber. I'm going to want a new toilet installed." Carl walked out and stood in the street struggling to comprehend what had just happened to him, dreading the inevitable phone call from his boss Mr. Whittaker.

14

Detective Sergeant Miller and D.C. Wainwright turned off the main road into Chalkhill, a uniformed officer opened the temporary tape barrier for them to pass. As they neared the Copse, a crowd of curious residents had started to form, and the council security guards, who had been called in on their day off, pushed the thirty or so spectators back to let the car pass. Wainwright grunted in contempt, "Rent-a-cops, not gonna be a lot of use when it all kicks off."

"If it all kicks off you mean," Miller corrected him.

"No, not really," he glanced at her with a shrug before pulling the car to the curb between the marked forensics van, and the blue tent that the forensics team had erected over the burnt-out shell of the car that Mitch was killed in earlier. Wainwright turned the car off, "Let's get on with it then."

A uniformed officer approached Miller, "Ma'am."

Miller rolled her eyes as she swung her door open, "Oh good grief."

The officer stepped back apologetically from the car, "Sorry ma'am."

She ignored him and continued, "Anything I should know before I go in there?"

On the far side towards the tower blocks a larger crowd had formed behind the police tape and phalanx of council guards. Perhaps a hundred residents milled around craning to see what was going on. The balconies of the blocks were packed three deep with young Black men, pushing and cajoling each other for a better view. He noticed her looking at the crowd, "The locals are getting restless ma'am."

The flap on the tent opened and a forensic detective in full length hazmat overalls and a mask stepped out and walked straight towards Miller. She walked past the unnamed officer and met the detective part way, stopping abruptly in front of him, “What do I need to know?” She asked as she pulled a notebook and pen from her back pocket.

“He’s dead. I’ve got everything I need; I can run all the tests I need back at the lab. The deceased has already been transported to the morgue. I’m getting out of here and you should too,” he nervously eyed the increasingly loud crowd that was gathering. Miller did what she normally did and ignored him, “I have an investigation to run, a man was murdered and there may be witnesses.”

“That’s your problem,” The forensics officer strode back to his van and climbed in the passenger side, the engine was already running, and the driver made a three-point turn and drove away.

Miller turned to Wainwright. “Get as many uniforms as you can and start a canvas of the crowd and then the flats,” she commanded.

“Do you think that’s wise?” Wainwright crossed in front of the car, approaching Miller.

“Mitchell Collins wasn’t one of them, why should they care,” she moved around, glancing over the burned car and peering around the crime scene, the pen tapping on the notepad.

“Very well,” Wainwright said following the order as he turned to the uniform who had greeted them on their arrival to relay the instructions.

Dejean leaned against the concrete railing on the third-floor balcony, directly overlooking the murder scene, surrounded by a gang of youths who circled him, eagerly waiting for his command. Dejean nodded his head before turning to stroll nonchalantly away. The gang reacted, pulling pre-made Molotov cocktails from inside their jackets. Samson snapped a Zippo off his thigh, exactly the way Terry did, and lit the first one up. The torch carrier, a boy of only thirteen, pushed his way through the crowd and threw the projectile. It arced through the air landing just before the tent, behind the line of security guards, and exploded in the road in a ball of flame. The crowd of onlookers, on the same balcony, immediately began shouting and cheering. The council guards, at the tower block end of the road, turned and ran past the crime scene, panicking their colleagues at the other end of the road into joining them in fleeing. The crowd in the street began to shout and cheer. Miller stepped out into the street to see what was going on. Wainwright grabbed her sleeve to stop her, "We have to leave."

She yanked her arm back, "Call for backup."

"Are you crazy? We are not riot cops!"

Up on the balcony, Dejean's army were laughing and jeering at the missile thrower for missing his objective. A second youth stepped forward and a second Molotov arced through the air, this time landing directly on top of the tent, which instantly erupted into a huge fireball. The rest of the youths shouted in approval and high five each other. A third missile landed and exploded in the street, then a fourth. Wainwright again pulled Miller back towards the car. The crowd in the street was growing larger and rowdier, at the front centre was a gang of young Black men with dustbins and dustbin lids banging on them with their hands and sticks in a loud booming rhythm.

"Fuck this! Let's go," Miller shouted as the two detectives climbed back into their car. As Wainwright started it, a brick smashed through the rear window. He jammed the car into reverse, and as he backed out, he saw the uniform who had greeted them, and another Constable, standing in the road, back-to-back, truncheons out, not knowing what to do. Wainwright slammed on the brakes, wound down his window and shouted, "Get in!" The two officers didn't need to be asked twice. They scrambled into the car and Wainwright backed out through the crowd, projectiles bouncing off the car as he did, "Might as well be back in Belfast, at least the trucks were armoured."

Miller looked at him with a curious look on her face, "I didn't know you were military?"

"Another time," he stated as he passed the crowd and backed into a side road to turn the car around. From the right a large crowd advanced on the estate. They displayed no anger or animosity, and it appeared more like they were going to a carnival, than a riot. One of the officers, in the back, spoke up, "Thanks for stopping by the way I thought we were done for."

Wainwright glanced over his shoulder intending to tell the man he is welcome but instead shouted, "Get your fucking helmets off, this lot sees them their moods gonna change mighty fucking quick!" Muttering apologies, the two quickly removed their headgear and Wainwright drove out of the estate as fast as he possibly could.

Ray arrived back at his house, slammed the door and ran straight up the stairs, into the toilet. After finishing, he came back out on the landing and turned to go into the bathroom where the sink was located. But the door was locked. He pounded on it, "Siobhan? You in the bath? I want in there."

"You'll just have to wait, won't you," Siobhan called back through the door.

Ray pounded again, "I had a shit, I wanna wash my hands!"

"Go downstairs!" She yelled back.

He jiggled the handle, "Bollocks, what are you up to?"

"Nothing!"

"Let me in then!" The lock on the inside unlatches with a loud click. Siobhan came out with a towel wrapped around her head. "What are you up to?"

"Just washed my hair," she pointed to the obvious towel on her head.

Ray sniffed, his eyes narrowing on her, "Bullshit, I can smell the henna." Without any warning, he whipped the towel off Siobhan's head. She stepped back in shock, as Ray stared at her hair. Where there had once been long, thick, curly, blonde locks, there were now short, spiky, bright orange spikes. He gasped, "What the fuck did you do?"

"It's my new look," Siobhan touched her hair proudly.

"New look?"

Siobhan was defiant, "Yeah! New look!"

He leaned in, his face almost touching hers, "This for Dave?"

She looked stunned, "You what? Don't be stupid."

Ray shook his head from side to side, "D'you two think I wouldn't recognise his boots the other day?"

Siobhan began to become frightened, not for herself, but for Dave, "Don't do anything stupid Ray. Please don't."

"That little prick!"

"It's not about him!" She desperately lied.

"Of course, it is. I was biding my time, trying to figure out what and when to deal with him, but this, this is it!" He was becoming more and more irate.

"Please Ray," she begged.

"Please Ray nuffin," Ray turned and ran back down the stairs, forgetting all about washing his hands, and stopped at the front door. He turned back casually adding, "By the way Mitch is dead."

Siobhan stared at him, completely shocked, "Dead?"

Enjoying how shocked she was, he smirked and added, "Yeah dead!"

Almost in a whisper, Siobhan gasped, "How?"

"He was found in Chalkhill, guess the coons did him in." Ray shrugged as he stepped out into the street, slammed the door behind him and set off to the Laureate. When he got to the pub, it was nearly empty. He sat at the bar and ordered a Whitetop, asked Gerry if he had seen Dave, and hearing that he hadn't, drained the beer and left, heading off to Wordsworth House to look for him.

Siobhan hurried to get dressed and headed out to Wobble's house. She pounded on the door in a panic, terrified that Ray might see her and find Dave before she could warn him, Wobble opened the door and immediately broke into a huge grin, "You're a sight for sore eyes. Like the hair."

She was a little taken aback, "Thanks, why are you so happy to see me?"

"You'll see!" Siobhan gave him a curious look and headed down the hallway into the living room that Dave was using as a bedroom. Wobble followed behind, taking the opportunity to run his eyes over her shapely rear end.

Dave was laying on the sofa, in a t-shirt, a blanket draped over his legs. He looked up as she entered, eyes widening in surprise, "What the fuck did you do to your hair?"

Siobhan rolled her eyes, "That's nice."

Dave laughed, and half-heartedly attempted to sit up, "It looks great, fabulous even, but your brother is going to kill me!"

"Yeah, about that..." Siobhan wasn't sure how to broach the subject.

Dave looked at her nervously, "What?"

Siobhan leaned in and gave Dave a kiss, resting her hand on his chest. Dave winced. "You been working out?" She lightly teased him.

Dave looked embarrassed, "No."

"You feel like you've been using a Bullworker for six months," Siobhan gave his chest a little squeeze, "and we know that ain't true!" Wobble smirked. She grew curious and needed to know what secret the other two were hiding from her, "What's going on?"

"I had a bit of an accident," Dave admitted, not wanting to reveal the full extent of his injuries.

"An accident?" She didn't know whether to believe him or not.

Dave could hear the concern in her voice, "Yeah, an accident." He was beginning to feel extremely nervous about showing her how bad it really was.

At this point, Wobble had enough of the game, "Just spill the beans Dave, d'you think she's never going to notice the scars?"

"What scars?" She glanced at Danny, and turned back to Dave, "What's going on Dave?" She asked him slowly as Dave gingerly slid his legs off the couch and stood up, wobbling slightly as he did, partly from the wounds, and partly from the tape wrapped round and round him making it near impossible to bend his limbs.

The blanket fell to the floor. He stood there in nothing more than a T-shirt that had the local hospital sports day logo on it, and his brown stained underwear. The silver tape wrapped around his arms, hands, and legs. Siobhan's mouth hung open as she stared, completely stunned into silence from the bizarre sight in front of her. “Take his shirt off, Wobble,” her voice was shaking as if she might cry.

Dave corrected her to distract her, “His name’s Dan.”

“Wobble,” she repeated, “do as I say.”

Wobble promptly stepped up right next to Dave, “Right, will do!” He grinned as he pulled the shirt up over his friend’s head. Dave shouted in pain as he did, and the rest of the tape wrapping was revealed.

“HELL TO THE NO!” Siobhan shouted at him. “You look like a skinny Michelin Man. What the fuck happened?”

Dave recounted the story. The entire time she stared at him, more and more bemused as the story went on. Finally, when he had finished, she turned to Wobble. “Give me the car keys,” she demanded, holding out her slender hand.

Wobble was naturally reluctant to hand the keys to his new motor over, “What for?”

Her eyes narrowed at his defiance, “Can you drive?”

“No,” Danny reluctantly admitted.

Siobhan shrugged and cocked her head to one side, “I can. Sort of.”

Danny was defeated, “Right then.”

Dave felt it was time to assert his authority. “It’s up to Wobble who drives his car, not you. Where d’you think you’re going anyway?”

“Not me… WE. We are going to the hospital to get you fixed.”

Dave waved his hands at the bandages, “Wobble already fixed me!”

Siobhan looked him over, a mixture of disgust, anger, and worry obvious in her gaze, “Great job Wobble, he’s leaking!”

Danny nodded his head sagely, "I warned him about that."

"Keys?" Siobhan again thrust her hand out demandingly. Wobble had no doubt that not handing the keys over would not end well for him, and he quickly turned to fetch them.

"I'm not dressed," Dave weakly protested.

Siobhan picked the blanket up from the floor. "Wrap yourself in the blanket, but for God sakes change those disgusting Y-fronts! I don't even want to think about what they look like you've done."

Dave desperately tried to think of an excuse, any excuse to avoid going to the hospital. "What if the police are looking for me?"

Siobhan was baffled as to why this might be, "For what?"

"I don't know," Dave's voice trailed off.

"No, because, Machine Gun Kelly, you didn't do nothing."

"Still."

Wobble walked back into the room, keys in hand. Siobhan turned to him, "Have you seen any police on the estate Danny?"

"No," he shrugged and tossed her the car keys.

"See," Siobhan gingerly took Dave's arm to help him walk, "if they were looking for you, we'd know, let's go."

Wobble looked confused, "Why would the police be looking for him?"

"They're not," she stated again, wrapping her arm around Dave's waist.

"But you said..." Danny moved to Dave's other side to help Siobhan.

The group slowly limped down the hall, Siobhan sighed, "Never mind. I'll explain in the waiting room. I'm sure we'll have plenty of time then. Let's go!"

The drive to the hospital was a painful one, the car jerking and bunny hopping most of the way as Siobhan had learned to drive in an automatic and really had no idea how to drive a standard. The triage nurse struggled to control a constant and urgent fit of the giggles as she took Dave's medical history and listened to the convoluted, and obviously false story, about how he had hung a mirror on the ceiling above his bed, only to have it come crashing down on top of him whilst he was wanking.

She looked at him skeptically, "Got any cuts on your dick then?"

"No," Dave could feel his ears reddening.

The nurse smirked, "Not that big a target then?"

Dave was stung by the inference, "You wouldn't want it as a wart on the end of your nose."

She laid her pen down and leant back, "Why do guys say that?"

Dave was embarrassed, "Well it's a way of saying they don't 'ave a small dick I guess."

She was clearly enjoying herself, "Yeah, but what girl would want any sort of wart on the end of their nose?"

Dave began to stammer, he knew he'd been outwitted, but didn't know what to do or say about it, "I guess..."

The nurse sensed victory, and moved in for the kill, "Dick shaped or not, would they?"

Dave was perplexed by the question; the obvious logic had never occurred to him before. The nurse directed him to sit and wait in the waiting room. He slowly crossed the room, still in a lot of pain, and sat next to Siobhan and Wobble, who had come more out of concern about his car, than about Dave's well-being. Dave ruminated and took in the conversation with the nurse before turning to Siobhan, eager to share his revelation, "You know the wart on the nose comment makes no sense!"

Siobhan rolled her eyes, "I could've told you that. Any girl could."

Danny didn't care, "Did they tell you how long we'll be here Dave?"

Dave looked irritated, "No Wobs they didn't. And you don't have to be here, either of you."

"I'm not having any boyfriend of mine going home on the bus wrapped in a dirty blanket with nothing but what look like shit-stained undies on. I told you to change them," Siobhan crossed her legs and folded her arms, rooting herself in her chair, determined not to leave.

A grin spread across his face, "D'you hear that Wobs? Her boyfriend, that's me." He regarded his girlfriend, "And I thought I told you, I couldn't get them off over the tape."

Siobhan smirked, "You don't usually have any trouble getting them off."

Wobble was bemused, "Oh I heard it, I'm just 'aving trouble calculating it."

Dave was now grinning ear to ear, "You're just jealous. Now be quiet I've gotta think up a better retort than the 'wart on your nose.'"

Wobble saw his opportunity to dig at Dave and maybe impress Siobhan at the same time, "Why d'you get a lot of small dick pokes then Dave? Get it pokes?"

She was not having any of this, "No he doesn't!"

Wobble shook his head in disgust, "I think I just threw up in my mouth!"

"Serves you right Wobs, serves you right." Dave rested his hand affectionately on Siobhan's lap and she took his hand in her hand. The intercom called, "NUMBER 77!"

"That's me," Dave tried to stand up, but the tape was by now really cutting into his legs which made it nearly impossible to bend them. He tipped sideways flailing his arms in a desperate attempt to remain upright, both Siobhan and Wobble jumped up grabbed his arms, steadied him, and he headed off stiff legged, across the room to where the nurse was waiting for him.

Danny looked at Siobhan as they sat back down, "How Long d'you s'pose he'll be in there Siobhan?"

She sighed, "No idea. 'Opefully long enough for me bruvver to calm down."

He looked concerned, "Bit het up, is he?"

A smile spread across Siobhan's face, "I love the way you talk Dan you know that? Het up."

He saw his chance, and half-jokingly added, "Well when you come to your senses and dump Dave, you know where I am."

"I'll keep that in mind."

Trying not to show disappointment, Danny continued, "I'm gonna go see if I can rustle up a cup of tea, you want one?"

Appreciating the gesture, and realising that he needed a moment to himself, Siobhan concedes, "Love one."

"Milk two sugars?" After all he figured, just about everyone takes their tea in the same fashion.

"Just black thanks."

This somehow made him feel even more crestfallen, "Oh, okay then."

Nearly three hours later, Dave finally reappeared, in a wheelchair. He was now wrapped almost head to toe in white bandages, the blanket hanging over his shoulders, wearing a pair of paper underwear. Behind him a huge, Black, male orderly pushed the wheelchair. Wobble saw him first, "'Ere he is, King Tut 'imself!" The orderly wheeled the chair across the waiting room, and over to Siobhan and Wobble.

They stopped in front of his friends, and Dave joked, "Thank you James, that will be all."

Siobhan, understandably embarrassed by his comment, looked up at the orderly to apologise, "Sorry, he's always like this." The orderly turned and walked away without saying a word. "I bet he's seen and heard worse," she thought. Standing, she walked around to the back of the wheelchair, "Let's go then." She began to push the chair towards the main doors.

Wobble limped off in the opposite direction, "This way Siobhan." He pointed down a hallway.

Siobhan stopped, looking over her shoulder at him, "Eh?"

"The car's around the back, this way's a lot quicker."

"You sure Wobs?" she looked unsure.

Danny perked up, "Course I am, no one's spent more time here who doesn't work here, than me!"

"I guess," she smiled and turned Dave's wheelchair around, she had to admit to herself, Wobble did make her smile with his infectious sense of humour.

"'Ere let me," Wobble took Siobhan's place, behind the wheelchair, and headed away down a side corridor with her falling in beside him.

"Steady Wobs, you don't 'ave a licence remember," Dave teased, and exaggeratingly grasped the arm rests.

"Very funny Dave, very funny," Wobble rolled his eyes.

"Ignore him Danny," Siobhan said, as she walked next to him, "and thanks for letting us use the car, we'd've been real stuck without it."

Danny blushed slightly from the attention being paid to him, "Let's have some fun!" As he spoke, he began to run, pushing the chair ahead of him. To be fair, with his condition, it wasn't exactly a sprint, but Dave didn't like it nevertheless and gripped the arms of the chair tighter and tighter. At this point, Danny was howling with laughter as he half limped, half ran, down the corridor. Siobhan casually jogged along beside him, giggling. Suddenly, Dave shouted, "WOBS!!" He saw what was directly ahead, the other two didn't.

A flight of eight concrete terrazzo steps heading downwards, right in front of him. Wobble couldn't stop in time and the chair tipped over the edge of the top step. Siobhan grabbed the handle on the back of the chair. The chair stopped but Dave didn't. He was launched out, over the steps, landing on his left thigh, halfway down, fell forward and crashed chest first onto the tile floor at the bottom of the steps. He screamed in pain. Wobble and Siobhan stopped, frozen at the top of the stairs, staring down at Dave who was now doubled over groaning in pain. "Shit, sorry Dave, I forgot about them."

Siobhan looked around in a panic, spotting an emergency pull lever on a nearby wall. Lifting the hinged, glass panel, she grabbed the lever and yanked it upward. A deafening klaxon alarm sounded, emitting a screaming, piercing wail, the lights turning on fully bright. Siobhan stepped back, her mouth hung open, stunned by what she had done. Wobble looked at her, “I don’t think you should have done that.”

It was nearly two hours later, after the nurses, doctors, and maintenance staff had responded to the alarm. Nearly two hours after the fire service had been called and notified that their presence wasn’t necessary. Nearly two hours after Siobhan and Wobble had given statements to an exasperated, bored policeman who had clearly heard it all before. “An innocent mistake” and “Could’ve ‘appened to anyone officer.” Nearly two hours later and they were thrown ignominiously out.

But not Dave, he was again admitted, over his objections, the cut on his head, caused by the latest accident, was stitched, and his left leg re-stitched. “One good thing,” he thought to himself, “Wobble can’t make a fuss about me not working now.”

15

Donnie awoke to the sound of his alarm beeping rhythmically and annoyingly. He reached out and slapped the oversized snooze button on the top and pulled the pillow over his head, closed his eyes to try to shield them from the sunlight pouring through the window. The alarm inevitably went off again, seven minutes later, and as always, Donnie was convinced that he had only just closed his eyes. He threw back the covers, knowing that without this grand gesture he wouldn't get up, but would spend his Sunday morning dozing in bed until 11:30, when he would finally get up just in time for The Laureate to open for lunch. However, there would be no pub lunch for him today. For the first time, in as long as he could remember, Donnie was going to church. He wasn't sure why he was going; it wasn't because he felt his soul needed saving. If such things as heaven and hell existed, he knew which he was bound for. No amount of praying would redeem him at this point, of that, he was sure. So, when Jimmy had asked, rather demanded, at the end of the day on Friday that he show up for service, Donnie had shrugged and said, "Sure why not?"

He was going to live up to his word and meet Jimmie at the Baptist church he attended in the East end. The reasons he had to go so far to be saved once a week, baffled Donnie, but so be it. He figured that if he got a move on, he could grab a quick breakfast at Abdul's before getting on the tube and trekking across the city.

He left his room; hurried down the stairs of the bedsit house he lived in and jogged down the street. Donnie was proud of how fit he was and threw a few punches right and left as he ran, just like back when he was training to box back in Glasgow. His aspirations as a boxer had been cut short, not because he couldn't fight, on the contrary, he was a natural. Unfortunately, there was one problem, Donnie had a fierce temper. As soon as an opponent hit him, all rules were out of the window. He didn't hear the bell, wouldn't let the referee stop him, or break the fight up. He felt head butts and low blows were fair play, and eventually the gym he trained at had dropped him. Albeit with huge regrets, they gave him his marching orders. That night, Donnie had gotten drunk and, in a fight over a pool game beer bet in a Glasgow boozer, had severely beaten a total stranger and caught the night train to London.

When he arrived at Abdul's it was, much to Donnie's chagrin, closed. It was always closed on Sundays, but having never tried to go before, he simply hadn't realised. He scoffed and jogged down to Kingsbury tube station. There was a McDonalds two doors down, but for reasons he couldn't fully articulate, Donnie wouldn't eat in a huge commercial outlet. He believed in supporting small local businesses and besides the way he saw it, Abdul was an immigrant trying his hardest to make good in a foreign land, and Donnie admired that. British or not, he often felt like a foreigner in London himself.

He boarded the train and headed for the East. The train didn't stop at Wembley Park as usual, and this confused Donnie. He wasn't aware that the riot on Chalkhill estate, opposite the tube station entrance, was still going full bore. He didn't know it had started in the first place. If he had, he most likely would have gone and joined in.

At the estate, the police were lined up at both ends in full riot gear, a phalanx of shields, truncheons drawn. In the centre, a mob of around five hundred youths, armed with sticks and bricks. The police would fire tear gas into the crowd and advance from both ends at the same time, beating rhythmically on their shields with their truncheons. They were pushed back each time by the angry crowd, beating the same rhythm on their dustbins and lids, mostly because of the hail of missiles raining down from the three levels of balconies on both sides of the street. The battle had gone on like this for the whole night, push and pull, give and take from both sides.

There were far more youth on the estate than lived there, and the police had closed all road and footpath access to try and stop the steady stream of support pouring in from all over the city. They were thwarted by the fact that the South side of the estate was bordered by the above ground tube tracks. If someone had been looking to join the riot, they could, simply by exiting the train one stop early at Neasden, dropping off the side of the platform, and walking down the tracks where the estate was easily reached.

At ten in the morning, the mayor, Hazel Mulligan, nicknamed "Do Over," partly because her policies were constantly overturned and partly because of her name, arrived with a group of councilors. She took a moment to consult with the police chief, before entering the estate. Equipped with a bullhorn, she had attempted to appeal to the protestors that if they would stop rioting, she would listen to their complaints. The police chief thought it highly unlikely that she could make a difference, after all the entire country was in uproar at the lack of decent jobs or support for the less fortunate, as well as the common abuse of the so-called "SUS laws," but he didn't see the harm in her trying.

From a vantage point on some raised ground by a slide and roundabout, the mayor cleared her throat and began speaking into the megaphone. What she said wasn't important, no one listened, no one even noticed her presence. The battle continued unabated below her.

Carl was asleep in bed with Sherry, when his mum burst into his bedroom and abruptly woke them up. "Carl, get up now," the panic rising in her voice.

He sat up, half asleep, and tried to focus his eyes, "What you doing mum?" He covered the half-naked woman up with his blanket, "I've got company."

"I can see that, get up, you got no time for that now," Queenie left the room, leaving the door wide open.

Sherry was not happy, "Jesus Carl what's going on?"

"I dunno. Stay here I'll be right back," Carl grumbled and climbed out of bed, pulled on a pair of jeans, and headed out, without a shirt, to see what all the fuss was about. In the living room Queenie was pacing, backwards and forwards, ringing a paper napkin in her hand. Carl stopped in the doorway, looking at her, his head tilted to the side inquisitively, “What’s going on?”

Queenie looked up, a worried expression on her face, “You gotta go get your aunt Beatrice, the whole estates erupted.”

“What?” Carl was briefly taken aback, “The Hill or Grahame Park?”

“The Hill of course, why would The Park riot?” His mum rolled her eyes, “They’re white, life isn’t so hard on them. And anyway, your Auntie doesn’t live in Grahame Park, does she? The Hill’s gone up like Brixton and Highgate.” She returned to her pacing across the floor.

“No way? Put the news on!” Queenie hurried to turn the television on, it being Sunday morning, a rerun of Songs of Praise was on BBC one. Carl pushed in front of her and twisted the tuning knob on the front of the set. ITV was showing a Bonanza rerun, BBC 2 a chamber orchestra.

She stepped forward and turned the set off, “Never mind the television, your aunt phoned. She’s stuck in her flat, can’t go outside. She’s afraid they’ll burn the place down around her.”

By this time, Sherry had entered and leaned on the wall listening, “Where’s Dejean?”

Queenie looked up at her and spat a response, “Him be the one lighting the fires, you can bet your sweet life on that!”

Sherry was taken aback by the vehemence in Queenie’s voice. “But his own mum, surely he’d look out for her?”

The older woman shook her head sadly, “How? He’ll have done his best to make sure the place went crazy and now no one will have any way of controlling what he let loose. It’s a runaway fire and he’ll be fanning the flames so he will.” She turned to Carl, on his left chest, between the nipple and the shoulder blade, was a black ink tattoo of a boxer. “And why you ever got that ridiculous drawing baffles me.”

Carl shrugged, “What? I like it.”

Queenie grew more riled up, taking her anxiety out on her son, “You can’t see it. What a waste of money!”

Carl became defiant, “It ain’t doing you any harm, and besides I’m getting another one next week.”

Her eyes narrowed on his face, “What on earth for?”

“I’m getting Sherry's name put under it right over my heart,” he pointed at his muscular chest, just above his nipple.

Sherry was stunned as was Queenie by this news. However, Queenie was, as always, the first to speak, “You put him up to dis child?”

Sherry sputtered, “No… I didn’t, I didn’t know any more about it than you did!”

His mother turned her attention back to the young man, “What you want to do that for?”

Carl was never much of one for displaying overt emotion, so still looking at Queenie, and not Sherry he replied, matter-of-factly, “’Cause I love her and I’m gonna ask her to marry me.”

His mother’s mouth hung open, looking almost wide enough to swallow the room, Sherry held her hands to her face and gasped as Carl turned to face her, “If she’ll have me that is.” She screamed in delight and leapt into his arms; Carl easily caught her. Queenie began to weep.

Sherry wrapped her arms around his neck and kissed him, long and hard, leaned her head back and looked at him lovingly, “Of course I will, I love you too babe!”

Queenie wiped her eyes and hurried across the room to plant a huge wet kiss on Carl's cheek, then another on Sherry’s, “And I love you both.” She smiled happily at the couple momentarily before taking a step back and allowing the worried frown to return to her face, “Now me and your fiancé got some planning to do, and you’ve gotta go get your Aunt Beatrice, she always throws the best parties.”

Donnie got off the tube in Bethnal Green and headed down the street. He felt like a fish out of water. He didn’t know anyone in this part of the city and constantly glanced around to make sure no one was following or watching him. Two streets down, he found the church, more an old community hall, the sound of singing audible from the street. He walked up the two steps and opened the doors, the singing of "Ezekiel Saw the Wheel" welling up as he entered. As soon as he stepped into the foyer, two large Black men in suits stepped toward him and placed a hand each firmly on Donnie's chest, stopping him dead. One of them leaned forward and spoke, "Can we help you son?"

Donnie looked puzzled. "I'm here for church," he replied, baffled as to why they had stopped him.

"Here?" The second man eyed him suspiciously, "You're here for church?"

Donnie grew impatient, "Yeah, why not?"

The two men glanced at each other before turning their attention back to Donnie, "Well have you noticed how you're dressed?"

Donnie looked down at his clothes. Fred Perry tennis shirt, his best red Harrington bomber jacket, Levi jeans with the cuffs rolled up to expose his twelve-hole Dr Marten cherry red boots. "What about it? It's my clean clobber."

The first man narrowed his eyes on Donnie's face, "You're a skinhead."

"Fucking right I am!" Donnie stood up straight, puffing his chest out.

The second doorman scoffed, and shushed him, "We don't swear in the house of the Lord!"

The skinhead coughed apologetically, lowering his voice, "Yeah sorry, I'll give you that one."

"Why are you, a skinhead, coming to church in a West Indian Baptist church?'

Donnie looked confused at all the questioning. "Jimmy," he stated, attempting to peer around the broad shoulders of the "bouncer."

The pair stepped closer together, obstructing his view of the church, "Jimmy?"

"Yeah" Donnie shrugged, "Jimmy's been on at me for weeks to come and get saved so here I am." The two men looked confused, and it was displayed all too clearly on their faces. Donnie noticed the looks and finally realised the gist of the problem. He continued quickly, "We're not all racists you know? Skinheads I mean. The originals listen to ska music." The two men again exchanged glances. Donnie looked hopeful, "You didne know that did ye?"

By now the singing had ended, the pastor was now standing on a low stage at the front of the church. He peered down the aisle to see what was happening at the entrance. The congregation slowly began to turn to see what he was looking at. One of the men left his spot at the door, and hurried to the front of the hall, whispering in the pastor's ear. They both glanced at Jimmy, and then back to the doorway. The pastor raised his hand, and with his forefinger, beckoned Donnie forward. The remaining doorman stepped aside and allowed Donnie to walk into the hall proper. He could hear the parishioners gasping and muttering to themselves as he walked up the aisle in the centre of the rows of fold-up chairs. Donnie had never felt so awkward and on display. Suddenly, a voice shouted, "DONNIE! YOU CAME! HALLELUJAH!"

Jimmy edged his way along the row of chairs he was halfway down, and out into the aisle where he hugged Donnie. He turned to the church, addressing them, "Everybody, this is my friend, Donnie."

The pastor raised his hands in greeting, "Any friend of Jimmy's is a friend of ours. Welcome Donnie."

As one, the parishioners' voices lift, "Welcome Donnie," they cried in unison.

Donnie looked around awkwardly, Jimmy still had his arm around his shoulders grinning from ear to ear as he again proclaimed, "WELCOME DONNIE!"

Donnie smiled awkwardly, "Watcha everyone."

The crowd began to laugh and repeat after him, "Watcha Donnie!"

The pastor clapped his hands, and the congregation turned their attention back toward him to listen "Make room for our new friend!" The people in Jimmy's row, stood to move down as Jimmy guided Donnie into the end. They sat, and the pastor continued, "Will Jimmy please come to the front."

Jimmy immediately rose, climbing over the legs of his fellow parishioners once more before starting for the front of the hall. Donnie stood to follow him, but Jimmy stopped him and sat him back down, before continuing to the front. When he reached the stage, he turned to face the room. The room slowly fell silent in anticipation, and Jimmy stood with his head bent in contemplation. Donnie's head pivoted from side to side, unsure of what was happening, the rest of the room stayed still in quiet expectation. In a deep baritone Jimmy began to sing, *"I'M ALONE AND MOTHERLESS EVER SINCE I WAS A CHILD."*

Voices throughout the room began to rise in background harmony and Donnie found himself swept up, in a way that he never would have expected, with the sadness and depth of the spiritual. *"EVER SINCE MY MOTHER WAS LIVING, I COULD TAKE THIS WHOLE WORLD WITH EASE, MOTHER RESTING IN GLORY GOT THE WHOLE WORLD TO PLEASE."* As the song continued to crescendo, Donnie felt a tightness in his chest. Jimmy sang loudly, tears pouring down his cheeks, *"JESUS SOMETIMES I WONDER, DID I TREAT MY MOTHER RIGHT?"*

When he and his fellow singers had hit the final notes the room jumped to their feet, cheering and clapping. Jimmy fell to his knees crying, the pastor stood behind him and placed his hands on his heaving shoulders. Donnie was overwhelmed, a tear slipped from his eye onto his cheek, and he reached up and wiped it away. Looking down at the wetness on his fingertips, he felt more anger than joy. "How could I let this happen? Why did I come here?" He thought and stood abruptly to step out of the row of chairs before turning to stride out of the hall. Outside he broke into a run towards the Tube station, fleeing as fast as his Dr. Marten booted feet would carry him.

16

Queenie watched as Sherry kissed Carl on the cheek and hugged him at the front door of the flat. "You be careful."

"Don't worry, piece of cake. I'll be back before you know it Treacle," he playfully teased her.

Sherry blushed, "You better be."

"Gotta go!" Carl kissed her on the lips, turned, and ran to the stairs.

His fiancé closed the door behind him, turned and slumped against it, "He better be okay."

"Don't you worry chile, my boy is special, they won't harm him," Queenie responded, attempting to reassure the girl and herself at the same time.

Sherry sighed, "You better be right."

"Let's sit and have some tea, we have so much to plan," Queenie stepped across the small flat, to her sink and began to fill the kettle.

Outside the front door of the Wordsworth house, Carl stopped and stood on the steps. In the distance, in the direction of Chalkhill, a black column of smoke was rising ominously into the air giving him pause for thought. He climbed into the van and drove away.

Across town, in the hospital, Dave lay in his bed in the ward and finished his hospital breakfast: A paper cup of juice that tasted vaguely like orange but with a strange bitter after taste, a perfectly circular scrambled egg that tasted nothing like egg, toast that had been shown the toaster just long enough to make it slightly harder than bread, barely buttered and then plonked dryly on the plate, and weak tea with milk and sugar already added. "I've had worse," he thought "and it was free, so it has that going for it."

An East Indian doctor approached with a group of interns that reflected the changing times in Britain, white, brown, black skins were all represented, and lifted the chart that was hanging off the bed frame reviewing it as he spoke, "My name is Dr. Patel and these fine people are medical students, now let me see..." he flipped quickly through the chart, "the patient suffered severe lacerations due to a mirror falling from the ceiling onto him whilst he was abusing himself." He lowered the folder and addressed the group, "At least he didn't go blind." Much to Dave's chagrin the students burst out laughing. The doctor continued, "Mr. Singh, what would you recommend for treatment?"

The intern straightened up upon hearing his name, beaming as he quickly responded, "Keep the wounds clean and treat with antiseptic."

"Very good," Patel commended him, his gaze returning to the chart, "he also has a head trauma from falling down some stairs, apparently whilst being discharged from the hospital." His brow furrowed and he looked at the patient, "Are you homeless?"

Dave was both surprised and stung by the question, "No, do I look homeless?"

Dr. Patel stared at Dave laying there, bandaged head to foot with his short pink spiky hair. "The only evidence I have to the contrary is the mirror falling on you whilst you were masturbating. Not many indigent people get hurt that way."

The students laughed louder and longer at this one. It was evident that Dr. Patel was enjoying himself. However, Dave wasn't, "Why would you ask someone that anyway?"

"Because it's the sort of trick that the homeless use to get another night's stay in a clean bed with two extra meals," the doctor scoffed in response.

Dave defended himself, "Well, I didn't, it was all Wobble's fault, I ain't homeless!"

"Good, because you will be discharged today," the doctor's voice was overly cheery.

Dave groaned and attempted to sit up in his bed, "What? But I can hardly walk!"

The doctor scribbled something in the chart and placed it back in its holder. “Regardless, we need the bed, perhaps you should think about getting a wife or a girlfriend.”

“I’ve got a girlfriend...” Dave’s voice trailed off in response, but Dr. Patel and the students had already moved on leaving him annoyed and humiliated. A moment later a nurse came walking through the ward carrying Dave's blanket, the large Black orderly beside her, pushing a wheelchair. They stopped next to Dave’s bed and the nurse held out the blanket. Dave looked shocked, “That’s it! You’re throwing me out with just a blanket?”

The nurse replied, sounding thoroughly bored, “Everyone comes naked from their mother’s womb and as everyone comes so they depart, they can take nothing from their toil that they can carry in their hands.”

“The Bible, you’re quoting the bible at me? Isn’t there something in there about charitable works and good deeds or summat?” Dave was desperate to stay in the hospital.

The nurse smiled at him, “I’m surprised that you recognised it. We’re giving you a bus pass, what more do you want?”

“Taxi fare maybe?” Dave asked, hopefully.

“Good luck darling, Mrs. Thatcher don’t cover no taxis, you’re lucky to get bus fare, Leon will get you to the door then it’s down to you,” The nurse chuckled and gestured to Leon, the orderly, who gave Dave a huge, toothy grin, “And you won’t fall out this time, not on my watch.”

Leon lifted Dave from the bed and into the chair in one easy motion and pushed him to the main doors and outside. After letting the patient pull himself awkwardly out of the chair, he turned and walked away, back through the hospital doors. Dave stood teetering on unsteady legs, staring at the bus stop through the drizzling rain. A 143 bus, the very bus he needed, pulled up to the stop and Dave took a step forward, ready to run for it, when the pain in his right leg stopped him cold. Wincing in pain, and stuck standing where he was, there was no more than twenty feet between Dave and the bus, but it might as well have been a mile. Dave watched as the door on the front of the bus slid closed and it pulled away. He took a limping step forward and again stopped in pain. It took twenty minutes but eventually he made it to the bus stop where he slumped, soaking wet against the post, wrapped only in his blanket, with a bus pass in his hand.

A second 143 pulled up and stopped, Dave made a move to limp to the front door as the other commuters, who had been waiting in the shelter, brushed roughly past him and got on first. Dave made it to the bus but couldn't bend his legs to get on. The bus driver, a middle-aged white guy who looked more bored than annoyed, glanced down at him and said, "You getting on or what?"

"I can't, I'd like to, but I can't," Dave held on to the side of the folded door.

The driver glared at him, his hand on the lever to close the door, "Well I ain't waiting all day, either get on or get out of the way!"

"Just a sec!" Dave turned and sat on the bottom step and used his legs, sore as they were, to push him up to the next step and the next. "There you go, I'm on."

The driver pointed to a sign, "Not yet you ain't, can't you read." Dave turned his head to read the sign posted on the wall above him. In bold black letters on a yellow background, it read: PASSENGERS MUST BE BEHIND YELLOW LINE WHEN BUS IS IN MOTION. Dave looked down; he was sitting on the yellow line. The bus driver continued, "And where's your fare?" He reached up, handing the driver his bus pass, and pushed himself once more with his feet until he was past the line. The bus pulled away with him lying on the floor.

At each of the nine stops from Edgware through Burnt Oak to Colindale, the bus stopped, and passengers got on, paid their fare and stepped over the bedraggled, soaking wet punk rocker without paying him a never mind, as if he didn't exist. At the end of Grove Park, the bus stopped. Dave went through his "push me, pull you" routine until he was left standing in a puddle, staring across one of the busiest roads in London. He wondered if he could get across the zebra crossing in one change of the lights, or if he would be best stopping at the centre island and waiting for a second change in the lights. He opted for the latter and began his slow journey out across the road.

Carl sped down Church Lane. Near the south end, he ran into a traffic jam and stopped. The police were diverting all traffic down into Neasden and onto the North Circular Road, away from Chalkhill estate. He pulled a quick U-turn and headed back into Kingsbury, down the high road to the roundabout, and up Fryent Way, past Barnhill, right on Forty Lane, and then Park Lane, where he was stopped by another roadblock. He was four cars back from the roadblock itself but could see officers leaning into the front two cars, questioning the occupants. Carl had nothing to hide, so he sat and waited as the officers got closer to his van. When they finally did, the officer on the driver's side signaled to his colleague on the other side to join him, but the other officer hesitated. The first policeman tapped on the window and Carl rolled it down. “Good afternoon, sir, mind if we ask where you’re going?”

Carl immediately knew that he had made a mistake staying and waiting and his response was deliberately evasive, “Work.”

The policeman narrowed his eyes suspiciously, “On a Sunday?”

Carl could feel his heart pounding, as if it was trying to escape his chest. He continued the lie he’d already begun, “Yeah. Emergency call out. One of our commercial clients.”

“Got a work order?”

“No,” Carl said dryly.

The officer straightened up, tapping the roof of Carl’s car, “You’re doing a commercial call out without a work order?”

“I got the call at home. I’m on weekend call out, so I fill out the paperwork on Monday at the office,” Carl responded quickly, making sure his hands remained visibly resting on the steering wheel.

The uniform placed his hands on his hips, “Well, you’re not coming through here.”

"What's going on?" Carl tried to look ignorant about what was happening on the estate.

"As if you don't know," the Constable was becoming more and more impatient.

"No. I don't," Carl hoped his voice sounded innocent.

"Couldn't hear the jungle drums then?" The policeman's voice was becoming more and more agitated each time he spoke, "Your lot are rioting again."

Carl struggled not to show his anger at the comment, "My lot?"

"Yeah, your lot," he leaned back and glared at Carl, "Is there a problem here?"

"No officer!" Carl was desperate to leave and collect his aunt.

In a quieter, even more threatening tone of voice the policeman growled, "Get out of the van!" He pulled at the door handle of the van.

Carl was stunned, "For what?"

"Cause I told you to, that's why! You Black, pickaninny bastard!" Seeing the situation escalating the other officer started to walk around behind the van. The policeman talking to Carl grabbed the door handle and tried to open the door, but it was locked. Carl slammed the van into reverse, slammed his foot down on the accelerator, and shot backwards. A car was pulling to a stop behind him as he did, the woman driving screamed. The female police officer, crossing behind the van, barely had time to glance up, before the van slammed into her face and crushed her legs between the van and the second car. She immediately collapsed, unconscious, pinned between the two vehicles, lying backwards over the bonnet of the car with the driver still screaming at the top of her lungs.

The first officer smashed Carl's window with his truncheon as more police came running from the barricade. People who had up to now stayed indoors, frightened by the events unfolding around them, came out of their houses to see what the commotion was. Carl, unaware he had run into anybody, let alone a police officer, had his arms curled around his head as three policemen dragged him from his van. Blows rained down on him from their truncheons, onto his hands, arms, back, head. His fingers shattered, his wrist was broken, his face smashed into the concrete curb as boots stamped on the back of his head, breaking his nose and knocking out a front tooth. He passed out, lying in the street. The three officers stopped and looked around at the watching bystanders, from the other cars and surrounding houses.

Three other police ran to the aid of their colleague still trapped behind the van. One of them positioned himself to block the bystander's views of the scene. "Get him across the barricade and put him in the prisoner transport van," he demanded as the other two officers grabbed Carl's limp body under the armpits and dragged him past the line of cars, past the barricade, and to the back of the paddy wagon. They tossed him in the back before climbing in the front and driving away.

Dave had finally limped back to Wobble's house, passing through the estate where he had dragged himself along the side of the high brick walls that line the alleyways, and down the street using the garden walls to prop himself up. He opened the front door and used the door frame to drag himself inside. The bandage on his right leg was now blood red, his wound leaking from the strain. "Oi Wobs, you here?" He called out weakly.

Wobble came out of the upstairs pool room and looked down the stairs. "They let you out then," he laughed at his own joke before starting down the stairs.

Dave joked back, "Nah, I did a runner, couldn't take anymore sleeping in a real bed with clean sheets. It was awful!"

Danny snorted, "If living here doesn't suit you..."

Dave rolled his eyes and slumped against the wall, "I was being sarcastic you plonker. Give me a hand, will ya?" Wobble ran down the stairs, as best he could considering his condition, and quickly wrapped his arm around Dave to hold him up and help him. The pair made their way slowly down the hallway to the couch where Dave collapsed onto the soft cushions. "Fuckin' Terry," he said with a sigh.

Wobble shrugged, as he helped Dave lift his legs onto the couch and lay down, "I'm sure he didn't mean it."

Dave winced, shooting Danny a quick glare, "Fuckin' Wobble."

"Me?" Wobble looked at him confused.

"Yeah you."

"For what?" He tilted his head to the side, wondering what he did now.

"For what?" Dave stared at him for a moment in disbelief that his friend already forgot, "For flying me out of that wheelchair and down the stairs that's what!"

"Oh yeah. That's fair enough I guess." Wobble didn't seem phased in the least, and quickly changed the subject, "Cup of tea?"

Dave saw an opportunity, "You got any Whitetop?"

Danny grinned, knowing Dave had one upped him, "Bit early, isn't it?"

"It's Sunday," Dave groaned as he attempted to prop himself up on the arm of the couch, wincing before he added, "And besides it's not like either one of us has to work tomorrow."

"You keeping a job was part of our agreement. If you want to stay living here remember?"

"Yeah, but that was before you turned me into an unwitting Evel Knievel, wasn't it?" Dave knew he had Wobble on the retreat.

"Yeah, I guess." Wobble turned to head upstairs to the fridge. Just as he returned, there was a knock at the door. Through the frosted glass he could easily tell it was Terry outside. He opened the door and handed Terry the two beers he was holding. Terry gratefully took them, "Thanks Danny! Now that's what I call service!"

"I'll get more," Danny turned and headed back up the stairs. Terry closed the door behind him and walked into the living room. He stopped in his tracks and stared in total disbelief at Dave, "What the fuck happened to you?"

"You did, that's what!"

Terry was confused, "Bullshit. I never did all this to you."

"You started it and well it just sorta took off from there," Dave pulled the grubby hospital blanket he was using tighter around himself, in a half attempt to cover his injuries.

Tel thrusted one of the cold bottles out towards Dave, "Here, have a beer." Dave slowly took it from his hand. "Thanks, I think."

Wobble returned, down the stairs once again, three more beers in his hands. There was another knock on the door. "Fuck," Wobble thought to himself with an audible groan. Through the glass he could see Donnie. He balanced the three drinks in one hand and opened the door.

Donnie stepped in, and without missing a beat, scooped a beer from Wobble's hand and stepped past him, "Thank you nicely, Wobs!"

"I'll just go back and get some more," Wobble sighed as he, yet again, headed back upstairs.

Donnie watched him for a moment before walking off down the hall. He stopped as soon as he saw Dave half propped up on the couch, "You look like you went to war and lost."

"I blame Terry."

"I told you it wasn't my fault!"

Terry and Dave both turned their attention to Donnie and instantly stop talking. Dave was the first to break the silence, "What are you wearing?"

Donnie glanced down at himself, he was wearing a plain white button up dress shirt, grey trousers, and running shoes. Clothes no card-carrying skinhead or punk would be seen dead in. Donnie proclaimed, "I ain't a racist"

Terry took immediate umbrage to the remark, "Neither am I!"

Donnie turned to him, "Aye, I know that."

Terry was confused, "Well then?"

"But other people don't, do they?" Donnie made his point. There was no arguing with his logic. People looked at skinheads and thought of one thing and one thing only. It hadn't always been that way, but it was now, in a way it was the end of an era.

Terry shrugged, "You still look like a right twat."

Donnie was embarrassed by his clothes, "It was all I had other than, you know, the gear."

Dave laughed, "Why would you have that though?"

Donnie thought the answer was obvious, "It's me court appearance clothes, why else?"

Terry looked at Dave with a scornful sneer, "Why else would he own them? You can be a right pratt sometimes Dave."

Dave cleared his throat, clearly embarrassed by the reprimand, "He still looks like a Tory cunt."

Donnie immediately defended himself, "Aye well I'll get some new gear tomorrow. You'll still look like a veteran from the First World war though." Wobble had finally returned as Donnie was speaking, and as one they all broke into a rousing rendition of The Green Fields of France:

> *"WELL, HOW DO YOU DO NOW YOUNG WILLIE MCBRIDE, DO YOU MIND IF I SIT DOWN BESIDE YOUR GRAVE SIDE, DID THEY BEAT THE DRUMS SLOWLY, DID THEY PLAY THE FIFE LOWLY, DID THEY SOUND THE DEATH MARCH AS THEY LOWERED YOU DOWN, DID THE BAND PLAY THE LAST POST AND CHORUS, DID THE PIPES PLAY THE FLOWERS OF THE FOREST?"*

Ray got off the bus in Ladbroke Grove, walked to the George and Dragon and pushed the door open. An undercover police officer in a delivery van parked opposite the pub snapped pictures of him as he did. As the bar door swung open, the room immediately fell silent. There were twenty or so biker types sitting at tables, the bar, or shooting pool at one of the three tables. They all turned and stared at the stranger, the tall muscular skinhead, who had come into their midst. From the bar a deep, commanding voice broke the silence. "He's with me." The bikers all returned to what they had been doing prior to the interruption. Ray turned and walked towards Greg, the source of the voice.

Greg laughed at him as he finished the remains of his beer, plunking the empty mug down, "You know how to make an entrance, I'll give you that."

"It's my worldly charm," Ray quipped as he leaned against the old wooden bar.

"Is that what it is? Give my friend here a beer and put it on my bill." The barman nodded and poured Ray a pint of Guinness and set it down heavily on the bar.

Ray was perplexed, "Guinness?"

"Is there a problem with that? I love Guinness."

"I guess not."

Greg started to laugh, "You stupid fuck have whatever you want, we're just fucking with ya."

Ray shook his head and smiled, "Lager thanks." The barman poured Ray a pint of lager and put it down on the bar.

"Let's sit." Ray and Greg moved to a table in a dark corner of the bar and take a seat. "I have to tell you, Ray, we were very appreciative of your help. I know it can't have been easy, family and all that." Greg watched Ray's expression carefully.

Ray shrugged, unmoved, "It had to be done."

"And it served its purpose. Mitch, without ever knowing it, advanced our agenda way further dead than he ever could alive," the man responded callously.

Ray raised his glass, "To Mitch."

Greg mimicked Ray's glass with his own, "To Mitch and the race war he helped to start!"

"Amen to that! I knew he'd be good for something someday," Ray smirked. The two men clinked their glasses together before taking large swigs.

Greg rubbed his chin before continuing, "So are you ready to do your part?"

Ray hesitated for a moment, looking for the proper words, "There's a problem."

"There better not be," his eyes narrowed on Ray's face. "I don't like problems,"

Ray interrupted him, blurting out, "I can fix it."

"What is it?" Greg's eyes were now burning into Ray's face.

"Me and Alex got pulled," Ray said as calmly and matter-of-factly as he could.

Now, Greg was struggling to keep his voice even, "I told you not to do anything to draw attention to yourself until after Wednesday."

"I know you did," Ray sighed, taking another sip of his beer.

"Well then?"

Ray folded his arms across his chest, "Alex got stupid, the other night in Willesden, he punched a Paki's turban off his head."

Greg looked a bit surprised, "Is that why they raided the club?"

"Seems so."

"Daniels is not impressed!"

Ray nodded in agreement, "I don't blame him."

"So how does this affect your duty on Wednesday?"

"Alex hasn't reappeared."

"D'you think he'll talk?" Greg clenched his teeth clearly annoyed at the story.

"NO!" Ray responded quickly, "no. He's good people."

The biker wasn't convinced Ray was telling him the truth, "Then why would they keep him?"

"I don't know," Ray shrugged, taking a swig from his mug, "but they were asking about Mr. Daniels and the meetings."

"What did you tell them?"

Ray scoffed, "Nothing, I'm not a grass!"

"You'd better not be, or you'll end up like your cousin Mitch!" Greg signaled to three bikers at a nearby table, they came striding across the room and grabbed Ray. As big and strong as Ray was, he didn't compare to these three. "Check him for a wire," Greg demanded, gesticulating at Ray. They bent Ray over the table, knocking his beer glass over and sending it rolling across the table and onto the floor and frisked him roughly and thoroughly. Not finding a wire, they let him go and stood back.

Ray stood up, took a deep breath and straightened his jacket, "Told you I wasn't a grass."

"We had to make sure." Greg waved at the bartender, not waiting for an answer, "Another beer."

Ray dismissed the bartender and looked at Greg, "I'll just take what I came for."

Greg nodded to the other bikers, and they returned to their table. "What about Alex? I thought he was the driver, and Mitch was supposed to steal the car, how you gonna get around that?"

Ray was quick with an answer, "I have an idea."

"You'd better," Greg stared long and hard at Ray, as he leaned back in his chair. He nodded to one of the three bikers who had restrained him. The biker crossed to the bar and was given a package by the barman that he then brought over to Ray. He thrusted it into his hand and Ray immediately began to open the package. Greg stopped him, "Don't. Everything you need is in there. A second World War vintage Luger preloaded with six bullets."

Ray stopped, "A Luger?"

"Yeah, I liked the symbolism," Greg smirked. Ray nodded as he shoved the package into his jacket, and pulled his jacket closed over it before standing up. Greg slid his chair back, standing as well, and they extended their left hands and shook, both exclaiming at the same time, "BLOOD!"

Ray looked straight into Greg's eyes, "Don't worry, no matter what happens, whether Alex talks or not, I won't let you down." He turned and left the pub; the undercover officer outside snapped more pictures of him.

Sunday night in "The Laureate," was always busy, there was Kevin's disco in the Lounge Bar, and a darts tournament in the Public Bar. The door to the Public Bar burst open, Donnie and Terry staggered in carrying Dave, who was waving a cricket bat above his head and shouting, “SIX AND OUT!” Wobble brought up the rear. The crowd in the bar took little notice, except for Dave’s parents. Stan shook his head in disgust. He hadn’t wanted to go to the pub, mostly because he didn’t want to see his son, and now he was feeling totally vindicated. The only reason he had finally agreed to go was because Jean had told him she needed a night out. Deep down, he knew she was lying, Jean didn’t care about going down to the pub. He knew she was hoping, against all hope, that there might be a reconciliation between father and son. The instant Dave entered in the manner he did, all parties knew that that was clearly off the table.

Terry and Donnie deposited Dave on a chair at Stan and Jean’s table and headed for the bar. Dave’s head swayed as he looked up at his parents through blood red eyes, “My dear mater and pater, how the devil are you?”

Stan’s face began to flush red, a vein in his temple began to pulse. “Your what? Speak English, you fool,” he bellowed at his son.

“Oh Papa, that is the very best of the Queen’s English, I thought you’d be pleased!”

Jean stared at the stitches in his hands. “What happened to your hands, son?”

“Well, you see I was having a wank and the mirror on the ceiling came crashing down on me.” He made a wanking motion with his right hand,” It’s God’s work.”

Stan grabbed his son by the front of his T-shirt and yanked him forward. “You ungrateful little prick,” he growled through clenched teeth, “How dare you speak to your mother like that?”

Jean started to cry. Dave winced in pain from the cuts on his chest. Noticing Dave’s pain, Jean sobbed, “Please Stan, don’t.”

Terry and Donnie returned from the bar with some drinks. Terry set the ones he was carrying down and placed his hand on Stan’s shoulder, “Leave him be Stan, he’s an idiot, you know how he gets. c’mon I got you a pint.”

Stan's grip tightened on Dave's shirt. "I know you mean well Terry. I swear I wish you was my boy. But I'll skip the drink if it's all the same to you." Relinquishing his grip on his son, Stan rose from his chair and turned to Jean to help her up, out of her chair, before leading her towards the door. He stopped, just beyond the tables, and turned toward his son one final time, "I hope you get everything you deserve in life, son. I really do." He took Jean's hand and led her across the bar, to the door and out.

Dave watched the door swing closed behind them and smirked, "Well, now that's out of the way we can have some fun!"

Donnie shook his head. "You dinna know you were born son, your own Ma?"

Terry looked at Donnie. "Let's head through." The two of them left, heading for the door into the Lounge Bar, where the disco was, leaving Dave and Wobble at the table.

Dave rolled his eyes as he watched them leave, before smiling at Danny, "You and me against the world Wobs."

"I don't think so!" Wobble stood abruptly and followed the other two.

Siobhan, who had been watching the whole scene from behind the bar, began to walk around the bar to gather up glasses from the tables. At the table next to Dave's, there was a group of six lads, in their mid-twenties, drunk and laughing. As Siobhan passed their table, one of them reached out and grabbed her butt, "Nice hair darling, does the carpet match the drapes?" He pulled her down, into his lap, as his friends shouted their approval and laughed.

Siobhan pulled away from him, her T-shirt ripping as she did. "Get off me!" She shouted.

The boy laughed and continued to hold her tightly against him, "You should come back to Burnt Oak with us, see what a good time is all abou..." Before the loudmouth could finish his head crashed to one side and he fell from his chair, tearing Siobhan's shirt further as he did. Dave had cracked him around the side of the head with the cricket bat. There was a moment of stunned silence broken by Siobhan.

"Shit," she said, moving from the group, pulling her torn shirt closed.

The other five jump up! Two of them smash pint glasses as they do, ready to "glass" Dave up with them. Suddenly they all stop. Ray was standing beside Dave, staring menacingly at first one, then another of them. Despite Ray's presence, which has given them pause for thought, they're still ready to trust in their numbers when Terry spoke, "Don't do anything stupid boys." The group turned, behind them stood Terry holding a Whitetop bottle, Donnie holding a pool cue, Bazza with his gigantic fists and Wobble who just looked scared. Terry continued, "Just take your friend and leave."

The would-be assailants dropped their weapons, helped their friend to his feet, and headed for the door. On the way out, one of them turned to shout, "We'll be back!"

Ray smirked at him, "Of course you will."

Siobhan sat in the chair next to Dave, trying her hardest not to cry in front of everybody, especially her brother. Despite her efforts, her shoulders started to shake, and she gave in to it. Dave pulled her close and hugged her. Ray towered over them, staring down, "Isn't that sweet."

"She's just a mate, Ray, I'm just trying to help," Dave defended himself.

Through her tears, Siobhan blubbered, "He knows, you idiot."

"He what?" Dave looked up at Ray nervously.

"I was coming here to do you Dave. But I gotta admit you had some balls clocking one of them Burnt Oak boys with that bat," Ray looked impressed.

Siobhan lifted her head, "Why the hell do you have a cricket bat anyway?"

"It's a crutch," Dave shrugged and continued, "Wobs wouldn't let me borrow a pool cue, so I got the bat instead."

"You're such an idiot," she laughed at him wiping at her tears.

"That's why you love me!"

"Yeah, I do." She leaned in to give Dave a long, deep kiss.

Ray was incredulous, "That's my sister you know?"

Dave ignored him and continued with the kiss until Gerry came over, "By Jesus you're supposed to be working, this isn't a Dublin brothel!"

"Sorry Gerry," Siobhan stood up, her shirt ripped at the collar, showing her bra strap.

Gerry looked at her disapprovingly, "You can't work looking like that."

"It's okay, I've got some safety pins in my bag. I'll look like a real punk then," she wiped her cheeks with her hands and smiled at Dave.

Terry and Donnie lifted Dave up onto their shoulders, and the three young men burst out in song, *"NOW HOW DO YOU DO NOW YOUNG WILLIE MCBRIDE."*

Later, near the end of the evening, the punters leave the pub in varying states of inebriation and head out into the estate. Siobhan and Wobble helped a now totally incapacitated Dave back to number 183.

Ray hung back until the crowds were gone and the streets were empty before heading to The Sunshine Cafe. In an alleyway beside the restaurant, he retrieved a brick and a petrol can he had secreted there earlier. Standing in front of the plate glass window of the Cafe, he hurled the brick through it. There was a deafening smash followed by a screeching alarm. Ray was unfazed, just as he was unfazed by the fact that Abdul and Louella lived above the cafe and were presumably asleep in bed. Ray poured the petrol through the broken window, onto the white and black tiled floor, lit a match, and tossed it in. The cafe exploded in a ball of flame. Ray turned and slowly walked away, singing, *"DID YOU DIE SLOWLY OR DID YOU DIE QUICKLY OR WILLIE MCBRIDE WAS IT SLOW AND OBSCENE."*

17

Alex sat in an interrogation cell. The entire wall in front of him a mirror, he had no doubt that it was a two-way mirror and that he was being watched from the far side. The drive to get there in the back of an armoured van had taken hours, at one point he had felt a rolling motion as if he were on a ferry. He was blindfolded when he had arrived, wherever it was he had arrived to, the blindfold had only been removed once he was in the cell that he now sat in. Later, he had been roughly manhandled by two very obviously powerful men and forced to sit at a table, his wrists were handcuffed to manacles on the desktop. He felt a deep foreboding fear, he had no idea why he was being held at all, never mind held in such a secretive, barbaric manner.

He was starving hungry, and sleep deprived and would have done anything to just be back in Kingsbury, in the Laureate, at his aunt's house, at work even, anywhere but here. He was surprised at the thought that suddenly occurred to him, "Work." They might even fire him for absenteeism, he had to get back there, had to explain, explain to Mr. Thrift that this, whatever this was, wasn't his fault, wasn't his doing. Surely, they would call his work for him, and let them know that he'd be back, back by tomorrow hopefully, as soon as this mess was settled, whatever this mess was.

He determined that the first thing he would ask was that they do that, call Mr. Thrift, and get it all sorted out. He looked up at the mirror, "Excuse me? Hello? Whoever you are, I need someone to call my work, I could get sacked and that's hardly fair..." The door burst open. In strode a man, a skinny man, in a shirt and tie. The tie tucked into his shirt halfway down the front, in the style that U.S Marines had worn them in photographs that Alex had seen from the war. "Which war though," he thought, "was it World War II? Korea? Vietnam?" All these questions raced incongruously through Alex's mind, incongruous as what Alex had also noticed, hard not to really, was that the man had a sack over his head, a black sack with eye holes cut in the front. The sleeves on the man's dark blue shirt were rolled up to his elbows and Alex noted that the hairs on his arms were ginger. In his right hand he held a heavy, black, rubber club. The man strode from the door straight at Alex, behind him came two other much larger men, carrying buckets of water. "Why would they have buckets of water?" Was the next thought that passed through Alex's mind.

The skinny man reached the table, and raised his right hand and with remarkable speed, smashed first Alex's right hand, then his left, the club crushing them against the desktop. Before Alex could make a sound, scream even, the club smashed him in the face knocking him stone-cold unconscious. Not a word had been said, since the men had burst into the room. The first words spoken, came from the skinny man, in a thick, Northern Irish accent, "Wake him up boys, let's see what he knows."

Alex groaned as he came around, soaking wet from the bucket of water that at that very moment was being poured slowly over his head. His head was in a total fog, pain coursed through his head and from his mangled broken fingers, "What's happening? Please don't hurt me anymore, where am I? What did I do?"

In front of him stood the lanky man, leaning forward toward Alex, against the desk. He spoke in his thick accent, "Oh we're not really concerned with what you did son. A little harmless Paki bashing doesn't concern us in the least. It's what you might know about what you and your associates plan to do that concerns us."

Alex stuttered, trying to make sense of the situation, "I, I have no idea what you're talking about?"

"Really? Do you expect us to believe that?"

"Yes!"

"Well, we don't," the well-dressed man stood up straight and continued, "What were you and your friend Raymond Collins doing, attending UVF meetings in London? Why are you supporting the paras?"

“I don’t even know what ‘paras’ are, what the fuck is the ‘UVF?’”

“Paramilitaries, son. The Ulster Volunteer Force. The people that want to drag this war on as long as they possibly can.”

“I really don’t know what you’re talking about,” Alex was totally terrified.

The man shrugged, uncaring, “Well I guess we’ll find that out!” Alex didn’t even see the cosh swing through the air, it slammed into his jawbone sending his head jerking backwards, to one side. The pain shot through his face and when his head slumped forward, he weakly spat a dislodged tooth out onto the desk. “Now young Alex, tell me about Seamus McCaffrey, why don’t you?”

“Who?”

“He was the guest speaker at one of the fascist meetings you and your friend Mr. Collins attended,” the voice continued relentlessly from behind the mask.

Now Alex was pleading with him to believe him, “I didn’t go to no Fascist meetings!”

“Aw c’mon lad, we not only have photographs of you at the meeting, we have photos of you shaking McCaffrey’s hand. Stop fucking lying to us!”

Alex cried out in response, “I’m no Fascist!”

“Really?” The man moved forward as if to hit Alex again. The skinhead began to blubber like a baby, tears pouring from his eyes, snot dripping from his nose, spit mixed with blood running down his chin. His chest heaved, his whole body convulsed, as he threw up down his chest, into his crotch, and across the table. The man took a step back, and watched impassively, his arms crossed across his chest waiting.

“Please,” Alex begged, “no more, I don’t know what you want from me!”

The masked man stepped back to the table across from him, “Tell me why you were at those meetings. If you’re not a Fascist, that is.”

"Ray! Ray told me to go," at this point, Alex hoped that this would be enough to make the beating and interrogation stop.

"Ray?" the interrogator paused for a moment, thinking, "Raymond Collins you mean?"

"Y-Yes," Alex stuttered as the mess dripped off his chin.

"And you always do what Ray says, do you?"

"I guess I just wanted to impress him, that's all," he coughed, nearly gagging on the taste in his mouth.

"Fancy him, do you?" the man sneered at him.

Alex's eyes opened wide, "What? No, nothing like that! I'm not a queer!"

"The only time I try to impress someone is if I meet a bird on a Saturday night, and think she might put out, is that what you were hoping for?" The two big men, standing towards the back of the room, start to chuckle at the comment.

"NO!" Alex continues to insist.

"Methinks the boy doth protest too much."

The bigger of the two men, stepped forward, and with a smirk, threw the bucket of water across the desktop and into Alex's chest, "Fucking faggot!"

The skinny man leaned over into Alex's ear and whispered, "Ignore him. It's okay I get it. We had men like you in the army, you're no less a man for it. But love him or not, you are going to explain to me what the connection between McCaffrey and Raymond Collins is if I have to beat you to death to get it. Do you understand me, Alex?"

Crying as he spoke, Alex blurted out, "I want to speak to a lawyer!"

"Too late for that, let me make something crystal clear here, No one knows where you are, Alex, no one. You're all mine. D'you hear me?"

Dave had woken up on the couch in Wobble's house, his head pounding and his vision blurry. There was a pressure on his chest causing him a fair degree of pain. He raised his head, realising that it was Siobhan's head, laying on his chest, that was causing the problem. He gently laid his head back on the arm of the couch and smiled. The discomfort was well worth it, knowing that she was there with him, knowing that for the first time, she had stayed overnight. He reached out to try and get a cigarette and his lighter from the coffee table beside the couch, but as he stretched, the pain became too much. He audibly groaned which caused Siobhan to wake up. "What are you doing?" She asked him sleepily, rubbing her eyes.

"I was trying to get a fag."

"Then why didn't you ask me?"

"I didn't want to wake you."

"Well, I'm awake now, aren't I?" She lay still on his chest.

After several more minutes, Dave was really craving a cigarette, "Er, if you're still awake, would you mind getting me a fag?"

"I like it here," she lightly wrapped her arm around him.

"And I like having you here, apart from the immense amount of pain it's causing me that is but could..." he reached out towards the table once more.

Siobhan suddenly realised what he meant and sat up, "Shit, I'm sorry Dave, I didn't think. Last night was so lovely and everything. What with you saving me from that guy and everything, and I just wanted to stay with you, but I didn't think about..."

"Siobhan," Dave cut her off, "can I please have a cigarette?"

"Oh. Right. Yeah. Sorry," she picked up the pack and found that there was only one cigarette left, "Sharesies I guess?"

"Course," he beamed, "I mean you're my bird now, ain't you?"

"Tweet tweet!" Siobhan put the cigarette in her mouth, lighting it for him.

"I was only joking," he grinned and waited impatiently for her to take a drag.

"You can be such an idiot," she said handing him the cigarette. He took a long haul from it, and she became deeply thoughtful.

Dave noticed her far-off expression, "What's wrong?"

"I was just thinking about those Burnt Oak blokes."

"Bunch of wankers, what about them?"

They passed the smoke between them. Siobhan continued, "They'll be back, they don't play games down there you know,"

"Fuck 'em, let 'em come back! They'll get the same as they did last night!"

She laughed and clapped her hands playfully, "Oh, listen to him, Joe Hawkins himself!"

The reference to the fictional skinhead "hard man" stung Dave, "You were quite happy to have me look after you last night."

Siobhan took another drag and moved away from him, "Of course I was, what would you expect? But this is today and it's different now in the cold harsh light of the morning."

"Are you breaking up with me?" Dave looked at her, confused.

"You what?"

He eyed her suspiciously, "You are, aren't you?"

"Of course, I'm not!"

"What is this then?"

Siobhan turned and took Dave's hand in hers, "Dave, I love you but..."

They heard the sound of Wobble came clumping down the stairs and into the living room. "Good morning you two, what a night that was!" He stopped dead in his tracks, seeing the pair of them holding hands, obviously caught in an awkward moment. He stammered and added, "I'll just head down the store and get some milk for the tea."

Siobhan smiled as he left, "Cheers, Wobs!"

Dave seized the opportunity, "Get me some fags Wobs, I'll get ya back later." Wobble muttered a response and limped down the hall and out of the front door. As soon as it was closed, Dave turned back to his girlfriend, encouraging her to continue, "You love me, but what?"

"Let's face facts," she paused for a moment, thinking.

"What?"

"You're not my brother," she stated bluntly.

Dave laughed in response, "Considering what we did last night I hope not!"

"Stop being you for a minute."

"That might be a little difficult..."

She groaned and smushed the cigarette into the ashtray, "Please, Dave, just listen."

"Go on," he pushed himself up into a sitting position in an attempt to appear more attentive.

"My brother," she finally continued, "you're not like him, or Terry, and you're certainly nothing like Donnie. He's completely insane!"

"You can say that again!"

"My point is, you're not a hard man, Dave," she sighed and looked at him lovingly, "and you need to stop pretending and acting like you are..."

"Again, you didn't complain last night," he teased her and reached out to gently stroke the curve of her shoulder.

She shooed his hand away from her, "You're going to end up getting hurt."

"Nah..."

Siobhan stared to cry, a warm tear ran down her cheek, "And I couldn't stand that!"

Dave's look softened and he pulled her closer to him, despite the stinging pain it caused in his chest. "Come 'ere don't be silly."

"I mean it Dave," she snuggled against him, "Ray, Terry, Donnie, even Carl can't always be around to protect you,"

"Hey, hey, hey, calm down." He kissed the top of her head, reassuring her, "I made it this far, didn't I? Nothing's going to happen to me, you'll see."

"You'd better be right."

Suddenly, the front door crashed open, and Wobble ran, as well as Wobble could, down the hallway and into the room. "You're not gonna believe this," he panted clearly out of breath.

Dave let Siobhan go, "What's up Wobs? Where's the milk?"

Wobble collapsed heavily into a chair, "The store's gone! The whole arcade! Burnt to the ground. Nothing left."

"Get the fuck out of here!" Dave was shocked and leaned forward hoping to hear more of the story. Siobhan's mouth fell open with surprise.

"Serious Dave, it's all gone," Danny continued, still trying to catch his breath.

"Then why didn't we hear the sirens or nothing?"

Siobhan turned back and looked at Dave, "Do you have any idea how drunk we all were?"

"Well, yeah, but..."

Wobble turned towards the door, "Will you two get a fucking move on? Let's go!"

Dave and Siobhan rushed to get dressed and the three of them left the house and hurried through the estate, it was slow going as Dave was limping as much as Wobble. They made their way towards where the shopping arcade had once been. Each crowd of people they passed grew larger and larger, everyone seemed eager to view the spectacle, the free entertainment at someone else's expense. When they got there, there were about fifty people gathered, staring at the wreckage from behind a hastily erected police barricade. Smoke still billowed from what had once been the three-storey building, now just a pile of smouldering debris. A single fire tender sprayed water over it, to keep any risk of the flames re-igniting at bay. The wreckage of the building was mixed with personal effects: A half-charred cookery book, bent kitchen implements with melted handles, a suitcase, empty and gaping open as if bearing witness to the hopelessness and tragedy of the situation, a child's doll completely untouched by the flames.

On the far side Abdul stood, talking to Detective Sergeant Miller and Detective Constable Wainwright. Louella, hung on his arm, her face a mask of fear and sorrow, the dried tracks of tears tattooed on her cheeks through the soot. Ray stood off to one side of the watching throng. The three new arrivals hurried across to see him. Ray was singing, *"Smoke on the water, Fire in the sky."*

Dave glanced at him, "Never took you for a heavy metal fan, Ray."

"I'm not Dave, it just seemed appropriate."

"I see Abdul got out, that's something at least."

Ray smirked, "Is it?"

Siobhan spun around to her brother, "That's not nice Ray, they're good people."

"They're fucking Pakis," he sneered, correcting her.

"They're Turkish actually." Big brother or not, Siobhan was determined to stand her ground.

Ray shrugged, unswayed, "Same difference."

Dave felt the need to change the subject, "What d'you think happened?"

Ray spat on the ground, "Can't say I care but probably some spillover from the Hill."

The trio turned towards Ray, confused as to what he meant. Siobhan was the first to speak up, "What do you mean?"

Ray continued with his theory, "Seems the jungle bunnies got out of their cages last night, as usual tried to burn their own house down, fucking morons."

At this point, a voice called Dave's name, the four of them turned to see Carl's girlfriend, Sherry, working her way through the crowd toward them, getting bumped and jostled as she did, but pushing relentlessly forward, "Dave, Dave, I've been looking all over for you."

"Alright," Dave furrowed his brow, "well you've found me now. What's up?"

"Carl's gone missing!"

Ray lets out a loud guffaw, "He's probably round at Vickie's giving her a good shagging." He snorted, "I hear she likes that kind of thing."

Sherry looked at him, stunned, "What are you talking about?"

Siobhan butted in, "Just shut up Ray. You can be a right 'eartless bastard sometimes. You know that?"

Sherry glared coldly at Ray and Dave put his arm around her, turning her away from Ray. "It's okay," he attempted to console her, "what happened?"

Sherry turned her attention back to Dave, "Queenie sent him to The Hill to get Beatrice, and he never came back."

"The Hill? There's a fucking riot going on over there."

"Why d'you think she sent him, huh?"

"Okay, okay, just let me think,"

Soon, Donnie came jogging up. "What the fuck happened here?"

Wobble shrugged, "No one knows, apparently there was some trouble on The Hill last night. Could have something to do with it."

Donnie turned harshly to Wobble, "Why the fuck would the two things be related Wobs? You lost what was left of your tiny mind?"

Wobble sputtered, clearly stung by the rebuke, "That's what Ray said."

Donnie turned to Ray, his eyes narrow, "I bet he did." He then turned his attention to his sister, "Hey Siobhan."

"Hey Don," she greeted in response, adding, "looks like Carl mighta got caught up in it."

"Ah bullshit," Donnie dismissed the thought with a wave of his hand, "he's too smart for that."

"Sherry says he went to get his aunt and never came back."

Ray guffawed, "I told you, he's giving Vickie a good rogering, fucking slut, loves some dark meat!"

Upon hearing this, Sherry lunged at Ray. Dave grabbed hold of her, as hard as he could, to pull her back as she screamed and kicked at him, despite the fact he was at least a foot taller than her, "You fucking bastard, you keep your nose out of this..."

Dave pulled her away, wincing from the pain in his chest as he did. Ray laughed, pointing his forefinger at her, "She's seen more helmets than Afghanistan that one!" Sherry struggled harder to get free from Dave's grip and confront Ray. Dave held on all the more tightly, despite the pain, "It's alright, calm down. He's winding you up deliberately." Sherry eventually broke free from Dave's grip and turned on him. "He's a fucking prick, why do you hang around with the racist pig anyway, Dave?"

Dave had never really thought about the answer to the question. He stopped, dead in his tracks, unable to put it into words, words like habit, laziness, cowardice even. That was it. Mostly, it was cowardice, a fear of rocking the boat, of not fitting in on the estate. A fear of Ray kicking his teeth in as well, the best he could come up with was, "Well, I am shagging his sister."

"Shagging me, are you Dave? That's what we're doing is it?" Siobhan took Sherry by the arm, "Come on darling I'll walk you back." The two girls turned and left, heading back toward the tower blocks that loomed high above.

Dave shook his head and let out a long sigh, watching them leave, "Fuck."

Ray grabbed Dave by the front of the shirt and pulled him up onto his tiptoes. "Shagging my sister? Nice one Dave," he growled at him.

Dave closed his eyes ready for the inevitable onslaught of violence, "at least I won't have to worry about the Burnt Oak boys killing me now," the thought passed momentarily through his head. But he suddenly released Dave, and pushed him backward, sending him toppling to sit in a puddle caused by the fire hoses.

Dave looked up, as two figures stepped forward between him and Ray, Detective Sergeant Miller and Detective Constable Wainwright, "Good morning, Mr. Collins. D.S. Miller, remember me?" Wainwright glanced down at Dave and then back to Ray, leaving Dave sitting with his hand held out vainly hoping for the policeman to help him up. Instead, Donnie stepped forward and pulled Dave to his feet. "We could charge you with assault for that." the officer added.

Ray ignored him, "Good morning, Detective Sergeant. Nice to see you again."

"Is it? Not my sentiment exactly," she surveyed the scene, "I don't suppose you know what happened here?"

"Why would I?"

"Just a little coincidental, apparently you had a disagreement with the cafe owner and then his business goes up in flames."

Ever the innocent, Ray responded, "No idea what you're talking about."

"Fortunately, his wife had a chronic toothache," Miller recounted, "and he was up taking care of her otherwise this could have been a real tragedy. They managed to wake the occupants of the other flats, and everyone made it out alive."

"That's nice," the hardened man added dryly.

"Isn't it?" her tone matched his.

"If you don't mind," Ray turned to leave, "I've got to go now."

Miller nodded in his direction, "We'll be watching you."

"That's nice," he took out a cigarette and lit it, adding, "perhaps you and your lot should be figuring out why those Black bastards on The Hill killed my cousin Mitch!"

"Oh, we'll figure out who killed him. You can take my word on that."

Miller, Wainwright, Dave, and Donnie watched as Ray turned and loped quickly away. After he was out of sight, Wainwright turned to Dave, "I don't suppose you have anything you'd like to share?"

Dave wasn't about to say a word and stared at the ground, "I really don't. No."

Wainwright put his hand on Dave's shoulder, "You could press charges against him."

"Oh yeah and sign my own death warrant? I don't think so." Without another word, Dave turned and hurried after Siobhan and Sherry. Donnie fell into step beside him. Wobble still smarting from Donnie's rebuke, hung back waiting for an invite to join them that never came.

Donnie bent down to pick up a rock, and threw it a couple of feet to the side, as he addressed Dave, "Ya dinny think Ray's right, do you?"

Dave stopped dead in his tracks and spun towards Donnie, "No I don't. Are you accusing me of being a racist now as well? Cause you should know better Donnie."

"I meant about Carl being at Vickie's shagging her you fucking eediot!"

"Oh, fuck. Sorry Don."

"You're alright Dave. Anybody who knows you, knows better than to accuse you of that, you fucking numpty," Donnie laughed and slugged Dave on the bicep.

"Cheers Don!" Dave slugged him right back, "Now, let's get a move on and catch up with the girls, we've gotta do whatever we can to help Carl. If he's not at Vickie's that is."

"You'd better not let Sherry hear you saying that" Dave added as they hurried to catch up with Sherry and Siobhan, who were disappearing through the doors of Wordsworth.

When they caught up with the girls, they were exiting the lift back out into the lobby of the block of flats. Siobhan was holding her hand over her nose and mouth in shock. Sherry shook her head and smirked, "I told you we'd be better off walking."

Siobhan stared at her in disbelief, "I know you did but Jesus, I didn't think it could possibly be that bad!"

Dave laughed, "Every Monday it's the same thing. Holiday Express, I call it, better start climbing." Dave, Siobhan, and Donnie started climbing to the ninth floor. Sherry stopped at the bottom of the stairs, reluctant to join them, uncertain as to whether she was ready to forgive Dave yet.

Siobhan looked back at her, noticing her hesitation, and turned to Dave, "Dave, I think you need to talk to Sherry."

Dave agreed and slowly limped back to the bottom step, "Listen Sherry, you know Carl is my mate, right?"

"Of course, I do," Sherry said, placing her hands firmly on her hips.

Dave leaned against the railing, "Then how can you possibly think I think like Ray? I mean it doesn't make any sense, does it?"

"But you hang around with him Dave, WHY? He's a fucking monster," she paused for a moment, casting a glance to Ray's sister, "no offense Siobhan but he is."

Siobhan shrugged, "None taken. I know he is better than anyone."

"Well then, and you Donnie, you're no better."

Donnie scoffed, "How did I get dragged into this?"

For the first time Sherry noticed Donnie's clothes, "And what are you dressed like?"

"It's me court clobber, I'm changing the way I look, I'm bothered about what people think, you know, when they see me." Donnie straightened up and awkwardly adjusted the collar on his shirt.

Dave stepped forward and took Sherry's hands into his own, "Listen, none of us are perfect, but no one here is a racist and what's important now is that we all do all we can to try and help Carl and find out where he is."

Sherry nodded her head, adding sternly, "You're right, but don't think for a minute this is over with."

Dave stepped back to the railing to let Sherry pass. She brushed abruptly past him, her head held high, and they all continued up the stairs in silence. When they finally reached their destination, Sherry opened the door, and they all entered the flat. As the door opened, Queenie rushed over hoping it was Carl, the disappointment evident on her face upon seeing the others. Dave attempted to cut the awkwardness as he began to make introductions, "Queenie, this is Donnie and Siobhan."

"I'm sick of telling you, it's Mrs. Bartrum to you. And who exactly are they?"

"Donnie's a mate of Carl's and Siobhan's my girlfriend,"

"You?" Queenie laughed, "She's YOUR girlfriend?"

Dave shrugged, "Yeah, I know."

Siobhan stepped forward with her hand extended ready to shake Queenie's. "Hi Mrs. Bartrum,"

"You can call me Queenie, you're not him. What on earth are you doing going out with a boy like him? You look like a nice girl."

Siobhan leaned closer in, lowering her voice slightly, "Well don't tell him I said so, but I think I kinda love him."

Queenie looked stunned, Donnie snorted in the background, but no one was more shocked by the public revelation than Dave, who blurted out, "You what?"

Before Siobhan could answer, Sherry cut in, "Can we get back to why we're here?"

Siobhan speaks first, "Yeah sorry, didn't mean to..."

"You love me?"

Donnie dug his elbow into Dave's side, "Really?"

Dave snapped out of it, shrugged and looked at Carl's mother, "Sorry Queenie, what can we do?"

"Thank you, Dave, I won't bodder telling you how to address me correctly anymore. My Carl went down to The Hill to get his Auntie, and never came back. And I'm afraid something terrible happened to him." She wrung her hands nervously.

Sherry stepped forward and hugged Queenie who was struggling to hold her tears in, a handful of scrunched up tissues held to her quivering lips. Dave and Donnie stood awkwardly, not knowing what to do or say. Siobhan stared at Dave, mouthing, "Well, do something."

Dave looked uncomfortably at Donnie who shook his head in exasperation at Dave before adding, "Me and Dave will go down to the Hill and see what we can find out."

"We will?" Dave looked surprised.

Donnie's eyes narrowed on his friend's face as he repeated slowly, "Aye, we will."

Much as he didn't want to go near The Hill during a riot, Dave knew it was the right thing to do. "Right," he chimed in.

Siobhan joined Sherry in hugging Queenie trying to assure her, "Listen, maybe he got picked up on SUS or something. What with all the trouble they're bound to be casting a wide net. I'm sure it's just a misunderstanding."

Queenie nodded her head in a rapid up and down motion, "I hope you're right, chile. It's not easy being Black and having a son in this country, you know?"

Siobhan shook her head sadly, "I don't, no."

Dave decided this was his time to assert himself, "Okay sweetheart, you stay here with Queenie, and me and Donnie will head over to The Hill and see what we can find out. Okay?"

Siobhan turned away from Queenie with a look of confusion on her face, "That's Mrs. Bartrum to you. And if you think I'm letting you head down to The Hill without me you've got another think coming. You're liable to get yourself killed!" Queenie guffawed at her comment, "you tell him chile! The boy's a damn fool!"

Dave stood, completely stunned by the turn of events, Siobhan shook her head and headed for the door. "Well, come on then."

The group headed for the door and out into the corridor. At the top of the stairs, Dave turned to Sherry, "Don't you think that you should stay here and look after Queenie?"

Sherry looked at him with a quizzical look on her face, "Why's that Dave? Don't you want to be seen with me?"

"What?" Dave faltered, quickly adding, "No."

Sherry continued to stare at him and shook her head, "That's what I thought."

"Nah, nah, I meant no," Dave stumbled trying to find the right words, "that's not what I want!"

"What?" the Black woman glowered at him.

"Oh fuck! I have no problem with being seen with you Sherry, you got it all wrong!"

Siobhan realised that she was going to have to dig him out of the hole he had inadvertently dug for himself, "He just misspoke Sherry that's all, you know what an idiot he can be."

"I'm learning real fast," Sherry rolled her eyes.

Donnie continued down the stairs, "Can we get on with this now?"

Sherry and Dave still had their eyes locked on one another at the top of the stairs. Sherry shook her head, "I'm probably the only one of us who's safe on The Hill right now anyway."

Dave smiled, "You're probably right." They all turned and headed down the stairs, none of them certain as to what they might be heading into. Sherry, scared, but mostly for Carl. Siobhan, embroiled with mixed emotions, knew this could well be the end of any friendly relationship between her and her brother. Dave, scared of what they might be heading into, scared that Ray was now going to be out for his blood. Yet, at the same time, feeling an urgent need to make things up to Sherry, to prove he's not who she thinks he is. Donnie, as always, looking forward to a crack, thinking, "a riot might be fun."

They continued down Church Lane planning to catch the 83 bus down to Wembley Park and the main entrance to The Hill. As they reached the bus stop, Gimpish and Sally came limping up, both looking the worse for wear. They wore scabs on their faces, and on the exposed flesh on their arms and hands and were scratching at their upper bodies as if infested by some kind of parasite.

Gimpish approached the group, "Hey Dave, listen, I don't suppose that I could borrow a tenner, could I?" He scratched his forearm and sniffled, "I know it's a lot to ask but we're really hurting, and Sally's been sick, real sick, so she can't get any work. If you get what I mean?"

During the entire speech, Gimpish was sniffling and rubbing his already red, raw nose with the back of his hand, making it redder and more sore looking. Sally had slowly slid down the side of the bus shelter, emitting a low whimpering sound, and muttering curses as if she had an early form of Tourette's syndrome. Sherry curled her lips in disgust, "'Ow the fuck d'you know these people, Dave? They're disgusting!"

Siobhan was taken aback by the outburst, "Jesus Sherry, don't be so judgmental, Gimpish and Dave were friends back before..." She stopped mid-sentence.

"Before what?" Sherry asked curiously.

"Before he became..."

Gimpish's head swiveled, seeing Siobhan had no idea how to finish the sentence, from somewhere deep down inside he dragged up one of the few shreds of decency he had left and said, "Sick. before I became sick."

Sherry stared at him and without trying to hide her disgust, "And what sort of work is it that your girlfriend is too sick for? As if I couldn't guess."

Gimpish smiled, not a fake smile, there was nothing forced about it at all, "She's a lady in waiting at Buckingham fucking Palace." He started to laugh, a deranged manic cackle from somewhere deep down in his chest, Sally joined in with a hysterical screeching laugh, his head fell back, and he cried at the sky, "She's a fucking lady in fucking waiting!" He stepped suddenly forward, and his face is just an inch from Sherry's, "And we're invited to the Royal wedding, ARE YOU? YOU FUCKING CUNT!"

Spit flew in Sherry's face as he screamed into her face, without even thinking Dave punched Gimpish, knocking him flat, he fell in front of the bus. It screeched to a halt before nearly running over his chest. Sherry began to cry, completely shocked at what had just happened. Sally, completely oblivious about Gimpish nearly being flattened was still wailing a totally deranged song of desperation and sorrow. Gimpish curled into a ball against the curb and started to cry. The bus doors opened, Siobhan grabbed Sherry and pulled her on. "Four please to Wembley Park," she announced to the driver.

The driver shook his head, "We're not stopping at Wembley Park today, we've been detoured."

"Well as close as you can get us."

"That'll be two quid."

The four of them climbed the stairs and sat down, Sherry and Siobhan together in one seat, Dave sat across the seat in front of them, and Donnie across the aisle. The bus was almost empty, and the two boys saw no point in squashing up together on the same seat. Dave spoke first, "Don't s'pose you've got a fag 'ave ya Donnie?"

"Aye I do."

Dave reached out his hand, "Thank fuck I'm desperate." Donnie pulled out a crumpled half empty pack of Benson and Hedges and tossed one to Dave, another to Siobhan and then offered the pack to Sherry.

She turned her nose up at the offer, "No thanks I don't!"

Donnie shrugs, "Your loss."

"I normally sit downstairs; I find the smoke hurts my eyes." As she spoke, both Dave and Siobhan were leaning across the aisle toward Donnie who was holding out a lit Zippo as they took long draws on their cigarettes to light them.

Siobhan turned to Sherry, "Well this is awkward."

"It's okay I'll move," Sherry stated as she climbed over Siobhan and moved forward three seats to the front of the bus. The group sat in awkward silence. Donnie was quiet as well except he knew nothing of feeling awkward, that just wasn't part of his make-up.

As the bus made its way down Church Lane, Dave had an idea, "Let's get off at the Blackbirds and head into the Hill the back way. That way it don't matter about the detour."

Siobhan nodded, "Good idea Dave."

Sherry drew in a long deep breath and let it out slowly, ignoring the smell of cigarettes, "Thanks for what you did back there Dave."

"What? With Gimpish you mean?"

"Yeah."

Dave shrugged, "Don't sweat it, he had it comin'."

"Still, thanks, he was really scaring me."

"Hey like I said, don't sweat it," he dismissed the notion with a wave of his hand turning his attention out the window, "we'd better get going, our stop's coming up." The four of them jumped up and ran down the stairs and waited at the back door, none of them knew what they were heading into until the bus turned the corner, the door opened, and they stepped off.

They could hear the shouts and yells long before they saw the crowds. They stood on opposite corner from Church Lane, the same corner where Ray had been saved by Mitch in the stolen car. The crowd of about a hundred demonstrators, the majority of them skinheads, were chanting "Sieg Heil" over and over again, while thrusting Nazi salutes into the air with their right arms. Many of them wore swastika armbands or waved flags with the National Front NF symbol on them. In the centre was Ray, his right arm thrust high in the air as he screamed; his hatred infecting the very air around him.

Across Forty Lane stood another crowd, compromised of mostly Black people, but with a smattering of white and East Indian youths some of whom waved Anti-Nazi League and Rock Against Racism banners. They were shouting back at the skinheads equally as loud and passionate. Both groups were held back by lines of police who struggled to contain them.

On the third corner stood the four friends totally stunned by the scene playing out in front of them. Ray's eyes were fixed on them, and he drew deep hate filled breaths at his sister and his so-called friends standing there with Sherry, his sworn enemy. Dave locked eyes with Ray momentarily and his heart sank. There was no going back now, he was the enemy, he knew what it meant, and in a way, it was a relief. He nudged Siobhan and signaled with his head across the road, she spotted her brother and instantly knew that her life was about to change as well.

Donnie noticed them staring across the road and followed their eyelines. Seeing who they were looking at, he smirked, "Well I guess you two have some decisions to make." He gave Ray the two-finger 'fuck off' salute and grinned at him. The veins in Ray's neck bulged out through the skin, he looked ready to kill somebody.

Sherry stared across the road at the hate filled throng and screamed, "Fuck you! You fuckers!" Dave and Siobhan glanced at each other and without a thought joined in, screaming at the top of their lungs, letting all the pent-up fear loose in one long screamed tirade aimed at Ray, at the skinheads, at everything they stood for. The police line broke and the skinheads poured across the street. Most of them ran at the opposing crowd but Ray and another group broke ranks and went straight for Dave and the others.

Ray felt someone grab him by the arm and drag him backwards, spinning around he found one of the huge bikers from the George and Dragon, where he'd met with Greg, pulling him. He turned and followed the man back to where Greg stood leaning against a lamppost.

Watching the other skinheads running toward them, Dave shouted, "Fuck this, let's go!" He grabbed Siobhan and Sherry by the arms, and they legged it out across Forty Lane. Dave glanced back and saw a police van pulling up in the centre of Church Lane and officers in riot gear jumping out. Donnie stood in the centre of the road fists swinging, fighting two skinheads.

Dave, Siobhan and Sherry ducked around the back of the opposite crowd, a confused mass of surging policemen who tried to hold back the left-wing and Black protesters and stop the onrushing right-wing thugs. The three of them hurried to the back gate of Chalkhill where they were stopped by another line of policemen, three deep, riot shields at the ready. Dave approached, gasping for breath, the two girls hanging back behind him. A policeman stepped forward, "Where d'you think you're going?"

Dave pointed to a distant location, "Visit my mate."

"Your mate?" The policeman didn't believe him for one second.

The man was determined, "Yeah."

The cop nodded and held his position, "Where's he live?"

Dave pointed again, "On the Hill."

The policeman's eyes followed the direction as he responded, "You're not going in there."

"Why not," Dave inquired, "looks to me like the riots behind me, not in front."

"Access is restricted to residents and essential personnel only!" The officer sounded like he was reading the line from a manual.

"You're kidding," Dave looked at him totally stunned, attempting to change his mind, "look it's probably safer for me to keep going forwards than head back to what we just left!"

"I don't care, this entire area is subject to a double murder investigation and access is restricted."

Sherry stepped in front of Dave, "What do you mean double murder?"

"That's all I'm at liberty to say," he raised his shield and stepped back from the group, "now you have to leave before I arrest you."

Unswayed by his words, Sherry continued, "My boyfriend has gone missing; I'm trying to find him!"

The policeman stared past them into the distance as if he couldn't see them any longer, showing his disinterest in their plight, "File a report at the station then, now do you want to get arrested or are you going to leave?" With no other choice, the trio turned and walked slowly back towards the shouting and the chaos outside The Blackbirds.

Greg stared into Ray's eyes and shook his head, "What the fuck do you think you're doing? And why aren't you at work?"

"Standing up for what's right!"

He screamed in Ray's face, "You fuckin' idiot!"

“What?” Ray squared off at him, “We’re at war! You said so yourself. These are our people!”

“True, very true, but you are a soldier, and you have a duty to follow through on your orders and your orders don’t include getting arrested in a stupid street fight.” Greg folded his arms over his chest and continued, “That’s what we have the idiots for, you’re a combat specialist Ray, and you have a mission to complete.”

Ray stared back at him breathing long, deep breaths trying to calm down, “I guess I wasn’t thinking.”

“You leave the thinking to me.” His eyes narrowed on Ray’s face, “And again, why aren’t you at work?”

“I called in sick” Ray responded and shrugged.

Greg scoffed, “That’s a parole violation just waiting to happen.”

“Like I said I guess I wasn’t thinking.”

“If you go in now, you might not get reported, get the fuck out of here before you get yourself into trouble.” Ray nodded and turned to stride away a huge scowl on his face, enraged by the dressing down he had just been given.

18

Alex woke up in a windowless cell, a scratchy woolen blanket wrapped around him, his head on the lumpy thin mattress, no pillow. He took in a long breath, through his nose, the stench of urine from the blanket causing him to bolt quickly upright. The pain in his hands and jaw instantly reminded him where he was. He exhaled, and watched the damp, cold air fill with his breath, feeling as if his life was leaving him one breath at a time. A key rattled in the door and the big man, the one who had poured water over his head, entered. "Get up," he bellowed in a demanding tone.

"Where am I?"

The man wouldn't respond and simply repeated, "Get up." He stepped back out into the hallway to wait.

Alex stood up slowly beside the bed, on shaky legs. He took a step forward, his legs gave out from under him, and he crashed into the opposite wall of the cell, thankful that it was there to stop him from collapsing completely. He called out to the guard, "I can barely walk."

"Not my problem."

"Please, where am I?" Alex repeated, as he pushed himself off the wall, using one broken hand to support himself. The untreated wounds from the day before caused him to scream and slump against his arm.

The guard looked in the room, agitation crossed his face, "I don't have all day." Alex once more forced himself off the wall and staggered out of the cell. The man walked ahead of him, seemingly impervious to Alex's pain and problems walking.

The corridor was lined on both sides with similarly windowless cells all of which were unoccupied, their doors, entrances to their own untold hells, hanging wide open as witness to how alone Alex really was. The sudden realisation of just how isolated he was and how true his interrogator's statement the day before were. "No one knows where you are," the words reverberated around Alex's head as he limped to the end of the corridor where the man stood, waiting, holding another heavy, metal door open. The room where Alex had been the day before, it's door gaping wide open. A feeling of dread and terror swept over him when he saw it. He stopped and stared, an audible gasp escaping from his lips again filling the air with mist. "Get in."

Alex stood stuck, feeling as if his feet were dried in concrete, unable to make his legs move. His head spun, and the pain in his hands suddenly became intolerable. He wanted to cry, to beg the man, "Just let me go back to the cell. Never mind home, just let me go back to the urine-stained mattress. Anything but this room."

"Get in!" The man commanded in a voice that echoed off the concrete walls.

Alex forced himself to focus on the door, forced his legs to move, to carry him to his fate, a fate that, he was convinced, would be worse than death. Why wouldn't it be? After what he had suffered in that very room just yesterday, "If it was yesterday," he thought, realising that he had no way of knowing how long he was in that bed. He used his elbow against the doorjamb to support himself and watched himself in the mirror on the opposite wall as he staggered into the room, barely recognising the gaunt figure that stood before him. The desk sat waiting for him, the chair he was sitting in the last time he was in the room lay on its side, he had no idea why, no memory of leaving the room or what had transpired toward the end of last time he was here. The door clanged shut behind him, and he turned toward it, finding himself alone, awaiting his fate.

In the Poets, Gimpish and Sally limped through the estate heading for Coleridge house. A week before, one of the flats had become vacant after its elderly occupant had died. Andy the Weasel, through some nefarious means that he would never confess to, had come into possession of the keys. Andy Junior had, in exchange for sexual favours from Sally, given the keys to Gimpish. Now, he and Sally had somewhere temporary to sleep and get high.

They caught the lift up the seven stories, oblivious to the ubiquitous stench. Sally rocked backwards and forwards muttering gibberish. Gimpish feverishly scratched at his arms desperate for the fix he clutched tightly in his left hand to bring him relief from the all-encompassing craving that consumed his brain, his soul, his entire being. This was the only thing that would shut out the truth about his life and the state Sally was in. No matter how deep he sank, how bad the terrors became, she was always haunting his subconscious. The fact that no matter who introduced who to what, he felt overwhelmingly responsible for the state into which she sank.

The lift doors opened on the seventh floor, and they stepped out onto the landing. Outside their "flat," as they had come to think of it, waited Andy Junior and Bazza's kid brother, Sammy. Andy grinned his weasel-like grin, as they approached, "Gimp, Sally, how are you?"

Gimpish shook his head manically, he wanted to scream, he had to get in the flat, "Not now, Andy!"

"Yes, now! Or I'm gonna call the council and you two will be out of here faster than you can think."

Gimpish glared at him, gesturing wildly towards Sally, "She's not in a good way. This isn't a good time!"

Andy sucked his teeth, "I'll decide that, not you!" He looked at Sally, she was slumped against the wall, doubled over muttering and crying. Sammy cocked his head sideways to match the tilt of Sally's, "What's wrong with her?"

Andy put his hand on Sammy's shoulder, "Nuffin' she's fine." He cast a glance at the addict, "Ain't that right Gimp?"

Gimpish coughed and wiped his nose, "She just needs five minutes." He hated himself, but he had to kill the pain, he would do anything to just get in the flat and fix up.

"You've got five minutes, and no more Gimp." Andy took a step to the side, clearing the door's entrance for them, "I made the kid here a promise. You hear me?"

"I got it," Gimpish quickly opened the door and pulled Sally in with him, "five minutes okay!" He tried to slam the door behind him, but Andy stepped in and stopped him by jamming his booted foot in the door. Gimpish had more important issues on his mind than arguing with Andy and he pulled Sally into the living room, where she collapsed onto the sofa. He immediately tied an old necktie, that he kept for just this purpose, around his calf muscle and started to heat a spoon with a Zippo.

As soon as he had injected himself between his toes, he undid the tourniquet, a warm all-encompassing feeling of joy mixed with hatred poured through him. He knew he had a very limited amount of time left before he was totally incapacitated, so he quickly turned to Sally's needs, repeating the entire process. As soon as he was done, he flopped backwards on the couch.

Moments later, Andy and Sammy stepped into the room and stared at the seemingly comatose couple. Sammy sneered at the state of Sally, "Are you sure?"

"Fucking right," Andy tittered, "we can do whatever we want with her." Sammy hesitated and Andy added, "What are you waiting for, this is going to be fuckin' fantastic!" He lurched forward and grabbed Sally under one arm and started to pull her up off of the sofa. Despite her small size he was shocked at how heavy her dead weight seemed. He looked back at Sammy, "Com'on give me a hand." Sammy stepped forward and grabbed the sleeping woman under her other arm. They dragged her into the bedroom and dumped her on the bed. The last thing Gimpish saw before he lost consciousness, was the two young men pulling off Sally's clothes before Andy kicked the bedroom door closed.

Donnie woke up in a communal cell and slowly surveyed his surroundings. There were five other young men in the room, two of them skinheads, three of them Black. He sat up and grinned, "Morning." The skinheads and the Black guys glared at each other from opposite ends of the cell. Donnie had been asleep on a cot along one of the side walls. One of the skinheads, sporting a swollen black eye, glared at him, "Fuckin' race traitor."

Donnie smirked at the man's bruised face, "Did I do that?"

The other man leaned forward, still sitting on his cot, "Yeah and I'm gonna do you for it."

"I doubt it somehow," Donnie laughed in response.

One of the Black guys smirked, "'Ow the fuck did you manage to sleep so heavily?"

Donnie shrugged, "Clean conscience?"

"Been 'ere before then?"

"Yeah, but never in the same cell as the enemy," Donnie gestured at the skinheads.

The Black man smiled at his new and unexpected ally, "The place is over run, what with the riot and then this lot, they're packin' us in wherever they can."

"Not surprised" Donnie nodded toward the skinheads, "Thanks for watching over me."

One of them rolled his eyes, "No sweat."

A key clanked in the door and a policeman entered, "Alright you lot out." Everyone, except Donnie, stood and began making their way to the door. Donnie remained seated. The policeman looked at him, "You coming?"

"Depends. What are we charged with?"

"Nothing."

Donnie looked at him with surprise, "Nothing?"

"That's right, you lot are the least of our troubles, collect your stuff from the Sergeant and get the hell out of here!"

"Ya don't have to tell me twice!" He quickly jumped up and walked quickly out of the cell, a big grin on his face, unable to believe his luck. After the group had collected their personal effects, and a warning about staying out of trouble or next time the law wouldn't be so lenient, they all headed out through the back door of Wembley police station. Donnie was the last out into the parking lot, the Black men had already disappeared. The two skinheads had stopped and were standing in the open gateway, 'Black Eye' was lighting a cigarette. Never having been one to care about authority, or to pass up the chance for a fight, Donnie shouted, "Oi!" The two skinheads looked up to see him striding towards them across the parking lot. Before they could speak, Donnie reached 'Black Eye' and punched him straight in the mouth as hard as he could, knocking him flat on his back. "Gonna do me are ya? You fuckin' cunt?"

The other skinhead stepped quickly back, wanting nothing to do with the crazed Scotsman. Donnie kicked his prostrated friend in the bollocks, causing him to curl up in a groaning ball on the ground. He bent down to pick up the cigarette his victim had dropped, "Waste not want not," he took a drag from it as he strolled away, glancing up and down Ealing Road, looking for a bus back to Kingsbury.

When he reached the bus stop, an 83 bus pulled up and Donnie jogged up the stairs. Sitting two seats back from the stairs, he spotted Terry, chatting to a young man that was holding a bag of tools and a four-foot spirit level. "Oi up Terry."

Terry looked up from his conversation with surprise, "Donnie? What are you doing here? Shouldn't you be at work?"

"Spent the night at Her Majesty's pleasure, just got out."

"What did you do this time?"

Donnie flung himself into an empty seat as the bus lurched forward, "Punched some gob shite racist in the mouth down The Blackbirds yesterday."

"You were in that?" Terry leaned forward suddenly interested in the story.

"Not deliberately."

Terry's companion spoke up, "I heard it went mental over there."

"It did," Donnie agreed, leaning over on the seat as the bus accelerated.

Terry suddenly remembered his manners, "This is Doug." He nodded to the man with the tools, "Donnie, old mate of mine."

"Hey Doug, d'you get fired?"

Doug looks confused, "What? No, why?"

Donnie glances down at Doug's bag, "The tools."

"Oh right. Nah mate, I'm off to Germany, leaving this afternoon."

Donnie regarded him with a puzzled look, "Germany?"

"Yeah!" Doug continued excitedly, "you can make three times what they're paying on the sites here."

"Get the fuck out of here!" Donnie leaned against the side of the bus in faked surprise.

"Nah really."

Terry furthered the introduction, "Donnie here's a hoddie, best there is."

Doug looked Donnie up and down, he was still in his court clothes and didn't look much like a bricklayer's labourer. "You got work gear?" He asked curiously.

"Aye, of course!"

"You might wanna think about coming with us then, easier to get hired as a crew."

"A crew?" The interest was written all over Donnie's face.

"Yeah, me and my mate, Tony, are going. If we had a labourer we could get piece work, even better money."

Terry looked at Donnie, "Get you away from spending your nights at Her Majesty's pleasure."

Donnie scoffed, "Aye I've had enough of that to last me a lifetime."

The bus lurched to a stop, the doors squeaking loudly as they opened, Doug gathered his tools, "This is my stop." He stood and added, "we're leaving at three. Tony's got a motor, be outside The Blackbirds at three and you can hitch a ride with us."

"I'll think about it," Donnie replied to Doug's back as the man made his way to the front of the bus.

Doug started down the stairs, glancing back at the pair, "See ya Tel!"

"Yeah, take care mate," Terry called back as the doors closed behind him.

Donnie moved to take the vacant seat beside Terry, "Seems like a nice guy."

Terry glanced out the window in the direction Doug was heading, "He is, you could do a lot worse than taking his offer."

"I'll think about it."

"What's to think about?"

Donnie sank deep into thought, before suddenly realising that Terry wasn't with them yesterday. He quickly changed the subject, "Carl's gone missing."

"What d'you mean missing?"

"He went to The Hill in the middle of the riot and neither hide nor hair of him has been seen since."

"Carl was rioting?"

"Nah he was running an errand for his ma."

Terry frowned, "Does Dave know?"

Donnie nodded, "Aye, he was out looking for him when I got arrested."

"He didn't get…?"

"Nah. Siobhan was looking out for him."

Terry chuckled, "Best thing that ever happened to him, that girl."

Donnie agreed and scoffed, "If Ray doesn't kill him that is."

"True enough!" Terry admitted as the bus pulled to a stop at the top of Church Lane. The two men rose from their seats, headed down the stairs and jumped off. They walked past the police cordon tapes, around what was left of the shopping arcade and the Sunshine Cafe, and into the estate. Outside Wordsworth they spotted a marked police car, not an unusual sight, but on this occasion, one that filled them both with foreboding. They continued toward the tower block, watching as D.C Wainwright and D.S Miller exited from the lobby and climbed in the police car and sped away. Donnie and Terry exchanged glances, Terry shook his head, "That doesn't look good."

Donnie stopped in his tracks, his eyes widening with a grim realisation, "He's dead!"

Terry interrupted immediately, "You don't know that."

"Don't I?" Donnie muttered and the pair quickly entered the lobby and ran up the stairs, all the way to the ninth floor. They gasped for breath as they found Siobhan, sitting on the floor outside the apartment, holding Dave, his body heaving, wracked with sobs.

Terry stepped forward, a look of concern across his brow, "You okay Dave?"

Dave pulled his head up from Siobhan's shoulder, tears rolled down his cheeks, "Why wouldn't I be?" He could barely get the words out, in one hand he held an unlit cigarette, "I just had to come out because Queenie won't let me smoke in there." No matter how hard he tried, he couldn't hold the sobbing in. Both Donnie and Terry, the two supposedly hard men, stepped forward to hug him and Siobhan. They stood for a few moments, holding each other. Despite his grief, Dave started to laugh, "What if them Burnt Oak boys could see us now?" The other three laughed in response, the only release they could find at that tense moment.

Hearing their laughter from inside, Sherry flung open Queenie's door and stepped out into the hallway. She stared at them quizzically, angrily before stepping back inside and slamming the door shut.

In his interrogation room, Alex righted the chair and sat down, exhausted, in pain and totally confused. He turned his head and stared at the mirror over his shoulder convinced that he was being watched. Hoping desperately that this would soon all be over with, however it was going to end, he just hoped that it would end soon. The familiar sound of keys in the lock caused him to start gasping in one deep breath after another in anticipation of the three men, the cosh, the buckets of water. Instead, a young woman entered; about thirty years old, if that, slim, attractive, with long, strawberry blonde hair. He remembered that strawberry blonde on a billboard at the bus stop outside his aunt's house that always seemed to advertise hair and beauty products. He had always thought it was stupid, strawberries were bright red, not blonde. She walked across to the table and sat in the chair opposite him and dropped a packet of Rothmans and a lighter on the table. "Fag?" She had a faint Northern Irish accent.

The question caught Alex by surprise, "What?"

"You smoke, don't you?"

"Yeah."

She gestured at the pack of cigarettes, "Well then?"

"Sure, thanks," he stated cautiously as the young woman put two cigarettes in her mouth, clicked the lighter and raised it up to light them simultaneously. Alex noticed the way the light reflected in her green eyes, seeming to turn them more hazel in colour. She drew in the smoke from the two cigarettes, and let it out in a long deep breath, the cigarette smoke mixing with the vapour her breath caused in the cold room. She handed one to Alex, and he took it gingerly, "Thanks."

"You're welcome," she smiled at him and put the lighter back into her pocket, "I'm sure you understand we can't let you handle the flame. Just a precaution."

Alex held the cigarette between the little finger and thumb of his right hand, his other fingers mangled and useless and took a long deep drag. The mysterious woman introduced herself, "My name's Heather."

"Hi." Alex was tired of meeting people.

"Don't worry," Heather added with sweetness in her voice, "the man from yesterday won't be back."

"He won't?"

"No," she smiled kindly.

Alex sighed a breath of relief, "How come?"

Heather looked at Alex's disfigured hand with pity, "I don't agree with his methods, that's how come."

"You don't?" In his voice she could hear the surprise.

"No."

"You his boss?"

She shrugged, "Kinda."

Alex felt like he could cry with relief, "No torture today then?"

"No torture ever again. No."

He looked her features over slowly, taking a slow puff of the burning cigarette, "Is that why you don't care if I see your face?"

She nodded at him and smiled again, "Precisely."

Alex felt like he could trust her to help him, "Are you going to let me go?"

"Of course." She sorted through some papers in front of her.

The captor looked hopeful, "When?"

"Soon," she stated plainly.

Alex took another long haul from the cigarette, "What do I have to do?"

"You don't have to do anything. I would appreciate it if you would help me to understand some things, just so I can clean up some files. Just a small administrative matter."

"What things?" At this point Alex was more than willing to help.

"You already know that we're interested in your friend, Raymond Collins."

"I do, yeah."

"Well then," she leaned forward and poured him a cup of water from a nearly empty pitcher sitting on the table, "anything you can tell us about his connections to Seamus McCaffrey, Mr. Daniels, or anything else would be of help and then you can go."

Alex took the cup with both hands and slurped it greedily. As he finished he looked over the brim, suddenly suspicious at her kindness, "You're not going to let me go."

She never dropped the 'good cop' act, "What makes you say that?"

"I know too much!" He blurted out.

"Do you?" Heather chuckled.

"Yeah!"

She leaned back in her chair and tapped her fingers on the table, "Where are you?"

Alex looked around the grey coloured cement brick room, "I don't know."

Heather made a little 'hmm' sound and questioned him once more, "Who are we?"

"Again," Alex began to get the point, "I don't know."

"The man who beat you," she took his empty glass, poured him another cup of water, and pushed it back towards him, "what does he look like?"

"He was wearing a sack over his head." Alex looked suspiciously at the cup, for a brief moment, before thirstily grabbing and downing it.

Heather fiddled with the cuff of her shirt, adjusting the button, "What was his name?"

"Again," Alex groaned, "I don't know."

"Well then?"

Alex understood but was still confused. He added, "But, I know what you look like."

"I have plausible deniability."

"What?"

"Who do you think people will believe? Me or you?" She shrugged and Alex undeniably knew the answer.

He sat in silence for a few moments considering his stance. Determined to tell this nice woman everything he knew, he continued, "What do you want to know? I told the other guy I don't know who McCaffrey is, Daniels is a friend of Rays, I don't really know him though."

"You have to give me something Alex." She tsked at him, "I want to help you, but you have to give me something."

Alex took another pull from the cigarette, it burnt down to the butt, and burnt his thumb. Startled, he dropped it on the floor of the cell. Heather took out another one, lit it and passed it to him. Once again, he took the cigarette, took a long drag from it, all the time staring into her eyes, "If I tell you what we were planning, I could go to jail."

Heather gestured to the empty room, "Look around you, could it be worse than here? Whatever you tell me stays between you and me."

Alex didn't believe her, not for a second, but he was tired and in pain, and there was no other choice for him but to hope that she might be telling him the truth, no matter how unlikely it seemed. "We plan on robbing the Kentucky," he blurted out before he could overthink it.

She looked a little stunned at his absurd revelation, "What?"

"The Kentucky," he added, "the one in Colindale, on the Edgware Road. We planned on robbing it on the day of the Royal Wedding."

Heather was still unsure, "The Kentucky in Colindale?"

"Yeah."

"Why that particular Kentucky?" She picked up her pen and wrote some notes as he spoke.

"Ray says it's owned by Pakis and no one but Pakis work there. Says they got it coming."

Heather continued pressing him for more information, "On the day of Charles and Diana's wedding?"

"Yeah," he nodded, leaning forward with interest to show his willingness to help her, "Ray says the cops'll all be busy with the wedding, says we're in the clear."

"How much money do you think you'll get from robbing a Kentucky Fried Chicken?"

"Dunno," in reality Alex had never thought about how much money they would have made, "but he says we'll give it all to the cause anyway."

"The cause?"

"Yeah, I think that's where Daniels comes in, him and Greg."

"Greg?" She flipped through the file looking for the mentioned name.

"Yeah, he's a biker, leader of the Hangmen."

Finding nothing, she began to take notes once more as she furthered the questioning, "He's a friend of Ray's too then? This Greg?"

"Yeah!" Alex was happy that he was able to offer her some information she didn't appear to be aware of.

"You've seen them together?"

"Yeah, and one time with Daniels too, in The Laureate."

"The Laureate?"

"Yeah! The boozer on the estate, my local."

Heather nodded wisely, "The Poets estate?"

"Yeah!" he added excitedly.

Heather stood up, "Thank you, Alex."

Alex looked like a hopeful puppy, "Can I go now?"

"I just have to get some paperwork for you to sign and then yes you can go." She turned to head out the door, someone outside unlocked it, she stepped through and out of Alex's sight. The door slammed closed and, once more, the key turned in the lock. In the outside room sat the skinny man from yesterday, watching and listening through the mirror. He glanced up at her as she entered, "Nice work Sarah… or should I say, Heather."

Sarah smiled, "You know what to do. And try not to scare him, he's been through enough already."

Meanwhile, at The Poets, Dave, Siobhan, Terry and Donnie exited through the lobby door of Wordsworth and out into the estate. They stopped and stood awkwardly, glancing around, no one knowing what to do. Terry spoke first, "Pub?"

Donnie shrugged, "I'm skint."

"I'm paying," Terry added.

"In that case," Donnie turned quickly in the direction of the pub.

Terry placed his hand on Dave's shoulder, "A drink'll do you good."

Dave shrugged sadly and Siobhan spoke up for them both, "Maybe later. We're going to head back to Wobble's place for a while."

“Fair enough, if you change your minds, you know where we’ll be.” Terry and Donnie left towards the boozer as Dave and Siobhan headed down the road towards number 183. Donnie announced as they walked, “I’m just gonna head over to mine and have a quick shower and change. Get the stench of bird off me.”

“Fair enough,” Terry repeated, “I’ll keep the beer cold for ya.” Donnie jogged away and Terry rounded the corner around Wordsworth where he stumbled into Bazza dragging Sammy along by his arm. Terry looked the pair over, “What did the little prick do this time Baz?”

Baz stopped bluntly stating, “It’s not what he’s done, it’s what he’s had done to him, I reckon.”

“What d’you mean?” Terry looked Sammy up and down slowly.

“My aunt Carol saw him coming out of that flat in Coleridge, the one where Andy and Gimpish are squatting.”

“And?”

“Andy kissed him on the lips when they said goodbye and went back in,” Bazza fumed, “I’m gonna fuckin’ kill him, fuckin’ pervert.”

Terry glanced at the boy, “That true Sammy?”

Sammy glared and pulled at his arm still held tightly by his brother, “It ain’t what you fink, either of you!”

Terry eyes narrowed on Bazza’s face, “Can I have a word with him, Baz? Can’t do no harm.”

Bazza let go of Sammy’s arm, “You can ‘ave all the words you want. I’m still gonna fuckin’ kill that fucker.” Sammy grumbled and rubbed the spot on his arm. He followed Terry across to the wall above the loading dock. The window Dave had smashed earlier was now boarded up with plywood. He pulled out a packet of Rothmans and offered one to Sammy. Sammy took it, “Cheers Tel, it’s not what you fink.”

“What is it then?”

The younger brother looked down at the ground, “It’s nuffin’!”

"People only go in there to get high or rent Sally, nothing else," Terry paused for a moment, looking over the boy's figure suspiciously, "And why was Andy kissing you on the lips? He's a grown man."

"We were celebrating."

"Celebrating what?" Terry tilted his head curiously.

Sammy cleared his throat nervously, "It was my first time."

"With Sally or Andy?"

"Both," he winced anxiously noticing the look of disgust that was obvious on Terry's face.

"Both?"

"Yeah, but you can't tell my brother, he'll fuckin' kill me if he thinks I'm a queer!"

Terry turned to look around for him quickly realising that Bazza was nowhere to be seen. Terry groaned, "Fuck! Stay here." He ran towards Coleridge and in through the door. Sammy, despite Terry's instructions, was hard on his heels. Terry sprinted straight up the stairs, flight after flight and across the seventh-floor landing. The door to the squat was wide open, the lock smashed where Bazza had kicked his way into the flat. Terry hurried inside followed by Sammy.

In the flat, Gimpish was still passed out on the sofa, in front of him on the floor lay Andy Junior. He was holding his hands up to his smashed face, the nose he was named for broken, and his front two teeth were missing, the result of a single collision with Bazza's huge fist. He was crying and moaning plaintively. To his left, Bazza lifted a dining room chair and swung it, as hard as he could, against the kitchen window. The chair smashed into pieces, and the window only slightly cracked. Bazza picked up another chair. Recognising his intent, Terry shouted, "Bazza don't!"

Baz hesitated momentarily and held the chair in midair, ready to swing once more at the window. "Fuck off Terry," he barked back as he swung the chair with all of his substantial strength. The window shattered, glass flew out into the air, the stale stench of the flat being released at the same moment. Bazza turned and started towards Andy Jr once more.

Terry stepped forward to block his way, “Don’t do it Baz,” he begged.

Baz angrily punched Terry in the stomach, doubling him over forward. Sammy watched in horror as his brother grabbed Andy by the front of his green, bomber jacket. The rage boiled up from deep inside him, and Sammy called out desperately to his brother, “Leave him alone, you got no right!”

Andy begged and squirmed attempting to get away, “Please, don’t please! I didn’t do nuffin’!”

By now, Bazza was clearly engulfed by a red rage. He screamed in Andy’s face, “Didn’t do nothing? You fucking liar!” Bazza lifted him with both of his huge hands, walked two steps across the flat and, with one heft, hurled him out through the broken window. They could hear Andy screaming all the way down the seven stories before landing on the concrete with a sickening thud. Everything went silent.

A moment later, the bedroom door opened, and Sally walked out naked, oblivious to what had just transpired and to the people staring at her. She moved slowly, in a zombie-like trance, across the room to the window, and without the slightest hesitation, without saying a word stepped out and disappeared from sight. There were no screams this time and all the group heard was a second, sickening thud.

Terry slowly stood up, walked silently to the window and looked down at the pavement below. Andy was sprawled on the pavement, one of his legs bent jarringly backwards, where it broke upon landing, his arms splayed out to the sides. Even from seven floors up his eyes were visibly open, staring accusingly back up at the window he was thrown from, blood pooled around his head. Sally laid beside him, face down, arms by her side, a pool of blood slowly spreading out from her head mixing with Andy’s. He turned away from the scene and looked around the room: Gimpish was still laying comatose, oblivious on the sofa, Bazza stared at the window, pulling deep breaths in and out, seemingly unable to move, and Sammy slowly backed towards the open door before quickly spinning towards it and running off. Terry sighed and followed out the door behind him. The sound of approaching sirens wailed through the air.

19

Dave and Siobhan lay naked on the couch at Wobble's house, naked except for Dave's bandages, and his t-shirt. The lovemaking was the only thing that had managed to take their minds off the loss of Carl, and the way that he had been found. According to the police, his badly beaten body had been discovered in The Copse on The Hill. His death had been from a head wound, one of many that had been inflicted on him and they assumed that his death had occurred during the riot, presumably just a case of being in the wrong place, at the wrong time. His work van had yet to be found. The police assumed that the theft of the van was the reason for his demise, perhaps he had resisted the thieves and, in the heat of the moment, with the riot and everything, had paid with his life.

Despite the fact they were now very obviously an item, Dave still had trouble revealing not just his feelings but anything that would let Siobhan in, to the 'real' him. He much preferred to play the lovable rogue and hide behind the artifice. However, laying there now he thought it was time to share something with her. "Listen, if I show you something, do you promise not to laugh?"

"Of course, although I think I've seen everything you've got to offer!"

"I'm serious!"

"Yeah sorry, I know, what is it?"

"Pass my jeans over."

Siobhan reached down and pulled his Levi's from the floor. "There you go," she said, handing them to him before snuggling against him once more.

Dave reached into the back pocket and pulled out a crumpled piece of paper. He handed it to Siobhan, picked up a fag, and lit it.

She turned the paper over in her hands, looking at it curiously, "What's this Dave?"

He shrugged and stared up at the ceiling, hoping she would keep her word not to laugh, "Just something I've been working on."

Delicately, she unfolded the paper and found a poem titled "Scars."

"Promise you won't laugh," Dave once again stopped her, touching her hand gently.

She shushed him, "Quiet Dave! I want to read this!"

SCARS

The scars on my body
They run deeper inside
The pain of the flesh
Tears through my mind
I can't ever forget
The ones who left me behind
Some locked away
Quiet and stoic
Some no longer alive
To me vainly heroic
I mourn through my laughter
Capture my tears
How can I bear missing them
For lo all these years
They came and brought joy
Filled the life of the boy
Inspired my art
Even as they broke my heart
An emptiness a void
A pain I can't avoid
The memories tainted
Black pain painted
They leave me with fear
Of a drop too sheer
Of a life without

I just want to shout
To explode in rage
But instead I fill this page
Perhaps a whole book
While my smile is my look
Goodbye my friend
Til I see you at my end.

Siobhan sat stunned in silence, a tear slowly slid down her cheek and she hurried to wipe it away. Dave took a drag on his cigarette, waiting. "Well?" he finally asked.

"It's fucking beautiful," she smiled at him and held it against her chest, "did you write this for Carl?"

"Only if I'm psychic, been working on it for a while. He's not my first loss, you know?"

"I don't know what to say Dave, it's truly beautiful." She glanced over the crumpled paper once more, "it's the real you, isn't it?"

Dave grinned bashfully, "I guess, don't you go telling the others though."

"Do you think they don't already know? You idiot."

"I like to think I'm not that soft. You know how that would make me seem,"

"It's okay to have more than one side Dave. Time you learnt that you don't have to act the hard man all the time, you know, it's okay to be happy."

"You make me happy," he nuzzled her hair.

She leaned up and kissed him gently, "Good."

He could feel his heart swell as he kissed her back. "What now then?"

She winked playfully at him, "Well Wobbles gonna be awhile… I have an idea."

At Cooper's Olde fashioned butcher Shoppe, Nadia untied and removed her apron, pulled on her coat, and walked to the front door. She locked it, turned and walked through the store to the backroom. Abhijay was in the walk-in cooler, and Ray was at the back sink cleaning the knives. She called out to her husband, "I have to go, are you sure you don't mind getting the bus?"

From inside the cooler, he called back, "Not at all, you go have fun, I still have a lot to do here to be ready for tomorrow's celebrations."

"I love you."

"You too," he replied, "now go on and leave me be."

Nadia smiled in his direction before heading out the back door, "Goodnight Ray."

"'Night Nadia," Ray responded. He walked behind her to the door and watched as she climbed into the beat-up old Ford Cortina, put on her seatbelt, started the engine, and drove away. Once she was out of sight, he turned and strode back, across the room. Without the slightest hesitation, he lifted the bag of bones that were holding the cooler door open and threw it into the cooler. Abhijay spun around and saw Ray grinning crazily at him before slamming the heavy door shut. Everything went dark. Ray casually strode to the back door, took off his apron and threw it down onto the floor. He flung opened the back door, and walked out, leaving the door hanging wide open.

In his bedsit, Donnie hurriedly stuffed his clothes into a rucksack; it didn't take him long, he'd been travelling light for years. He knew Terry was right, there really wasn't anything to keep him here. "Maybe with a new beginning I could start to turn my life around, save some money, settle down," he thought to himself as he packed. He had lost count of how many times he had told himself that in the past, but he was sure this time it would be different. Donnie was the eternal optimist.

At the police station, D.C Wainwright hung up the phone and turned to D.S Miller. "That was our friend, Raymond Collins', probation officer, apparently he didn't show up for work yesterday," he said, tapping a pen on his desk.

Miller shrugged, "We already know that we have him on film at the demonstration."

"You didn't let me finish," Wainwright continued, "she was going to let it go as we have his file flagged but for some reason, he turned up mid-afternoon and started his shift. Mr. Singh reported back in, said he felt bad if he'd got Ray into trouble for no good reason. However, they called Mr. Singh back repeatedly today, no answer."

"Why would a reprobate like Collins bother, I can't imagine him caring about brownie points."

"Why don't we stop by, see what he has to say about it?"

Miller shook her head, "I don' think our friends at counter terrorism would look too kindly on that."

"No, I'm sure they wouldn't," he grinned at her, "so, shall we?"

She laughed and hopped out of her chair, grabbing her coat, "I don't see why not!"

Donnie turned the corner at The Blackbirds with his bag on his shoulder to find Terry already there, waiting with his own bag of clothes. He stopped, briefly surprised, and questioned, "What the fuck're you doing here?"

Terry nodded in greeting toward him, "Thought I'd see if there was room for one more, besides I wasn't sure if you'd show up or not."

"But you've already got a better job than most people I know." Donnie shifted the bag's weight from one shoulder to the other.

He scoffed, "It ain't about the job, Donnie."

"What then?"

"Life! This fucking place," Terry gestured wildly around the street.

"Oh!" Donnie agreed, "That I can understand."

"Don't worry," Terry continued, assuring him, "I'm not after the job Doug promised you."

"I was'ne worried. I'd just kick your arse if ye were. What about Dave?"

The question had been weighing on Terry's mind, "He'll survive. Time he learnt to look out for himself." He hesitated, knowing that Dave ever taking care of himself was highly unlikely, a thought struck him, "He's got Siobhan now. She'll straighten him out."

A car pulled up and after a brief explanation about Terry's presence the two young men tied their luggage to the roof rack and left, left for a brave new world across the English Channel where they felt there was still hope for a brighter future.

Wainwright pulled up in the alley beside Cooper's Fine Olde Butchery Shoppe. He and Miller climbed out of the car, headed around to the front of the shop, and found the front door locked, they headed back down the alley where they found the back door wide open. Miller stopped beside the sink and called through the plastic curtain, "Hello?"

Nothing.

"Mr. Singh?" she called once more.

Again nothing.

Wainwright and Miller exchanged glances, "Mr. Collins?" Wainwright took a step forward, "Shall we?"

They checked the front of the shop before returning to the back room. The knives lay on the draining boards, unwashed, the sinks still had unfinished chickens laying in them. Ray's blood covered apron lay, in a crumpled heap, in the centre of the floor, where he had dropped it. The two police officers spotted the wide-open door and checked the back alley, there was nothing untoward there either; some dust bins and a pile of crushed, fly covered, cardboard boxes that smelled of putrefied blood. As they re-entered the butcher's shop they looked around at the obviously abandoned, unfinished tasks that were at hand.

Wainwright stared curiously at the locked, freezer door. "You don't suppose?" He gestured towards the door, drawing Miller's attention. Gripping the handle, he pulled the door, and it flew open, partially propelled by the weight of Abhijay's body that was pressed against the other side of it. The force sent Wainwright crashing into the wall. “Christ! Call an ambulance ma’am!” Ignoring the slight, Miller hurried to pull out her radio and quickly called for an ambulance.

After the call, she turned back. Wainwright was desperately checking for a pulse. “And?” She inquired anxiously.

Wainwright nodded, “It’s weak, but it’s there.”

She fumed, glaring angrily towards the still open back door, “Guess we can add attempted murder to our friend Raymond Collin’s sheet.”

20

Sarah Donnelly, from the Royal Ulster Constabulary, stood at the front of the briefing room in Wembley Police Station. Despite the fact that she was in front of her own people, a room full of police, she still wore a mask, sunglasses and a hat that was pulled down tight hiding her face. No one in the briefing room had been told her true identity. On the board behind her were photographs of all the people she was about to discuss, at the centre was a blown-up picture of Ray Collins. "Doors will come down today, Raymond Collins, Eric Daniels, Greg Patterson of The Hangmen motorcycle club and his associates, Seamus McCaffrey and a whole host of other Ulster Volunteer Force supporters and enablers will be taken in. These are dangerous people, do not underestimate them. Your task is Raymond Collins, in the grand scheme of things he is not a big wheel, more a small cog. But we need him so that we can tie up loose ends. We consider him a fanatic, not about the Protestant cause so much, but about what it can do to help him and his Neo-Nazi compatriots."

She gripped the sides of the podium in front of her, leaning in toward the crowd, and added, "He is armed and dangerous and we will be ready for him. We have information, from an informer who will not be named, that Mr. Collins plans to rob the Kentucky Fried Chicken in Colindale..." A loud ripple of laughter and derisive comments spread through the room.

Detective Sergeant Miller immediately stood up from her seat beside the podium. "Calm down, let the young lady finish, please, and thank you." Once the laughter had subsided, she returned to her seat.

Ms. Donnelly waited a moment and continued, "Mr. Collins and his associates, one of whom we have in custody, thanks to the good work of members of The Metropolitan Police in this department...” Another murmur from the crowd, although not so loud this time, one of self-congratulation, rippled through the room. “Plan to rob said Kentucky at precisely the same time as Charles and Diana say their vows. Their thinking is that we will all be far too busy with the royal nuptials to take much notice of anything else. They then intend to donate the takings to Operation Warhead, their attempt to start a race war in this country through their friends in The Hangmen biker gang. We suspect that the self-same people were the catalyst for the recent riots on The Chalkhill Estate and in Handsworth, Birmingham. So, in case any of you feel that this is a Northern Irish problem, it’s not. The chickens have come home to roost ladies and gentlemen and today we intend to have them all rounded up.”

Wainwright leaned over to Miller and whispered, “Shouldn’t that be pigeons?”

Miller cast him a sideways glance, “What difference does it make?”

He sat up in his chair and straightened the buttons on his shirt, “Oh, don’t be so dolorous.”

Dave awoke with Siobhan again laying on his chest, he smiled and lifted his head to smell her hair. He could still smell the henna through the stronger scent of cigarette smoke. “Funny,” he thought as he loved smoking cigarettes, but the lingering aroma, not so much. Not wanting to wake her, he laid his head back down, his morning smoke could wait, right now, this is what made him happy. For the first time in his life, Dave was in love, plain and simple. Siobhan's happiness mattered to him more than his own did and that was that.

The door to Wobble's room upstairs slammed shut as Wobble emerged to go to the toilet. The noise caused Siobhan to stir and lift her head to look up at Dave, who had a huge smile on his face. She looked at him suspiciously, “What are you smiling at?”

“You,” he stated simply, leaning forward to kiss the top of her head.

She leaned happily into the kiss, "Why?"

"Cause you're here, with me. And that makes me happy."

"Soppy pratt," she teased him, "put the kettle on."

"But then I'd have to get up."

"I want a cuppa and besides it'll be a nice surprise for Wobble," she insisted moving away from him.

"For fuck sakes, alright then!" He slid off the couch and went into the kitchen to do as he was told. Siobhan watched him leave, dressed as always in his T-shirt, underwear on, his legs still bandaged.

"You could've put some trousers on Dave."

Dave looked down at his bandaged legs, "I kinda already do really."

"Idiot."

Meanwhile, Wobble had come down the stairs to find Dave standing semi-dressed in his kitchen. He wrinkled his nose in disgust and shook his head, "That's enough to put me off my tea."

"I was trying to be nice."

"Siobhan put you up to it?"

"What d'you think?"

"Thanks Siobhan," Danny called out towards the other room, "but get him to put something on next time."

"You're welcome Wobs," Siobhan replied from the couch, "I tried."

Wobble opened the door to the fridge and looked inside, "Out of milk again, I see. Your turn Dave."

Dave found some old mugs, placed them on the countertop, and sighed heavily, "That's not fair. I'm injured."

"Not too injured to go to the pub or down to Chalkhill yesterday."

The comment stung Dave and without thinking he spun around and shouted at Wobble, "If I had to crawl down there on stumps I would have! Carl was my friend, he deserved that much."

Danny quipped back quickly, "And I'm your friend Dave, don't forget that. I do let you live under my roof, remember?"

Siobhan came out from the living room to see what was going on and realised that if she didn't intervene this could easily get out of control. "Hey, come on you two. No need for this, you're both upset about Carl, we all are." As she spoke, she walked to the middle of the kitchen, placing herself between them. The two young men stood staring at each other, in a stand-off.

After what seemed like an eternity, but was probably only about ten seconds, Dave slowly extended his hand. "Sorry Wobs, you didn't deserve that, I'm just gutted about Carl that's all. You understand right?"

"Of course, I do, Dave, only natural."

Dave stepped forward and grabbed Wobble in a big embrace. "You're a good mate," he said, hugging him tightly.

Wobble pushed him back, embarrassed, "Get off me you bloody idiot! You've still got no trousers on and you ain't my type."

"That's better you two," Siobhan interrupted them, "why don't I go down the shops and get us some milk, and then we can watch the Royal Wedding on the tele."

Dave burst out laughing, "You hear that Wobs? Royal fucking wedding, not very punk that is it?"

Danny let out an awkward laugh, "I wouldn't mind watching it."

"You? You're kidding me?"

"Always had a soft spot for Lady Diana." He suddenly had a better idea, "Tell you what, Dave, you go down the store and me and Siobhan will watch the royal nuptials together."

Dave bristled at the idea. "You trying to get in with my bird, Wobs? And it's not nuptials, whatever they are, it's a wedding, you nonce."

At this point, Siobhan began to feel agitated, "Enough you two, Wobs, thanks for the offer, but Dave you should want to watch it with me, if only because it makes me happy. Now, I'll leave you to think about that, while I go get the milk."

Wobble stepped forward, “It’s alright Siobhan, I’ll go. I need some Rothmans anyway. You two clear the couch off so the three of us can play happy families and watch the big event together.”

Dave and Siobhan returned to the living room to start cleaning up as Wobble headed out of the door. They had no sooner started to pull the covers off the couch when there was an enormous crash from the front door. They ran back out into the kitchen and found Ray barreling down the hallway dragging Wobble by his jacket collar. He threw Wobble flying across the room, crashing into the fridge. Siobhan stared at her brother feeling nothing but hatred, despite their sibling bond, “What the fuck are you doing Ray?”

“Good morning to you too sis!”

Dave puffed out his chest, “You can’t do this.”

“Oh, shut up Dave,” Ray looked Dave slowly up and down with disgust, “And put some trousers on for Christ’s sake, what do you think this is a brothel?”

His words made Siobhan more enraged than ever, “Just get the fuck out of here, will you?” She yelled at her brother.

“Calm down sis and put the kettle on,” he slid a chair out from under the table, plopped down in it and made himself comfortable, “I’m dying for a cuppa tea or coffee. Some arsehole burnt the cafe down.” Wobble groaned and slowly pulled himself up from the floor. He, Dave, and Siobhan nervously glanced at each other. The mention of the fire at Abdul’s made the atmosphere in the room even more menacing than before. Ray glared at Wobble, then Dave, then his sister. “The kettle?”

“We don’t have any milk.” Wobble spoke, or more stammered, for the first time since he and Ray had come crashing through the door. “That’s where I was just going. To... to get the milk.”

Ray stared at him and addressed his sister, “Go get the milk Siobhan.”

Dave chimed in, “Why her?”

"Cause I said so. Cause I know she won't do anything stupid. At least not while I've got you two, especially you Dave. Now you go get some trousers on." He regarded his sister coldly, "and you go get the milk."

Defeated, Dave slinked into the living room to retrieve his jeans. Siobhan followed behind him, grabbing her purse, and gave Dave a quick kiss on the cheek before turning to the front door. As she pulled it open, Wobble called out, "Don't forget my Rothmans."

Ray spun towards him, "D'you give her any money?"

"N-n-no," Danny swallowed nervously.

"Is she your girlfriend too then? What is this? Some kinda swingers club?"

"N-n-n-n-no," Wobble stammered.

Ray stared at Wobble with contempt in his eyes, "Give her some dosh then and put the kettle on so that we can have a brew up ready for when she gets back."

Wobble hurried to pull a ten pound note out of his pocket and thrust it out to Siobhan. Ray grinned as he saw how much money he gave her and added, "Get me a packet too. Benson and Hedges."

Siobhan looked at Wobble for approval, as if there was a chance of him saying no, Wobble, of course nodded, and she exited out the door. Ray reached over and patted Wobble on the cheek, "Good lad, now about that kettle?"

Wobble limped over and grabbed the kettle off the stove, hurrying to fill it with water. In the other room, Dave rushed to get dressed. Ray watched Wobble for a moment and then stood from his chair and entered the living room, surveying it. The couch that Wobble's mother had bought second hand, that Dave and Siobhan now used as a bed, had definitely seen better days. There was a conspicuous sag in the centre and one of the arms was ripped. The dining table was covered in piles of papers, old chip bags, an old ketchup bottle and empty Whitetop bottles. There was a glass fronted corner cabinet that housed souvenirs from The Costa Del

Brava and Butlins trips to Morecambe, none of which Wobble had been on. Directly across from the couch was an old cabinet style television that had an ashtray full of butts and more empty beer bottles on top of it, beside them was an empty Baby Cham bottle, the only evidence of Siobhan living there. Everything about the room aged it by ten years or more. Ray looked around with disgust, "Quite the dump you've got my sister living in here, Dave."

Wobble took offense. "They don't have to live here."

"Don't they? She's not moving back in with me and mum, not now I know she's a race traitor."

Dave was growing more and more nervous by the second, "What d'you want here anyway, Ray?"

Ray stepped directly into Dave's space, staring him blankly in the eyes, "I've got some work to do today, and you are gonna help me, Dave."

Dave swallowed anxiously, "What sort of work?"

"Work for the cause, a chance for you to redeem yourself."

"Why would I?"

"Because Dave, like it or not, you're English and white and when your country and Saint George calls you, it is your duty to answer that clarion call."

Dave knew it was insane to argue with Ray, but he felt the need to assert himself, to stand up, for once, for his own beliefs. Without realising what he was doing, he blurted out, "I dance to the tune of a different drummer though, Ray."

The backhand was so swift it sent Dave flying backwards onto the couch with his lip split open. Wobble took two steps back, up against the glass front cabinet, knocking into it and causing one of the cheesy matador dolls to fall from the shelf. Ray glared sharply at Danny before growling through clenched teeth, "I will knock some sense into you Dave, or kill you trying. How can you desert your country in its time of need?"

"Need? The people in need in this country are mostly not white Ray. You're on the wrong side." Dave touched his lip lightly, examining the blood on his fingers while he flicked his tongue over his lip.

"That's where you're wrong Dave, the people you seem to care about, this isn't their country, and it's time they, and you, learned that." From the kitchen, the kettle started to whistle. Dave and Wobble stared at Ray as he angrily glanced from one to the other. "Well, who usually plays Mum?"

Wobble coughed, "I do."

Ray sneered in response, "Well get on with it then." Wobble left the pair and returned to the kitchen. He poured some boiling water into the teapot to warm it and tipped it down the sink, took down the tea caddy and spooned four spoons of loose tea into it, one for each person and one for the pot. Then filled the pot with boiling water. Ray chuckled, his attention returning to Dave, "He really is a mother, isn't he?"

"Wobble makes a good cup of Rosie."

"Right then gents," Ray paced about the dingy living room, stopping briefly in front of the TV, "we have an hour to kill before me and Dave have to go to work. Might as well watch some of the build up to the wedding." He stopped midthought, glanced around and realised that Wobble was no longer in the kitchen. While Ray had been talking Wobble had snuck down the hall, to the front door and at that very moment his hand was turning the handle to open it. Ray dashed down the hall, pulled the Luger from his waistband and leveled it at him, "I wouldn't do that if I was you."

Wobble froze mid-action, turned slowly and stared straight down the barrel of a gun for the first, and he hoped, the only time in his life. He was frozen in his spot, but his right leg wouldn't stop shaking. Ray's arm stayed pointing straight at him, his hands unwavering. "Let go of the handle," he commanded slowly.

Wobble did as he was told, his hands lifting up near his shoulders. Dave felt a desperate need to do something to diffuse the situation. He slipped out into the hall, behind Ray, and gave Wobble a reassuring nod. "You don't want to do this Ray," he said quietly, attempting to reason with him.

"Why not? Getting rid of a crippled welfare bum seems like a patriotic social service to me."

The door was suddenly flung open, sending Wobble staggering awkwardly forward towards Ray. Siobhan had returned, milk in her hand, "Sorry it took so long. I had to go to Hay Lane…" She found herself staring straight down the barrel of the gun her brother was holding, "what the fuck, Ray?"

"The gimp was trying to escape." He shifted so the gun was once more pointing at Danny, instead of his sister.

"Yeah well, he's not now, is he?"

"N-n-no, I'm not," Wobble again stammered nervously in response.

"He can't even speak proper," Ray snarled at Wobble repulsed, "maybe I should put a cap in him, put him out of his misery. Shut the door, Siobhan."

Siobhan closed the door behind her and finally, Ray slowly lowered the gun. She walked straight past her brother, stopping next to him, "Why the fuck do you have a gun, Ray?"

He responded with a shrug, foreseeing an upcoming lecture, "I'm gonna need it at work later."

She stared directly into his eyes, "What sort of work is that Ray?"

He hated when she spoke to him like a child, "A patriot's work Siobhan, for Queen and St. George."

While he was speaking, Siobhan noticed Dave's split lip, "And what happened to Dave's face?"

"He forgot his place."

"His place?"

"That's right, his place!" The four of them stood in silence. After a pause, Ray grunted, shoved the gun back in his waistband, and immediately changed the subject, "Milk's here, so what about that cup of tea? Hmmm, no one else thirsty?"

Wobble shuffled forward, volunteering, "I'll pour it."

Ray reached out and grabbed him by the arm, "Siobhan can pour it. You and I are going upstairs." Wobble, Dave, and Siobhan exchanged glances, but no one spoke. Ray shoved Wobble across to the stairs, "Let's go." Wobble limped his way upstairs followed by the hulking skinhead. Once on the landing, Ray started opening doors, first the bathroom, then the toilet, next Wobble's room, and finally the games room. Finding the door opened outward he muttered, "Perfect. In here, you." He shoved Wobble roughly into the games room, pulled out the Luger and clubbed Wobble on the back of the head, sending him crashing to the floor unconscious. Ray stepped out of the room taking one of the shortened pool cues, closed the door, and wedged the cue between the door and the banisters, securing it shut. Satisfied with his work, walked back downstairs and into the kitchen. He picked up his cup of tea before walking into the living room.

Dave and Siobhan sat on opposite ends of the couch, Siobhan spoke first, "What was that thumping sound?"

Ray took a slow sip of his tea before responding, "Your gimpy friend is having a little siesta that's all, nothing to worry about."

Dave and Siobhan glanced nervously at each other, before she looked up at her brother, "What now?"

Ray plopped himself down on the couch, between them, "Now we get to drink our tea while we watch a piece of history, a one-time moment in English pomp and pageantry, turn the tele on Dave, we're missing it."

Detective Sergeant Miller pulled to a stop and parked in Silkfield Road, two streets down and across on the other side of The Edgware Road from the Kentucky Fried Chicken in Colindale. In the passenger seat sat Sarah Donnelly, still wearing a mask, sunglasses, and a hat. Miller turned to her, "You're going to have to at least lose the bandana. You look like you're about to commit a robbery."

Donnelly shrugged in response, "Aye, but I'm not, am I?"

"No but some poor old lady is likely to come by with her shopping trolley full of groceries, cream crackers, and Tetley tea, and the like, see you and call the police. They'll show up, lights and sirens blaring, and the whole thing's a waste of time."

"Fair enough." She pulled the bandana down from her face. "That's quite a relief actually, it's awfully warm today." They sat in silence for a few minutes, before Donnelly continued, "I need to ask you something."

Miller glanced at her curiously, "Go ahead."

"How come you and Constable Wainwright knew to enter Mr. Singh's shop to find him in the freezer, if we'd given a directive for Collins to be left alone?"

The Detective thought for a moment, "I don't know, call it intuition maybe? A cop's instinct."

Sarah pursed her lips in response, "Feels more like defiance to me."

Before Miller could answer, the police car radio crackled. Wainwright's voice came through the static, "In position, ma'am."

"Good enough," she replied, adding, "and enough with the Ma'am."

Another crackly response over the speaker, "Yes Ma'am."

Wainwright sat parked in Rydal Gardens, one road back from the Kentucky. With him were five heavily armed, tactical squad officers. On the far side of The Edgware Road, opposite the Kentucky, were two plain clothes officers with concealed firearms, one, Constable Roddy, dressed as a homeless man, the other, lounged in the doorway of a closed store, dressed as a biker. All of them were waiting for Ray. It was eleven in the morning, on the twenty ninth of July 1981, twenty minutes until Charles and Diana were due to say their vows.

Back at Wobble's house, as Charles and Diana began their walk down the aisle in St. Paul's Cathedral, Ray stood up, and abruptly turned off the television. "Shall we Dave?" Dave and Siobhan stared at him, not moving, not speaking. Ray sighed, his eyes narrowing on Dave's face, "That wasn't a question David, we have work to do, and I don't want to be late."

Dave slowly stood up, "But I have no idea what it is you want me to do."

"You're my getaway driver."

Dave stared at Ray, completely dumbfounded, "Getaway driver?"

"You heard me. Now Mitch has gone, after serving the cause as best he could, and Alex has been captured by the enemy." He reached back, his hand resting on the butt of the gun, "I need someone else."

Siobhan looked at her brother, confused "But Dave can't drive."

Letting go of the gun, Ray folded his arms across his chest, "I don't care if he has a licence or not. We're going to commit a robbery, so the legalities of it ain't exactly relevant. Are they?"

"No, I mean he can't drive, he's an idiot when it comes to anything mechanical."

Ray paused, stunned. It hadn't crossed his mind, when he had hatched his plan, to check whether his planned getaway driver could actually drive or not. Something suddenly occurred to Dave, "Drive what?"

By this point, Ray was reaching the end of his tether, "A car you fuckin' idiot! What else? A fuckin' elephant?"

Dave and Siobhan exchanged glances, and she inquired, "What car?"

"The gimp's car, of course."

"You're going to steal Wobble's car?"

Ray paced anxiously back and forth, "Shut up, I've got to think." Striding into the kitchen, he started kicking the fridge in anger. Suddenly, something occurred to him, he stopped kicking the fridge and turned to Siobhan, "You had driving lessons, I remember cause I was mad mum paid for them."

"Yeah, but I was shit at it. So, I quit."

"You'll do. Let's go, both of you," he gestured at them and began searching the room, "Where's the keys?"

Dave pointed, "On the hook, by the front door."

Ray pulled the gun from his waistband and pointed it at them both. Siobhan was desperate and scared, but not for herself, "What d'you need Dave for, if he can't drive?"

"He's coming in with me." Ray waved the gun between Dave and the door, "Make sure there's a getaway car outside to make a getaway in."

"But you know how to drive Ray, that's why you were mad mum paid for my lessons 'cause she didn't yours."

"I can't be my own getaway driver though, can I?" He pulled a balaclava helmet out of his Harrington pocket, and threw it to Dave, "Here you'll need this." Dave caught it and quickly put it on, Ray snatched it off his head, "Not now, you idiot! When we get there."

With Siobhan in the lead, Dave second, and Ray following up at the rear, the three of them left through the front door of number 183, and into the street. Siobhan and Dave glanced up and down, desperately hoping for some kind of help. Ray did the same making sure there were no cops around. He figured Mr. Singh would have been found, frozen in the freezer by now, and that he would be wanted for murder, but wanted to pull off the robbery before the law caught up with him. Siobhan climbed into the driver's side, Dave scrambled into the back through the passenger side door, and Ray jumped in the front. Siobhan started the car, put it in first gear, and slipped the clutch. The car bunny hopped forward and stalled. Ray stared at her, totally exasperated, "'Ow fuckin' much money did mum waste on your drivin' lessons?"

She held tightly to the steering wheel, "Shut up Ray, you're makin' me nervous. I told you I was shit at this."

Ray glowered, "You better try it again."

Siobhan once more restarted the car and slipped the clutch. This time, the engine sputtered once, and the car pulled forward onto the street. Siobhan let out a sigh of relief, "Where am I going?"

"The Kentucky."

"The Kentucky?" she repeated him, not sure where he meant.

"Yeah, down in Colindale. Take the Kingsbury Road, to the Edgware Road, and turn left. That way you'll be facing the right way to make a getaway."

Siobhan drove out of the estate on Kingsbury Road desperately hoping she didn't hit a red light at the junction with Church Lane and have to risk stalling the car again. To her relief, the light was green, and she continued through, up the hill past Holy Innocents Church on the left. Dave watched quietly out the window, remembering how his parents had made him go to that church as a kid, and join the Scout group. As they passed Silver Jubilee Park on the right, Siobhan remembered when life was innocent, and she and Ray had played catch and tag there as kids. They drove down the other side of the hill, and left at the lights, where luckily, she had hit another green light before turning onto the Edgware Road, one of the busiest roads in London. Ray was clearly agitated at the amount of traffic, and even less happy at the number of parked cars that were lining the side of the road.

Miller picked the radio off the dash in her unmarked car, "Anything?"

Wainwright responded first, "Nothing." The homeless man, next, "Nothing here."

Donnelly checked her watch, "Should be any minute now."

Miller nodded, "If your informant told you the truth. Who was it? Alex Wheeler?"

"I can't tell you that, you should know better than to ask."

Miller continued to press her for information, "He never reappeared after we handed him over to a mysterious man in a dark trench coat. All very John le Carré."

"What's that got to do with me?"

"You suddenly show up with information on his best friend provided by an informant," the policewoman eyed her suspiciously, "I don't believe in coincidences."

Sarah shrugged, "Maybe the luck of the Irish then."

The Ford Capri with Ray, and his two reluctant accomplices inside, drove slowly past the Kentucky. There were no available parking spaces anywhere near the front door. Siobhan was beginning to feel desperate, she needed to get out of the car, get away from the steadily mounting pressure. She felt as if she would implode if she didn't. "What are we going to do Ray?" She asked, the panic growing in her tone, "There's nowhere to fucking park. Maybe we should just give up on it, head back to the estate."

He scowled at her, "Shut up and let me think! Go round the block again." Siobhan turned left onto Wakemans Hill and gunned the engine trying desperately to mount the steep hill while staying in third gear. The engine screamed as the car mounted the crest of the hill. Ray stared at her, "For fuck sakes Siobhan, try not to kill the car, not 'til the robberies over at least."

"I'm trying," she responded, her voice flustered.

Dave leaned forward, "Leave it out Ray, you're only making things wor..." He didn't finish before Ray had pulled out the Luger and pressed it roughly against his cheek.

"What was that, Dave?"

Siobhan hurried to butt in, "He didn't mean anything by it, Ray. He was just sticking up for me."

Ray lowered the gun, setting it on his leg, as he addressed his sister, "Maybe you should concentrate on your driving, before you get us all killed."

Wainwright lifted his radio, "Do we have any idea what he's supposed to be driving? Over."

Miller turned to Donnelly who had clearly heard the call. Donnelly shrugged, and Miller replied, "None whatsoever."

In his car, Wainwright shook his head, "Great."

The Capri pulled back on to the Edgware Road and cruised slowly back past the Kentucky. There were still no spots. Siobhan was now sweating with nervousness, "What now?"

It was clear how angry Ray was becoming, "Let me think." At that point they are about ten shop doorways past the Kentucky, at the corner of Wakemans Hill, when Ray spotted an empty parking spot on the corner. Realising where they were he suddenly blurted out, "Pull in, in there, quick!"

Siobhan yanked the steering wheel and pulled the car into the spot and slammed on the brakes, causing the car to lurch, sputter, and die. She turned her head to look at Ray, "You can't be serious, the Kentucky's a mile away."

"I know," he flung open his door and stepped out, "we ain't doing the Kentucky anymore."

He turned back to the car, lifting the seat forward, as he addressed Dave, "Come on you." Before Dave could respond, Ray reached in, grabbed him by the arm and dragged him out, shouting at Siobhan as he did, "Make sure the engine's running when we come out."

The pair stood outside Andy's kebab shop. Ray pulled out his balaclava, and pulled it over his face, Dave's eyes darted nervously from side to side as he copied Ray, pulling his on as well. He was terrified that he would be seen, and someone would call the police, and just as terrified that he wouldn't be, and no one would do anything. The busy high street continued on, life as usual.

Ray drew the gun out with his right hand, grabbed Dave's elbow with his left, and strode straight in through the shop doorway, dragging the terrified Dave with him. As soon as they were in the shop, Ray raised the gun and fired a shot through the mirror, behind the counter. The explosion of the shot and the shattering mirror glass caused the only two customers, a pair of young white girls out to get lunch from their jobs at Woolworths, the proprietor, who was in the process of cutting a donair kebab, and even Dave, to duck in shock. The only one who didn't was Ray. He stood there, a huge maniacal grin on his face, in his glory. The two girls were doubled over, their hands on their heads, peering through their fingers in sheer terror. The proprietor, a Lebanese national from Beirut, and no stranger to the horrors of war, had backed up against the wall with the shattered mirror, his hands held up at shoulder height, the long, sharp kebab knife in one hand, a half-filled pita bread in the other. Dave slowly stood up.

Constable Roddy, heard the shot, turned his head and spoke into his concealed radio, "There seems to be some sort of disturbance at the kebab shop at Wakemans Hill, shot fired."

Miller immediately replied, "Roddy checks it out, everybody else keeps eyes on the Kentucky." She turned to Donnelly, "Great, now we're gonna lose Collins 'cause the drug dealers at the kebab are at war again."

Donnelly strained to look down the road towards the out of sight kebab shop, "Happens a lot, does it? Gunfire in Colindale."

"Three or four times a year."

"Oh, you poor thing, don't know how you manage."

Roddy hurried towards the kebab shop on the opposite pavement. Meanwhile, inside the shop, Ray completely ignored the two girls, they were of no interest to him. "Get the cash Dave," he demanded, his gun still held steady on the proprietor.

Dave rushed behind the counter and stared at the register; he had no idea how to open it. He turned to the man who stood near him, knife still in hand. "What do I do?"

The man swallowed hard and barely managed to whisper, "Turn the key." Dave spotted the key, turned it, and the drawer popped open. Quickly, he grabbed all the money he saw and turned to leave. Ray stopped him, speaking with a calm and collected voice, "There's always more in the bottom of the draw."

Dave pulled out the insert and found the larger notes, the ten- and twenty-pound ones. He grabbed them too, before heading back around the counter, "Let's go."

Ray still had a calm, totally unperturbed look on his face, "Not yet."

Dave glanced nervously out the window, "Are you crazy?" He knew the answer to his own question and added a quick, "Never mind."

Constable Roddy crossed the road towards the shop, the first thing he noticed was the Ford Capri, parked at a somewhat erratic angle and sticking out past the corner with the engine running. There was a crowd of onlookers gathering to his left, people who had heard the shot but were too scared to advance any further. He noticed Siobhan behind the wheel, staring straight ahead, transfixed. He called over his radio, "Robbery in progress at Andy's kebab shop, request assistance."

Miller's head sagged, she looked at Donnelly, "Shit, I have to do it."

Donnelly shook her head, "We'll lose him,"

"You said he was a small cog."

"But he's my small cog."

Miller lifted her radio, "Wainwright, go see what's happening at the kebab shop. The rest of you stay where you are."

From inside the shop, Ray stared into the shopkeeper's eyes, the shopkeeper returned his stare. "I want the drugs too," Ray stated bluntly.

The proprietor looked at him quizzically, "What drugs?"

"You know what drugs," Ray held the gun steadily in his direction and continued, "the drugs you're poisoning my people with."

"There are no drugs."

Dave was coming apart and the two girls were softly crying. "Come on Ray," he begged the gunman, "we have to go."

Ray's steely eyed glaze hadn't left the shopkeeper's face for even a second. He looked at the knife in the man's hand, "Are you threatening me?"

Before he had any chance to answer Ray shot him in the face, sending a cascade of blood flying up the wall, the man's body slid down the wall to the floor. The two girls started screaming at the top of their lungs. Wainwright heard the shot but could only see the crowd of onlookers as people began to scramble away from the sound of the shot.

Roddy knocked on the driver's window with his gun, Siobhan's trance was broken. He signaled for her to get out of the car, she opened the door and turned to get out. In her nervousness, she had forgotten the car was in gear and when she lifted her foot off the clutch, it lurched forward, sending her flying into Constable

Roddy's arms, knocking him flat with Siobhan landing on top of him. He quickly pulled himself out from under Siobhan handcuffed her and dragged her off down the street.

Ray calmly strolled out of the store with Dave in tow. As he crossed the street, he noticed Siobhan was gone and shouted at Dave, "Get in, I'll drive!" He ran to the far side of the car and as he climbed in, Roddy shouted from further up the street, "Stop! Police!"

Ray lifted the Luger and fired, hitting Roddy in the stomach, Roddy dropped his gun and fell to his knees with his hands on his stomach. Siobhan stood in the street, handcuffed and screaming as loudly as she could, there were no words, just a primal scream. Dave heard Siobhan and attempted to get out of the car, but, as he did, Ray grabbed him and yanked him back, and in the same instant roared away, tyres squealing, into Wakemans Hill.

Wainwright reached the corner and pointed his service revolver at the rapidly shrinking target of the car. He couldn't get a safe shot off. Lowering the gun he turned to Roddy, who was on his knees in the road, blood pouring from his stomach, oozing through his fingers. Siobhan was still screaming. Traffic in both directions had stopped and horns were blasting. A new crowd had begun to gather, staring curiously at the bleeding, homeless man, the screaming girl, and the armed policeman. Wainwright ran over to Roddy, calling over his radio, "Officer down, need an ambulance, suspect fled North on Wakemans Hill."

Siobhan hurried to Wainwright, who knelt down, and was holding Roddy, trying to console him, "You'll be alright mate, the ambulance is..."

"You've got to go after them," she interrupted him, "it's my brother Ray, he's got Dave."

Surprised, Wainwright looked up at her, "Ray who?"

"Ray Collins, you've got to help..."

Wainwright grabbed his radio, "It was Collins, he got away."

Miller turned to Donnelly, "If my officer dies, I'll ruin you."

Donnelly shrugged and pulled her mask back over her face, "How? I was never here. Remember?"

The Ford Capri tore along Church Lane towards Wembley. Dave couldn't believe what just happened, what he just witnessed. He started to retch and brought his hands up rapidly to his mouth, "Pull over, I'm going to be..." But it was too late, Dave was violently sick, spraying through his fingers onto the dash, down his chest into his lap. He pulled the now soggy balaclava off, over his head.

Ray shook his head in disgust. "You useless coward, look at you, you're pathetic."

Dave coughed and sputtered, wiping his hands on his pants, "You blew his fucking head off!"

Ray grinned, "Serves him right."

At this point Dave was hysterical, he screamed, "You blew his fucking head off!"

"Calm down Dave."

"There was fucking blood everywhere," Dave continued to shout.

"Shut up Dave!"

"It was all over..." Ray reached across and backhanded Dave in the face, hard, causing Dave to curl up defensively. He started to cry, sobbing and sniffling, and couldn't stop himself.

Ray rolled down the window, attempting to air the car out, "Look at you, you're pathetic. I'm doing my sister a favour."

Dave peered out the passenger window, "Where are we going?"

"We have to dump the car."

He could feel himself grow more anxious by the second, "Yeah, okay, but where?"

"You'll see."

Siobhan sat in the back of the tactical squad vehicle, her legs hanging out the back, she was still handcuffed. Miller was interviewing her. Donnelly had gone, a car arrived, she got in, and disappeared, as if she had never been there. Siobhan told them of her and Dave's kidnapping. Tactical officers were dispatched with Wainwright to the estate to check Wobble's house. Miller leaned forward, questioning her about her brother, "Where are they going?"

"I don't know."

"He must have said something."

"Just the usual claptrap about Queen and country."

"Nothing else?" she pressed the young woman again, "nothing out of the ordinary?"

Siobhan strained to think, there had to be something she could say or do to help Dave. Sadly, there was nothing she could think of, "I'm sorry, I'm really sorry." She felt like she was about to fall apart.

"It's okay you did your best," Miller turned away, defeated. However, a thought suddenly occurred to Siobhan, "There was one thing."

"Go on." Miller stopped, looking at her hopefully.

"It's probably nothing."

"We'll be the judge of that, you'd be surprised how these things add up."

"He said something about Mitch."

"Mitch Collins? Your cousin?"

"Yeah. Something about how Mitch had served the cause the best he could. I didn't know what he meant by that; Mitch was never political."

Miller immediately picked up her radio, "Send cars to The Chalkhill estate. Collins is heading there."

The Capri screeched to a stop on the service road beside The Copse on the estate. Dave threw the passenger door open and fell out, struggling to scramble to his feet. Halfway up, he realised Ray was standing in front of him. He had no idea what Ray intended to do to him, but he knew it couldn't be good. He balled up his fist and punched Ray as hard as he could in the bollocks, sending him doubling over and letting out a gasp of air. Dave rolled to one side and stood, pushing away with his right foot into a run, still hampered by the bandages and the damage to his legs, it wasn't much of a run, more a fast walk.

As soon as he made it around the corner to the back of the nearest building, Ray was upon him. He grabbed Dave by the collar of his jacket, threw him face first into the concrete building and pinned him there. They stood gasping for breath, the hulking skinhead pinning the skinny, punk rocker in place. Ray spun hi around and pushed the Luger under his chin, "Any last words Dave?"

Dave desperately struggled for something to say, something that would play on Ray's conscience, anything that might save his skin, but all he could come up with was, "Please, Ray, please, don't. I thought we were mates."

Ray chuckled, a mirthless cruel guttural sound, "Mates? You're a race traitor Dave, how could we be mates? I knew you'd come in handy in the end. Didn't know how. But knew you would." Sirens could be heard approaching in the distance.

"The police will be here soon, Ray," Dave pleaded, "let me go. I won't say anything!"

"I know that Dave, you have one job left to do for us, just like Mitch, you're gonna help us burn this place to the ground!" Dave hadn't taken his eyes off the gun, he saw Ray's finger begin to tighten on the trigger, he knew it was all over, there was nothing left for him to do. He sensed a warm, wet feeling in his trousers as he wet himself. He couldn't help it, he was terrified.

There was a strange thunk sound, Ray's face went suddenly tense, a stunned grimace passed across it, he abruptly dropped to the ground in front of Dave. Standing directly behind him was Samson, a blood covered machete in his hands. Samson looked over his shoulder at Dejean standing there. Dejean spit on the ground and stared directly into Dave's eyes. "Don't come back," Dejean muttered and turned away before he and Samson disappeared quickly from sight.

The sirens grew louder and louder.

THE END

Printed in Great Britain
by Amazon

53993116R00155